BRET HARTE
—From a Portrait taken in 1872

"ARGONAUT EDITION" OF
THE WORKS OF BRET HARTE

MRS. SKAGGS'S HUSBANDS

BY

BRET HARTE

ILLUSTRATED

VIGILANS ET AUDAX

P. F. COLLIER & SON
NEW YORK

813
H25

3772

CONTENTS.

LEGENDS AND TALES.

MRS. SKAGGS'S HUSBANDS.

PART I. — WEST.

THE sun was rising in the foot-hills. But for an hour the black mass of Sierra eastward of Angel's had been outlined with fire, and the conventional morning had come two hours before with the down coach from Placerville. The dry, cold, dewless California night still lingered in the long cañons and folded skirts of Table Mountain. Even on the mountain road the air was still sharp, and that urgent necessity for something to keep out the chill, which sent the barkeeper sleepily among his bottles and wineglasses at the station, obtained all along the road.

Perhaps it might be said that the first stir of life was in the bar-rooms. A few birds twittered in the sycamores at the roadside, but long before that glasses had clicked and bottles gurgled in the saloon of the Mansion House. This was still lit by a dissipated-looking hanging-lamp, which was evidently the worse for having been up all night, and bore a singular resemblance to a faded reveller of Angel's, who even then sputtered and flickered in *his* socket in an arm-chair below it, — a resem-

blance so plain that when the first level sunbeam
pierced the window-pane, the barkeeper, moved
by a sentiment of consistency and compassion, put
them both out together.

Then the sun came up haughtily. When it had
passed the eastern ridge it began, after its habit,
to lord it over Angel's, sending the thermometer
up twenty degrees in as many minutes, driving the
mules to the sparse shade of corrals and fences,
making the red dust incandescent, and renewing
its old imperious aggression on the spiked bosses
of the convex shield of pines that defended Table
Mountain. Thither by nine o'clock all coolness
had retreated, and the "outsides" of the up stage
plunged their hot faces in its aromatic shadows as
in water.

It was the custom of the driver of the Wingdam
coach to whip up his horses and enter Angel's at
that remarkable pace which the woodcuts in the
hotel bar-room represented to credulous humanity
as the usual rate of speed of that conveyance. At
such times the habitual expression of disdainful
reticence and lazy official severity which he wore
on the box became intensified as the loungers
gathered about the vehicle, and only the boldest
ventured to address him. It was the Hon. Judge
Beeswinger, Member of Assembly, who to-day
presumed, perhaps rashly, on the strength of his
official position.

"Any political news from below, Bill?" he asked, as the latter slowly descended from his lofty perch, without, however, any perceptible coming down of mien or manner.

"Not much," said Bill, with deliberate gravity. "The President o' the United States hez n't bin hisself sens you refoosed that seat in the Cabinet. The ginral feelin' in perlitical circles is one o' regret."

Irony, even of this outrageous quality, was too common in Angel's to excite either a smile or a frown. Bill slowly entered the bar-room during a dry, dead silence, in which only a faint spirit of emulation survived.

"Ye did n't bring up that agint o' Rothschild's this trip?" asked the barkeeper, slowly, by way of vague contribution to the prevailing tone of conversation.

"No," responded Bill, with thoughtful exactitude. "He said he could n't look inter that claim o' Johnson's without first consultin' the Bank o' England."

The Mr. Johnson here alluded to being present as the faded reveller the barkeeper had lately put out, and as the alleged claim notoriously possessed no attractions whatever to capitalists, expectation naturally looked to him for some response to this evident challenge. He did so by simply stating that he would "take sugar" in his, and by walking un-

steadily toward the bar, as if accepting a festive
invitation.   To the credit of Bill be it recorded
that he did not attempt to correct the mistake, but
gravely touched glasses with him, and after saying
" Here 's another nail in your coffin," — a cheerful
sentiment, to which " And the hair all off your
head," was playfully added by the others, — he
threw off his liquor with a single dexterous movement of head and elbow, and stood refreshed.

" Hello, old major !" said Bill, suddenly setting
down his glass.   " Are *you* there ? "

It was a boy, who, becoming bashfully conscious that this epithet was addressed to him, retreated sideways to the doorway, where he stood
beating his hat against the door-post with an
assumption of indifference that his downcast but
mirthful dark eyes and reddening cheek scarcely
bore out.   Perhaps it was owing to his size, perhaps
it was to a certain cherubic outline of face and figure, perhaps to a peculiar trustfulness of expression,
that he did not look half his age, which was really
fourteen.

Everybody in Angel's knew the boy.   Either
under the venerable title bestowed by Bill, or as
"Tom Islington," after his adopted father, his was
a familiar presence in the settlement, and the
theme of much local criticism and comment.   His
waywardness, indolence, and unaccountable amiability — a quality at once suspicious and gratui-

tous in a pioneer community like Angel's — had often been the subject of fierce discussion. A large and reputable majority believed him destined for the gallows; a minority not quite so reputable enjoyed his presence without troubling themselves much about his future; to one or two the evil predictions of the majority possessed neither novelty nor terror.

"Anything for me, Bill?" asked the boy, half mechanically, with the air of repeating some jocular formulary perfectly understood by Bill.

"Anythin' for you!" echoed Bill, with an overacted severity equally well understood by Tommy, — "anythin' for you? No! And it's my opinion there won't be anythin' for you ez long ez you hang around bar-rooms and spend your valooable time with loafers and bummers. Git!"

The reproof was accompanied by a suitable exaggeration of gesture (Bill had seized a decanter) before which the boy retreated still good-humoredly Bill followed him to the door. "Dern my skin, if he hez n't gone off with that bummer Johnson," he added, as he looked down the road.

"What's he expectin', Bill?" asked the barkeeper.

"A letter from his aunt. Reckon he'll hev to take it out in expectin'. Likely they're glad to get shut o' him."

" "He's leadin' a shiftless, idle life here," interposed the Member of Assembly.

"Well," said Bill, who never allowed any one
but himself to abuse his *protégé*, "seein' he ain't
expectin' no offis from the hands of an enlightened
constitooency, it *is* rayther a shiftless life." After
delivering this Parthian arrow with a gratuitous
twanging of the bow to indicate its offensive
personality, Bill winked at the barkeeper, slowly
resumed a pair of immense, bulgy buckskin
gloves, which gave his fingers the appearance
of being painfully sore and bandaged, strode to
the door without looking at anybody, called
out, "All aboard," with a perfunctory air of su-
preme indifference whether the invitation was
heeded, remounted his box, and drove stolidly
away.

Perhaps it was well that he did so, for the conversation at once assumed a disrespectful attitude
toward Tom and his relatives. It was more than
intimated that Tom's alleged aunt was none other
than Tom's real mother, while it was also asserted
that Tom's alleged uncle did not himself participate in this intimate relationship to the boy to an
extent which the fastidious taste of Angel's deemed
moral and necessary. Popular opinion also believed that Islington, the adopted father, who received a certain stipend ostensibly for the boy's
support, retained it as a reward for his reticence
regarding these facts. "He ain't ruinin' hisself
by wastin' it on Tom," said the barkeeper, who

possibly possessed positive knowledge of much
of Islington's disbursements.   But at this point
exhausted nature languished among some of the
debaters, and he turned from the frivolity of conversation to his severer professional duties.

It was also well that Bill's momentary attitude
of didactic propriety was not further excited by
the subsequent conduct of his *protégé*.   For by
this time Tom, half supporting the unstable Johnson, who developed a tendency to occasionally dash
across the glaring road, but checked himself mid
way each time, reached the corral which adjoined
the Mansion House.   At its farther extremity was
a pump and horse-trough.   Here, without a word
being spoken, but evidently in obedience to some
habitual custom, Tom led his companion.   With
the boy's assistance, Johnson removed his coat and
neckcloth, turned back the collar of his shirt, and
gravely placed his head beneath the pump-spout.
With equal gravity and deliberation, Tom took his
place at the handle.   For a few moments only the
splashing of water and regular strokes of the pump
broke the solemnly ludicrous silence.   Then there
was a pause in which Johnson put his hands to
his dripping head, felt of it critically as if it belonged to somebody else, and raised his eyes to his
companion.   "That ought to fetch *it*," said Tom,
in answer to the look.   "Ef it don't," replied Johnson, doggedly, with an air of relieving himself of

all further responsibility in the matter, " it 's got to, thet 's all ! "

If " it " referred to some change in the physiognomy of Johnson, "it" had probably been " fetched " by the process just indicated. The head that went under the pump was large, and clothed with bushy, uncertain-colored hair ; the face was flushed, puffy, and expressionless, the eyes injected and full. The head that came out from under the pump was of smaller size and different shape, the hair straight, dark, and sleek, the face pale and hollow-cheeked, the eyes bright and restless. In the haggard, nervous ascetic that rose from the horse-trough there was very little trace of the Bacchus that had bowed there a moment before. Familiar as Tom must have been with the spectacle, he could not help looking inquiringly at the trough, as if expecting to see some traces of the previous Johnson in its shallow depths.

A narrow strip of willow, alder, and buckeye — a mere dusty, ravelled fringe of the green mantle that swept the high shoulders of Table Mountain — lapped the edge of the corral. The silent pair were quick to avail themselves of even its scant shelter from the overpowering sun. They had not proceeded far, before Johnson, who was walking quite rapidly in advance, suddenly brought himself up, and turned to his companion with an interrogative " Eh ? "

"I did n't speak," said Tommy, quietly.

"Who said you spoke?" said Johnson, with a quick look of cunning. "In course you did n't speak, and I did n't speak, neither. Nobody spoke. Wot makes you think you spoke?" he continued, peering curiously into Tommy's eyes.

The smile which habitually shone there quickly vanished as the boy stepped quietly to his companion's side, and took his arm without a word.

"In course you did n't speak, Tommy," said Johnson, deprecatingly. "You ain't a boy to go for to play an ole soaker like me. That 's wot I like you for. Thet 's wot I seed in you from the first. I sez, 'Thet 'ere boy ain't goin' to play you, Johnson! You can go your whole pile on him, when you can't trust even a bar-keep.' Thet 's wot I said. Eh?"

This time Tommy prudently took no notice of the interrogation, and Johnson went on: "Ef I was to ask you another question, you would n't go to play me neither, — would you, Tommy?"

"No," said the boy.

"Ef I was to ask you," continued Johnson, without hooding the reply, but with a growing anxiety of eye and a nervous twitching of his lips, — "ef I was to ask you, fur instance, ef that was a jackass rabbit thet jest passed, — eh? — you 'd say it was or was not, cz the case may be. You would n't play the ole man on thet?"

"No," said Tommy, quietly, "it *was* a jackass rabbit."

"Ef I was to ask you," continued Johnson, " ef it wore, say, fur instance, a green hat with yaller ribbons, you would n't play me, and say it did, onless," — he added, with intensified cunning, — "onless it *did ?* "

"No," said Tommy, "of course I would n't; but then, you see, *it did.*"

"It did ?"

"It did !" repeated Tommy, stoutly; "a green hat with yellow ribbons — and — and — a red rosette."

"I did n't get to see the ros-ette," said Johnson, with slow and conscientious deliberation, yet with an evident sense of relief; "but that ain't sayin' it warn't there, you know. Eh ? "

Tommy glanced quietly at his companion. There were great beads of perspiration on his ashen-gray forehead and on the ends of his lank hair; the hand which twitched spasmodically in his was cold and clammy, the other, which was free, had a vague, purposeless, jerky activity, as if attached to some deranged mechanism. Without any apparent concern in these phenomena, Tommy halted, and, seating himself on a log, motioned his companion to a place beside him. Johnson obeyed without a word. Slight as was the act, perhaps no other incident of their singular companionship indicated as completely the dominance of this careless, half-effeminate, but self-possessed boy over this doggedly self-willed, abnormally excited man.

"It ain't the square thing," said Johnson, after a pause, with a laugh that was neither mirthful nor musical, and frightened away a lizard that had been regarding the pair with breathless suspense, — "it ain't the square thing for jackass rabbits to wear hats, Tommy, — is it, eh?"

"Well," said Tommy, with unmoved composure, "sometimes they do and sometimes they don't. Animals are mighty queer." And here Tommy went off in an animated, but, I regret to say, utterly untruthful and untrustworthy account of the habits of California fauna, until he was interrupted by Johnson.

"And snakes, eh, Tommy?" said the man, with an abstracted air, gazing intently on the ground before him.

"And snakes," said Tommy; "but they don't bite, — at least not that kind you see. There! — don't move, Uncle Ben, don't move; they're gone now. And it's about time you took your dose."

Johnson had hurriedly risen as if to leap upon the log, but Tommy had as quickly caught his arm with one hand while he drew a bottle from his pocket with the other. Johnson paused, and eyed the bottle. "Ef you say so, my boy," he

faltered, as his fingers closed nervously around it;
" say ' when,' then." He raised the bottle to his
lips and took a long draught, the boy regarding
him critically. "When," said Tommy, suddenly.
Johnson started, flushed, and returned the bottle
quickly. But the color that had risen to his cheek
stayed there, his eye grew less restless, and as they
moved away again, the hand that rested on Tommy's shoulder was steadier.

Their way lay along the flank of Table Mountain, — a wandering trail through a tangled soli-
tude that might have seemed virgin and unbroken
but for a few oyster-cans, yeast-powder tins, and
empty bottles that had been apparently stranded
by the " first low wash " of pioneer waves. On
the ragged trunk of an enormous pine hung a few
tufts of gray hair caught from a passing grizzly,
but in strange juxtaposition at its foot lay an
empty bottle of incomparable bitters, — the *chef-
d'œuvre* of a hygienic civilization, and blazoned
with the arms of an all-healing republic. The
head of a rattlesnake peered from a case that had
contained tobacco, which was still brightly pla-
carded with the high-colored effigy of a popular
danseuse. And a little beyond this the soil was
broken and fissured, there was a confused mass of
roughly hewn timber, a straggling line of sluicing,
a heap of gravel and dirt, a rude cabin, and the
claim of Johnson.

Except for the rudest purposes of shelter from rain and cold, the cabin possessed but little advantage over the simple savagery of surrounding nature. It had all the practical directness of the habitation of some animal, without its comfort or picturesque quality; the very birds that haunted it for food must have felt their own superiority as architects. It was inconceivably dirty, even with its scant capacity for accretion; it was singularly stale, even in its newness and freshness of material. Unspeakably dreary as it was in shadow, the sunlight visited it in a blind, aching, purposeless way, as if despairing of mellowing its outlines or of even tanning it into color.

The claim worked by Johnson in his intervals of sobriety was represented by half a dozen rude openings in the mountain-side, with the heaped-up *débris* of rock and gravel before the mouth of each. They gave very little evidence of engineering skill or constructive purpose, or indeed showed anything but the vague, successively abandoned essays of their projector. To-day they served another purpose, for as the sun had heated the little cabin almost to the point of combustion, curling up the long dry shingles, and starting aromatic tears from the green pine beams, Tommy led Johnson into one of the larger openings, and with a sense of satisfaction threw himself panting upon its rocky floor. Here and there the grateful dampness was condensed in quiet pools of water, or in a monotonous and soothing drip from the rocks above. Without lay the staring sunlight, — colorless, clarified, intense.

For a few moments they lay resting on their elbows in blissful contemplation of the heat they had escaped. "Wot do you say," said Johnson, slowly, without looking at his companion, but abstractly addressing himself to the landscape beyond, — "wot do you say to two straight games fur one thousand dollars ? "

"Make it five thousand," replied Tommy, reflectively, also to the landscape, "and I 'm in."

"Wot do I owe you now ? " said Johnson, after a lengthened silence.

"One hundred and seventy-five thousand two hundred and fifty dollars," replied Tommy, with business-like gravity.

"Well," said Johnson, after a deliberation commensurate with the magnitude of the transaction, "ef you win, call it a hundred and eighty thousand, round. War 's the keerds ? "

They were in an old tin box in a crevice of a rock above his head. They were greasy and worn with service. Johnson dealt, albeit his right hand was still uncertain, — hovering, after dropping the cards, aimlessly about Tommy, and being only recalled by a strong nervous effort. Yet, notwithstanding this incapacity for even honest manipulation, Mr. Johnson covertly turned a knave from the bottom of the pack with such shameless inefficiency and gratuitous unskilfulness, that even Tommy was obliged to cough and look elsewhere to hide his embarrassment. Possibly for this reason the young gentleman was himself constrained, by way of correction, to add a valuable card to his own hand, over and above the number he legitimately held.

Nevertheless, the game was unexciting, and dragged listlessly. Johnson won. He recorded the fact and the amount with a stub of pencil and shaking fingers in wandering hieroglyphics all over a pocket diary. Then there was a long pause, when Johnson slowly drew something from his pocket, and held it up before his companion. It was apparently a dull red stone.

" Ef," said Johnson, slowly, with his old look of simple cunning, — " ef you happened to pick up sich a rock ez that, Tommy, what might you say it was ?"

" Don't know," said Tommy.

" Might n't you say," continued Johnson, cautiously, " that it was gold, or silver ?"

" Neither," said Tommy, promptly.

" Might n't you say it was quicksilver ? Might n't you say that ef thar was a friend o' yourn ez knew war to go and turn out ten ton of it a day, and every ton worth two thousand dollars, that he had a soft thing, a very soft thing, — allowin', Tommy, that you used sich language, which you don't?"

"But," said the boy, coming to the point with great directness, "*do* you know where to get it? have you struck it, Uncle Ben?"

Johnson looked carefully around. "I hev, Tommy. Listen. I know whar thar's cartloads of it. But thar's only one other specimen — the mate to this yer — thet's above ground, and thet's in 'Frisco. Thar's an agint comin' up in a day or two to look into it. I sent for him. Eh?"

His bright, restless eyes were concentrated on Tommy's face now, but the boy showed neither surprise nor interest. Least of all did he betray any recollection of Bill's ironical and gratuitous corroboration of this part of the story.

"Nobody knows it," continued Johnson, in a nervous whisper, — "nobody knows it but you and the agint in 'Frisco. The boys workin' round yar passes by and sees the old man grubbin' away, and no signs o' color, not even rotten quartz; the boys loafin' round the Mansion House sees the old man lyin' round free in bar-rooms, and they laughs and sez, 'Played out,' and spects nothin'. Maybe ye think they spects suthin now, eh?" queried Johnson, suddenly, with a sharp look of suspicion.

Tommy looked up, shook his head, threw a stone at a passing rabbit, but did not reply.

"When I fust set eyes on you, Tommy," contin-

ued Johnson, apparently reassured, "the fust day
you kem and pumped for me, an entire stranger,
and hevin no call to do it, I sez, 'Johnson, Johnson,' sez I, 'yer 's a boy you kin trust. Yer 's a boy
that won't play you; yer 's a chap that 's white
and square,' — white and square, Tommy: them 's
the very words I used."

He paused for a moment, and then went on in
a confidential whisper, " ' You want capital, Johnson,' sez I, 'to develop your resources, and you
want a pardner. Capital you can send for, but
your pardner, Johnson, — your pardner is right
yer. And his name, it is Tommy Islington.'
Them 's the very words I used."

He stopped and chafed his clammy hands upon
his knees. " It 's six months ago sens I made you
my pardner. Thar ain't a lick I 've struck sens
then, Tommy, thar ain't a han'ful o' yearth I 've
washed, thar ain't a shovelful o' rock I 've turned
over, but I tho't o' you. 'Share, and share alike,'
sez I. When I wrote to my agint, I wrote ekal
for my pardner, Tommy Islington, he hevin no
call to know ef the same was man or boy."

He had moved nearer the boy, and would perhaps have laid his hand caressingly upon him, but
even in his manifest affection there was a singular
element of awed restraint and even fear, — a suggestion of something withheld even his fullest confidences, a hopeless perception of some vague bar-

rier that never could be surmounted. He may have been at times dimly conscious that, in the eyes which Tommy raised to his, there was thorough intellectual appreciation, critical good-humor, even feminine softness, but nothing more. His nervousness somewhat heightened by his embarrassment, he went on with an attempt at calmness which his twitching white lips and unsteady fingers made pathetically grotesque. " Thar's a bill o' sale in my bunk, made out accordin' to law, of an ekal ondivided half of the claim, and the consideration is two hundred and fifty thousand dollars, — gambling debts, — gambling debts from me to you, Tommy, — you understand ? " — nothing could exceed the intense cunning of his eye at this moment, — " and then thar's a will."

" A will ? " said Tommy, in amused surprise.

Johnson looked frightened.

" Eh ? " he said, hurriedly, " wot will ? Who said anythin' 'bout a will, Tommy ? "

" Nobody," replied Tommy, with unblushing calm.

Johnson passed his hand over his cold forehead, wrung the damp ends of his hair with his fingers, and went on : " Times when I 'm took bad ez I was to-day, the boys about yer sez — you sez, maybe, Tommy — it 's whiskey. It ain't, Tommy. It 's pizen, — quicksilver pizen. That 's what 's the matter with me. I 'm salviated ! Salviated with merkery.

"I 've heerd o' it before," continued Johnson, appealing to the boy, "and ez a boy o' permiskus reading, I reckon you hev too. Them men as works in cinnabar sooner or later gets salviated. It 's bound to fetch 'em some time. Salviated by merkery."

"What are you goin' to do for it?" asked Tommy.

"When the agint comes up, and I begins to realize on this yer mine," said Johnson, contemplatively, "I goes to New York. I sez to the barkeep' o' the hotel, 'Show me the biggest doctor here.' He shows me. I sez to him, 'Salviated by merkery, — a year's standin', — how much?' He sez, 'Five thousand dollars, and take two o' these pills at bedtime, and an ekil number o' powders at meals, and come back in a week.' And I goes back in a week, cured, and signs a certifikit to that effect."

Encouraged by a look of interest in Tommy's eye, he went on.

"So I gets cured. I goes to the barkeep', and I sez, 'Show me the biggest, fashionblest house thet 's for sale yer.' And he sez, 'The biggest, nat'rally b'longs to John Jacob Astor.' And I sez, 'Show him,' and he shows him. And I sez, 'Wot might you ask for this yer house?' And he looks at me scornful, and sez, 'Go 'way, old man; you must be sick.' And I fetches him one over

the left eye, and he apologizes, and I gives him
his own price for the house. I stocks that house
with mohogany furniture and pervisions, and thar
we lives, — you and me, Tommy, you and me!"

The sun no longer shone upon the hillside. The
shadows of the pines were beginning to creep over
Johnson's claim, and the air within the cavern
was growing chill. In the gathering darkness
his eyes shone brightly as he went on: "Then
thar comes a day when we gives a big spread.
We invites govners, members o' Congress, gentlemen o' fashion, and the like. And among
'em I invites a Man as holds his head very high,
a Man I once knew; but he does n't know I
knows him, and he does n't remember me. And
he comes and he sits opposite me, and I watches
him. And he 's very airy, this Man, and very
chipper, and he wipes his mouth with a white
hankercher, and he smiles, and he ketches my eye.
And he sez, 'A glass o' wine with you, Mr. Johnson'; and he fills his glass and I fills mine, and
we rises. And I heaves that wine, glass and all,
right into his damned grinnin' face. And he
jumps for me, — for he is very game, this Man,
very game, — but some on 'em grabs him, and he
sez, 'Who be you?' And I sez, 'Skaggs! damn
you, Skaggs! Look at me! Gimme back my
wife and child, gimme back the money you stole,
gimme back the good name you took away, gimme

back the health you ruined, gimme back the last
twelve years! Give 'em to me, damn you, quick,
before I cuts your heart out!' And naterally,
Tommy, he can't do it. And so I cuts his heart
out, my boy; I cuts his heart out."

The purely animal fury of his eye suddenly
changed again to cunning. "You think they
hangs me for it, Tommy, but they don't. Not
much, Tommy. I goes to the biggest lawyer there,
and I says to him, 'Salviated by merkery,— you
hear me, — salviated by merkery.' And he winks
at me, and he goes to the judge, and he sez, 'This
yer unfortnet man is n't responsible, — he 's been
salviated by merkery.' And he brings witnesses;
you comes, Tommy, and you sez ez how you 've
seen me took bad afore; and the doctor, he comes,
and he sez as how he 's seen me frightful; and
the jury, without leavin' their seats, brings in a
verdict o' justifiable insanity, — salviated by merkery."

In the excitement of his climax he had risen to
his feet, but would have fallen had not Tommy
caught him and led him into the open air. In
this sharper light there was an odd change visible
in his yellow-white face, — a change which caused
Tommy to hurriedly support him, half leading, half
dragging him toward the little cabin. When they
had reached it, Tommy placed him on a rude
"bunk," or shelf, and stood for a moment in anx-

ious contemplation of the tremor-stricken man before him. Then he said rapidly: "Listen, Uncle
Ben. I'm goin' to town — to town, you understand — for the doctor. You're not to get up
or move on any account until I return. Do you
hear?" Johnson nodded violently. "I'll be back
in two hours." In another moment he was gone.

For an hour Johnson kept his word. Then he
suddenly sat up, and began to gaze fixedly at a
corner of the cabin. From gazing at it he began
to smile, from smiling at it he began to talk, from
talking at it he began to scream, from screaming
he passed to cursing and sobbing wildly. Then
he lay quiet again.

He was so still that to merely human eyes he
might have seemed asleep or dead. But a squirrel, that, emboldened by the stillness, had entered
from the roof, stopped short upon a beam above
the bunk, for he saw that the man's foot was
slowly and cautiously moving toward the floor,
and that the man's eyes were as intent and watchful as his own. Presently, still without a sound,
both feet were upon the floor. And then the
bunk creaked, and the squirrel whisked into the
eaves of the roof. When he peered forth again,
everything was quiet, and the man was gone.

An hour later two muleteers on the Placerville
Road passed a man with dishevelled hair, glaring,
bloodshot eyes, and clothes torn with bramble and

stained with the red dust of the mountain. They pursued him, when he turned fiercely on the foremost, wrested a pistol from his grasp, and broke away. Later still, when the sun had dropped behind Payne's Ridge, the underbrush on Deadwood Slope crackled with a stealthy but continuous tread. It must have been an animal whose dimly outlined bulk, in the gathering darkness, showed here and there in vague but incessant motion; it could be nothing but an animal whose utterance was at once so incoherent, monotonous, and unremitting. Yet, when the sound came nearer, and the chaparral was parted, it seemed to be a man, and that man Johnson.

Above the baying of phantasmal hounds that pressed him hard and drove him on, with never rest or mercy; above the lashing of a spectral whip that curled about his limbs, sang in his ears, and continually stung him forward; above the outcries of the unclean shapes that thronged about him, — he could still distinguish one real sound, — the rush and sweep of hurrying waters. The Stanislaus River! A thousand feet below him drove its yellowing current. Through all the vacillations of his unseated mind he had clung to one idea, — to reach the river, to lave in it, to swim it if need be, but to put it forever between him and the harrying shapes, to drown forever in its turbid depths the thronging spectres, to wash away in its yellow flood all stains and color of the past. And now he was leaping from boulder to boulder, from blackened stump to stump, from gnarled bush to bush, caught for a moment and withheld by cling-ing vines, or plunging downward into dusty hollows, until, rolling, dropping, sliding, and stumbling, he reached the river-bank, whereon he fell, rose, stag-gered forward, and fell again with outstretched arms upon a rock that breasted the swift current. And there he lay as dead.

A few stars came out hesitatingly above Dead-wood Slope. A cold wind that had sprung up with the going down of the sun fanned them into momentary brightness, swept the heated flanks of the mountain, and ruffled the river. Where the fallen man lay there was a sharp curve in the stream, so that in the gathering shadows the rush-ing water seemed to leap out of the darkness and to vanish again. Decayed drift-wood, trunks of trees, fragments of broken sluicing, — the wash and waste of many a mile, — swept into sight a moment, and were gone. All of decay, wreck, and foulness gathered in the long circuit of mining-camp and settlement, all the dregs and refuse of a crude and wanton civilization, reappeared for an instant, and then were hurried away in the darkness and lost. No wonder that as the wind ruffled the yellow waters the waves seemed to lift their unclean hands toward the rock whereon the fallen man lay, as if eager to snatch him from it, too, and hurry him toward the sea.

It was very still. In the clear air a horn blown a mile away was heard distinctly. The jingling of a spur and a laugh on the highway over Payne's Ridge sounded clearly across the river. The rattling of harness and hoofs foretold for many minutes the approach of the Wingdam coach, that at last, with flashing lights, passed within a few feet of the rock. Then for an hour all again was quiet. Presently the moon, round and full, lifted herself above the serried ridge and looked down upon the river. At first the bared peak of Deadwood Hill gleamed white and skull-like. Then the shadows of Payne's Ridge cast on the slope slowly sank away, leaving the unshapely stumps, the dusty fissures, and clinging outcrop of Deadwood Slope to stand out in black and silver. Still stealing softly downward, the moonlight touched the bank and the rock, and then glittered brightly on the river. The rock was bare and the man was gone, but the river still hurried swiftly to the sea.

"Is there anything for me?" asked Tommy Islington, as, a week after, the stage drew up at the Mansion House, and Bill slowly entered the barroom. Bill did not reply, but, turning to a stranger who had entered with him, indicated with a jerk of his finger the boy. The stranger turned with an air half of business, half of curiosity, and looked critically at Tommy. "Is there anything for me?" repeated Tommy, a little confused at the silence and scrutiny. Bill walked deliberately to the bar, and, placing his back against it, faced Tommy with a look of demure enjoyment.

"Ef," he remarked slowly, — "ef a hundred thousand dollars down and half a million in perspektive is ennything, Major, THERE IS!"

MRS. SKAGGS'S HUSBANDS.

IT was characteristic of Angel's that the disappearance of Johnson, and the fact that he had left his entire property to Tommy, thrilled the community but slightly in comparison with the astounding discovery that he had anything to leave. The finding of a cinnabar lode at Angel's absorbed all collateral facts or subsequent details. Prospectors from adjoining camps thronged the settlement; the hillside for a mile on either side of Johnson's claim was staked out and pre-empted; trade received a sudden stimulus; and, in the excited rhetoric of the "Weekly Record," "a new era had broken upon Angel's." "On Thursday last," added that paper, "over five hundred dollars was taken in over the bar of the Mansion House."

Of the fate of Johnson there was little doubt. He had been last seen lying on a boulder on the river-bank by outside passengers of the Wingdam night coach, and when Finn of Robinson's Ferry admitted to have fired three shots from a revolver at a dark object struggling in the water near the ferry, which he "suspicioned" to be a bear, the

question seemed to be settled. Whatever might
have been the fallibility of his judgment, of the
accuracy of his aim there could be no doubt. The
general belief that Johnson, after possessing himself of the muleteer's pistol, could have run amuck,
gave a certain retributive justice to this story, which
rendered it acceptable to the camp.

It was also characteristic of Angel's that no
feeling of envy or opposition to the good fortune
of Tommy Islington prevailed there. That he was
thoroughly cognizant, from the first, of Johnson's
discovery, that his attentions to him were interested,
calculating, and speculative was, however, the general belief of the majority, — a belief that, singularly enough, awakened the first feelings of genuine
respect for Tommy ever shown by the camp. "He
ain't no fool; Yuba Bill seed thet from the first,"
said the barkeeper. It was Yuba Bill who applied
for the guardianship of Tommy after his accession
to Johnson's claim, and on whose bonds the richest
men of Calaveras were represented. It was Yuba
Bill, also, when Tommy was sent East to finish his
education, accompanied him to San Francisco, and,
before parting with his charge on the steamer's
deck, drew him aside, and said, "Ef at enny time
you want enny money, Tommy, over and 'bove your
'lowance, you kin write; but ef you 'll take my
advice," he added, with a sudden huskiness mitigat-
ing the severity of his voice, " you 'll forget every

derned ole spavined, string-halted bummer as you
ever met or knew at Angel's, — ev'ry one, Tommy,
— ev'ry one ! And so— boy — take care of yourself — and —and — God bless ye, and pertikerly
d—n me for a first-class A 1 fool." It was
Yuba Bill, also, after this speech, glared savagely
around, walked down the crowded gang-plank
with a rigid and aggressive shoulder, picked a
quarrel with his cabman, and, after bundling that
functionary into his own vehicle, took the reins
himself, and drove furiously to his hotel. " It cost
me," said Bill, recounting the occurrence somewhat
later at Angel's, — " it cost me a matter o' twenty
dollars afore the jedge the next mornin' ; but you
kin bet high thet I taught them 'Frisco chaps
suthin new about drivin'. I did n't make it lively
in Montgomery Street for about ten minutes, —
O no ! "

And so by degrees the two original locaters of
the great Cinnabar Lode faded from the memory
of Angel's, and Calaveras knew them no more. In
five years their very names had been forgotten ;
in seven the name of the town was changed ; in
ten the town itself was transported bodily to the
hillside, and the chimney of the Union Smelting
Works by night flickered like a corpse-light over
the site of Johnson's cabin, and by day poisoned
the pure spices of the pines. Even the Mansion
House was dismantled, and the Wingdam stage

deserted the highway for a shorter cut by Quicksilver City. Only the bared crest of Deadwood
Hill, as of old, sharply cut the clear blue sky, and
at its base, as of old, the Stanislaus River, un-
wearied and unresting, babbled, whispered, and
hurried away to the sea.

A midsummer's day was breaking lazily on the
Atlantic. There was not wind enough to move
the vapors in the foggy offing, but where the vague
distance heaved against a violet sky there were
dull red streaks that, growing brighter, presently
painted out the stars. Soon the brown rocks of
Greyport appeared faintly suffused, and then the
whole ashen line of dead coast was kindled, and
the lighthouse beacons went out one by one.
And then a hundred sail, before invisible, started
out of the vapory horizon, and pressed toward the
shore. It was morning, indeed, and some of the
best society in Greyport, having been up all night,
were thinking it was time to go to bed.

For as the sky flashed brighter it fired the clus-
tering red roofs of a picturesque house by the sands
that had all that night, from open lattice and illu-
minated balcony, given light and music to the
shore. It glittered on the broad crystal spaces of
a great conservatory that looked upon an exquisite
lawn, where all night long the blended odors of
sea and shore had swooned under the summer
v. 17—A—Bret Harte

moon. But it wrought confusion among the
colored lamps on the long veranda, and startled
a group of ladies and gentlemen who had stepped
from the drawing-room window to gaze upon it.
It was so searching and sincere in its way, that, as
the carriage of the fairest Miss Gillyflower rolled
away, that peerless young woman, catching sight
of her face in the oval mirror, instantly pulled
down the blinds, and, nestling the whitest shoulders
in Greyport against the crimson cushions, went to
sleep.

"How haggard everybody is! Rose, dear, you
look almost intellectual," said Blanche Masterman.

"I hope not," said Rose, simply. "Sunrises are
very trying. Look how that pink regularly puts
out Mrs. Brown-Robinson, hair and all!"

"The angels," said the Count de Nugat, with a
polite gesture toward the sky, "must have find
these celestial combinations very bad for the *toi-
lette.*"

"They 're safe in white, — except when they sit
for their pictures in Venice," said Blanche. "How
fresh Mr. Islington looks! It 's really uncomplimentary to us."

"I suppose the sun recognizes in me no rival,"
said the young man, demurely. "But," he added,
"I have lived much in the open air, and require
very little sleep."

"How delightful!" said Mrs. Brown-Robinson,

in a low, enthusiastic voice, and a manner that held
the glowing sentiment of sixteen and the practical
experiences of thirty-two in dangerous combination;
— "how perfectly delightful! What sunrises you
must have seen, and in such wild, romantic places!
How I envy you! My nephew was a classmate
of yours, and has often repeated to me those charming stories you tell of your adventures. Won't
you tell some now? Do! How you must tire of
us and this artificial life here, so frightfully artificial, you know" (in a confidential whisper); "and
then to think of the days when you roamed the
great West with the Indians, and the bisons, and
the grizzly bears! Of course, you have seen grizzly bears and bisons?"

"Of course he has, dear," said Blanche, a little
pettishly, throwing a cloak over her shoulders, and
seizing her *chaperon* by the arm; "his earliest infancy was soothed by bisons, and he proudly points
to the grizzly bear as the playmate of his youth.
Come with me, and I'll tell you all about it. How
good it is of you," she added, *sotto voce*, to Islington,
as he stood by the carriage, — "how perfectly good
it is of you to be like those animals you tell us of,
and not know your full power. Think, with your
experiences and our credulity, what stories you
might tell! And you are going to walk? Good
night, then." A slim, gloved hand was frankly extended from the window, and the next moment the
carriage rolled away.

"Is n't Islington throwing away a chance there?" said Captain Merwin, on the veranda.

"Perhaps he could n't stand my lovely aunt's superadded presence. But then, he's the guest of Blanche's father, and I dare say they see enough of each other as it is."

"But is n't it a rather dangerous situation?"

"For him, perhaps; although he's awfully old, and very queer. For her, with an experience that takes in all the available men in both hemispheres, ending with Nugat over there, I should say a man more or less would n't affect her much, anyway. Of course," he laughed, "these are the accents of bitterness. But that was last year."

Perhaps Islington did not overhear the speaker; perhaps, if he did, the criticism was not new. He turned carelessly away, and sauntered out on the road to the sea. Thence he strolled along the sands toward the cliffs, where, meeting an impediment in the shape of a garden wall, he leaped it with a certain agile, boyish ease and experience, and struck across an open lawn toward the rocks again. The best society of Greyport were not early risers, and the spectacle of a trespasser in an evening dress excited only the criticism of grooms hanging about the stables, or cleanly housemaids on the broad verandas that in Greyport architecture dutifully gave upon the sea. Only once, as he entered the boundaries of Cliffwood Lodge, the famous seat of

Renwyck Masterman, was he aware of suspicious scrutiny; but a slouching figure that vanished quickly in the lodge offered no opposition to his progress. Avoiding the pathway to the lodge, Islington kept along the rocks until, reaching a little promontory and rustic pavilion, he sat down and gazed upon the sea.

And presently an infinite peace stole upon him. Except where the waves lapped lazily the crags below, the vast expanse beyond seemed unbroken by ripple, heaving only in broad ponderable sheets, and rhythmically, as if still in sleep. The air was filled with a luminous haze that caught and held the direct sunbeams. In the deep calm that lay upon the sea, it seemed to Islington that all the tenderness of culture, magic of wealth, and spell of refinement that for years had wrought upon that favored shore had extended its gracious influence even here. What a pampered and caressed old ocean it was; cajoled, flattered, and *fêted* where it lay ! An odd recollection of the turbid Stanislaus hurrying by the ascetic pines, of the grim outlines of Deadwood Hill, swam before his eyes, and made the yellow green of the velvet lawn and graceful foliage seem almost tropical by contrast. And, looking up, a few yards distant he beheld a tall slip of a girl gazing upon the sea, — Blanche Masterman.

She had plucked somewhere a large fan-shaped

leaf, which she held parasol-wise, shading the
blond masses of her hair, and hiding her gray
eyes. She had changed her festal dress, with its
amplitude of flounce and train, for a closely fitting
half-antique habit whose scant outlines would
have been trying to limbs less shapely, but which
prettily accented the graceful curves and sweeping
lines of this Greyport goddess. As Islington rose,
she came toward him with a frankly outstretched
hand and unconstrained manner. Had she observed him first? I don't know.

They sat down together on a rustic seat, Miss
Blanche facing the sea, and shading her eyes with
the leaf.

"I don't really know how long I have been
sitting here," said Islington, "or whether I have
not been actually asleep and dreaming. It seemed
too lovely a morning to go to bed. But you?"

From behind the leaf, it appeared that Miss
Blanche, on retiring, had been pursued by a hideous
winged bug which defied the efforts of herself and
maid to dislodge. Odin, the Spitz dog, had insisted
upon scratching at the door. And it made her
eyes red to sleep in the morning. And she had
an early call to make. And the sea looked
lovely.

"I'm glad to find you here, whatever be the
cause," said Islington, with his old directness.
"To-day, as you know, is my last day in Greyport,

and it is much pleasanter to say good by under this blue sky than even beneath your father's wonderful frescos yonder I want to remember you, too, as part of this pleasant prospect which belongs to us all, rather than recall you in anybody's particular setting."

"I know," said Blanche, with equal directness, "that houses are one of the defects of our civilization; but I don't think I ever heard the idea as elegantly expressed before. Where do you go?"

"I don't know yet. I have several plans. I may go to South America and become president of one of the republics, — I am not particular which. I am rich, but in that part of America which lies outside of Greyport it is necessary for every man to have some work. My friends think I should have some great aim in life, with a capital A. But I was born a vagabond, and a vagabond I shall probably die."

"I don't know anybody in South America," said Blanche, languidly. "There were two girls here last season, but they did n't wear stays in the house, and their white frocks never were properly done up. If you go to South America, you must write to me."

"I will. Can you tell me the name of this flower which I found in your greenhouse. It looks much like a California blossom."

"Perhaps it is. Father bought it of a half-crazy

old man who came here one day. Do you know him?"

Islington laughed. "I am afraid not. But let me present this in a less business-like fashion."

"Thank you. Remind me to give you one in return before you go, — or will you choose yourself?"

They had both risen as by a common instinct.

"Good by."

The cool flower-like hand lay in his for an instant.

"Will you oblige me by putting aside that leaf a moment before I go?"

"But my eyes are red, and I look like a perfect fright."

Yet, after a long pause, the leaf fluttered down, and a pair of very beautiful but withal very clear and critical eyes met his. Islington was constrained to look away. When he turned again, she was gone.

"Mister Hislington, — sir!"

It was Chalker, the English groom, out of breath with running.

"Seein' you alone, sir, — beg your pardon, sir, — but there's a person — "

"A person! what the devil do you mean? Speak English — no, damn it, I mean don't," said Islington, snappishly.

"I sed a person, sir. Beg pardon — no offence — but not a gent, sir. In the lib'ry."

A little amused even through the utter dissat-

isfaction with himself and vague loneliness that had
suddenly come upon him, Islington, as he walked
toward the lodge, asked, " Why is n't he a gent ?

" No gent — beggin' your pardin, sir — 'ud guy
a man in sarvis, sir.   Takes me 'ands so, sir, as I
sits in the rumble at the gate, and puts 'em downd
so, sir, and sez, ' Put 'em in your pocket, young man,
— or is it a road agint you expects to see, that you
'olds hup your 'ands, hand crosses 'em like to that,'
sez he.   ' 'Old 'ard,' sez he, ' on the short curves, or
you 'll bust your precious crust,' sez he.   And hasks
for you, sir.   This way, sir."

They entered the lodge.   Islington hurried down
the long Gothic hall, and opened the library door.

In an arm-chair, in the centre of the room, a
man sat apparently contemplating a large, stiff,
yellow hat with an enormous brim, that was placed
on the floor before him.   His hands rested lightly
between his knees, but one foot was drawn up at
the side of his chair in a peculiar manner.   In the
first glance that Islington gave, the attitude in
some odd, irreconcilable way suggested a brake.
In another moment he dashed across the room, and,
holding out both hands, cried, " Yuba Bill ! "

The man rose, caught Islington by the shoulders,
wheeled him round, hugged him, felt of his ribs
like a good-natured ogre, shook his hands violently, laughed, and then said, somewhat ruefully,
"And how ever did you know me ? "

Seeing that Yuba Bill evidently regarded himself as in some elaborate disguise, Islington laughed, and suggested that it must have been instinct.

" And you ? " said Bill, holding him at arm's length, and surveying him critically, — " you ! — toe think — toe think — a little cuss no higher nor a trace, a boy as I 've flicked outer the road with a whip time in agin, a boy ez never hed much clothes to speak of, turned into a sport ! "

Islington remembered, with a thrill of ludicrous terror, that he still wore his evening dress.

" Turned," continued Yuba Bill, severely, — " turned into a restyourant waiter, — a garsong ! Eh, Alfonse, bring me a patty de foy grass and an omelette, demme ! "

" Dear old chap ! " said Islington, laughing, and trying to put his hand over Bill's bearded mouth, " but you — *you* don't look exactly like yourself ! You 're not well, Bill." And indeed, as he turned toward the light, Bill's eyes appeared cavernous, and his hair and beard thickly streaked with gray.

" Maybe it 's this yer harness," said Bill, a little anxiously. " When I hitches on this yer curb " (he indicated a massive gold watch-chain with enormous links), " and mounts this ' morning star,' " (he pointed to a very large solitaire pin which had the appearance of blistering his whole shirt-front), " it kinder weighs heavy on me, Tommy. Otherwise I'm all right, my boy, — all right." But he evaded Islington's keen eye, and turned from the light.

"You have something to tell me, Bill," said Islington, suddenly, and with almost brusque directness; "out with it."

Bill did not speak, but moved uneasily toward his hat.

"You did n't come three thousand miles, without a word of warning, to talk to me of old times," said Islington, more kindly, "glad as I would have been to see you. It is n't your way, Bill, and you know it. We shall not be disturbed here," he added, in reply to an inquiring glance that Bill directed to the door, " and I am ready to hear you."

"Firstly, then," said Bill, drawing his chair nearer Islington, "answer me one question, Tommy, fair and square, and up and down."

"Go on," said Islington, with a slight smile.

"Ef I should say to you, Tommy, — say to you to-day, right here, you must come with me, — you must leave this place for a month, a year, two years maybe, perhaps forever, — is there anything that 'ud keep you, — anything, my boy, ez you could n't leave?"

"No," said Tommy, quietly; "I am only visiting here. I thought of leaving Greyport to-day."

"But if I should say to you, Tommy, come with me on a *pasear* to Chiny, to Japan, to South Ameriky, p'r'aps, could you go?"

" Yes," said Islington, after a slight pause.

" Thar is n't ennything," said Bill, drawing a little closer, and lowering his voice confidentially, — "ennything in the way of a young woman—you understand, Tommy—ez would keep you ? They 're mighty sweet about here ; and whether a man is young or old, Tommy, there 's always some woman as is brake or whip to him !"

In a certain excited bitterness that character- ized the delivery of this abstract truth, Bill did not see that the young man's face flushed slightly as he answered " No."

" Then listen. It 's seven years ago, Tommy, thet I was working one o' the Pioneer coaches over from Gold Hill. Ez I stood in front o' the stage- office, the sheriff o' the county comes to me, and he sez, 'Bill,' sez he, 'I 've got a looncy chap, as I 'm in charge of, taking 'im down to the 'sylum in Stockton. He 'z quiet and peaceable, but the insides don't like to ride with him. Hev you enny objec- tion to give him a lift on the box beside you ?' I sez, 'No; put him up.' When I came to go and get up on that box beside him, that man, Tommy, —that man sittin' there, quiet and peaceable, was — Johnson !

" He did n't know me, my boy," Yuba Bill con- tinued, rising and putting his hands on Tommy's shoulders, — " he did n't know me. He did n't know nothing about you, nor Angel's, nor the quicksilver

lode, nor even his own name. He said his name
was Skaggs, but I knowd it was Johnson. Thar
was times, Tommy, you might have knocked me
off that box with a feather; thar was times
when if the twenty-seven passengers o' that stage
hed found theirselves swimming in the American
River five hundred feet below the road, I never
could have explained it satisfactorily to the company, — never.

"The sheriff said," Bill continued hastily, as if
to preclude any interruption from the young man,
—"the sheriff said he had been brought into Murphy's Camp three years before, dripping with water, and sufferin' from perkussion of the brain, and
had been cared for generally by the boys 'round.
When I told the sheriff I knowed 'im, I got him
to leave him in my care; and I took him to 'Frisco, Tommy, to 'Frisco, and I put him in charge o'
the best doctors there, and paid his board myself.
There was nothin' he did n't have ez he wanted.
Don't look that way, my dear boy, for God's sake,
don't!"

"O Bill," said Islington, rising and staggering
to the window, "why did you keep this from me?"

"Why?" said Bill, turning on him savagely, —
"why? because I warn't a fool. Thar was you,
winnin' your way in college; thar was *you*, risin'
in the world, and of some account to it; Yer was
an old bummer, ez good ez dead to it, — a man ez

oughter been dead afore! a man ez never denied
it! But you allus liked him better nor me," said
Bill, bitterly.

"Forgive me, Bill," said the young man, seizing
both his hands. "I know you did it for the best;
but go on."

"Thar ain't much more to tell, nor much use to
tell it, as I can see," said Bill, moodily. "He never
could be cured, the doctors said, for he had what
they called monomania, — was always talking
about his wife and darter that somebody had stole
away years ago, and plannin' revenge on that somebody. And six months ago he was missed. I
tracked him to Carson, to Salt Lake City, to Oma-
ha, to Chicago, to New York, — and here!"

"Here!" echoed Islington.

"Here! And that's what brings me here to-day.
Whethers he's crazy or well, whethers he's huntin'
you or lookin' up that other man, you must get
away from here. You must n't see him. You and
me, Tommy, will go away on a cruise. In three
or four years he'll be dead or missing, and then
we'll come back. Come." And he rose to his feet.

"Bill," said Islington, rising also, and taking
the hand of his friend, with the same quiet obsti-
nacy that in the old days had endeared him to
Bill, "wherever he is, here or elsewhere, sane or
crazy, I shall seek and find him. Every dollar
that I have shall be his, every dollar that I have

spent shall be returned to him. I am young yet, thank God, and can work; and if there is a way out of this miserable business, I shall find it."

"I knew," said Bill, with a surliness that ill concealed his evident admiration of the calm figure before him — "I knew the partikler style of d—n fool that you was, and expected no better. Good by, then — God Almighty! who's that?"

He was on his way to the open French window, but had started back, his face quite white and bloodless, and his eyes staring. Islington ran to the window, and looked out. A white skirt vanished around the corner of the veranda. When he returned, Bill had dropped into a chair.

"It must have been Miss Masterman, I think; but what's the matter?"

"Nothing," said Bill, faintly; "have you got any whiskey handy?"

Islington brought a decanter, and, pouring out some spirits, handed the glass to Bill. Bill drained it, and then said, "Who is Miss Masterman?"

"Mr. Masterman's daughter; that is, an adopted daughter, I believe."

"Wot name?"

"I really don't know," said Islington, pettishly, more vexed than he cared to own at this questioning.

Yuba Bill rose and walked to the window,

closed it, walked back again to the door, glanced at Islington, hesitated, and then returned to his chair.

"I did n't tell you I was married, — did I ?" he said suddenly, looking up in Islington's face with an unsuccessful attempt at a reckless laugh.

"No," said Islington, more pained at the manner than the words.

"Fact," said Yuba Bill. "Three years ago it was, Tommy, — three years ago !"

He looked so hard at Islington, that, feeling he was expected to say something, he asked vaguely, "Who did you marry ?"

"Thet's it !" said Yuba Bill; "I can't ezactly say ; partikly, though, a she devil ! generally, the wife of half a dozen other men."

Accustomed, apparently, to have his conjugal infelicities a theme of mirth among men, and seeing no trace of amusement on Islington's grave face, his dogged, reckless manner softened, and, drawing his chair closer to Islington, he went on : "It all began outer this : we was coming down Watson's grade one night pretty free, when the expressman turns to me and sez, 'There 's a row inside, and you 'd better pull up !' I pulls up, and out hops, first a woman, and then two or three chaps swearing and cursin', and tryin' to drag some one arter them. Then it 'pear'd, Tommy, thet it was this woman's drunken husband they was go-

ing to put out for abusin' her, and strikin' her in
the coach; and if it had n't been for me, my boy,
they 'd hev left that chap thar in the road.   But I
fixes matters up by putting her alongside o' me on
the box, and we drove on.   She was very white,
Tommy, — for the matter o' that, she was always
one o' these very white women, that never got red
in the face, — but she never cried a whimper.
Most wimin would have cried.   It was queer, but
she never cried.   I thought so at the time.

"She was very tall, with a lot o' light hair me-
andering down the back of her head, as long as a
deer-skin whip-lash, and about the color.   She
hed eyes thet 'd bore you through at fifty yards,
and pooty hands and feet.   And when she kinder
got out o' that stiff, narvous state she was in, and
warmed up a little, and got chipper, by G—d, sir,
she was handsome, — she was that!"

A little flushed and embarrassed at his own enthusiasm, he stopped, and then said, carelessly,
"They got off at Murphy's."

"Well," said Islington.

"Well, I used to see her often arter thet, and
when she was alone she allus took the box-seat.
She kinder confided her troubles to me, how her
husband got drunk and abused her; and I did n't
see much o' him, for he was away in 'Frisco arter
thet.   But it was all square, Tommy, — all square
'twixt me and her.

"I got a going there a good deal, and then one day I sez to myself, 'Bill, this won't do,' and I got changed to another route. Did you ever know Jackson Filltree, Tommy?" said Bill, breaking off suddenly.

"No."

"Might have heerd of him, p'r'aps?"

"No," said Islington, impatiently.

"Jackson Filltree ran the express from White's out to Summit, 'cross the North Fork of the Yuba. One day he sez to me, 'Bill, that's a mighty bad ford at the North Fork.' I sez, 'I believe you, Jackson.' 'It 'll git me some day, Bill, sure,' sez he. I sez, 'Why don't you take the lower ford?' 'I don't know,' sez he, 'but I can't.' So ever after, when I met him, he sez, 'That North Fork ain't got me yet.' One day I was in Sacramento, and up comes Filltree. He sez, 'I've sold out the express business on account of the North Fork, but it's bound to get me yet, Bill, sure'; and he laughs. Two weeks after they finds his body below the ford, whar he tried to cross, comin' down from the Summit way. Folks said it was foolishness: Tommy, I sez it was Fate! The second day after I was changed to the Placerville route, thet woman comes outer the hotel above the stage-office. Her husband, she said, was lying sick in Placerville; that's what she said; but it was Fate, Tommy, Fate. Three months afterward, her husband takes an overdose of morphine for delirium tremens, and dies. There's folks ez sez she gave it to him, but it's Fate. A year after that I married her, — Fate, Tommy, Fate !

"I lived with her jest three months," he went on, after a long breath, — "three months ! It ain't much time for a happy man. I 've seen a good deal o' hard life in my day, but there was days in that three months longer than any day in my life, — days, Tommy, when it was a toss-up whether I should kill her or she me. But thar, I 'm done. You are a young man, Tommy, and I ain't goin' to tell things thet, old as I am, three years ago I could n't have believed."

When at last, with his grim face turned toward the window, he sat silently with his clinched hands on his knees before him, Islington asked where his wife was now.

"Ask me no more, my boy, — no more. I 've said my say." With a gesture as of throwing down a pair of reins before him, he rose, and walked to the window.

"You kin understand, Tommy, why a little trip around the world 'ud do me good. Ef you can't go with me, well and good. But go I must."

" Not before luncheon, I hope," said a very sweet voice, as Blanche Masterman suddenly stood before them. " Father would never forgive me if in his absence I permitted one of Mr. Islington's friends

to go in this way. You will stay, won't you? Do!
And you will give me your arm now; and when
Mr. Islington has done staring, he will follow us
into the dining-room and introduce you."

"I have quite fallen in love with your friend,"
said Miss Blanche, as they stood in the drawing-
room looking at the figure of Bill, strolling, with
his short pipe in his mouth, through the distant
shrubbery. "He asks very queer questions, though.
He wanted to know my mother's maiden name."

"He is an honest fellow," said Islington, gravely.

"You are very much subdued. You don't
thank me, I dare say, for keeping you and your
friend here; but you could n't go, you know, until
father returned."

Islington smiled, but not very gayly.

"And then I think it much better for us to part
here under these frescos, don't you? Good by."

She extended her long, slim hand.

"Out in the sunlight there, when my eyes
were red, you were very anxious to look at me,"
she added, in a dangerous voice.

Islington raised his sad eyes to hers. Something glittering upon her own sweet lashes trembled and fell.

"Blanche!"

She was rosy enough now, and would have withdrawn her hand, but Islington detained it. She
was not quite certain but that her waist was also

in jeopardy. Yet she could not help saying, " Are
you sure that there is n't anything in the way of
a young woman that would keep you ? "

" Blanche ! " said Islington in reproachful horror.

" If gentlemen will roar out their secrets before
an open window, with a young woman lying on a
sofa on the veranda, reading a stupid French
novel, they must not be surprised if she gives
more attention to them than her book."

" Then you know all, Blanche ? "

" I know," said Blanche, " let 's see — I know
the partiklar style of — ahem ! — fool you was,
and expected no better. Good by." And, gliding
like a lovely and innocent milk snake out of his
grasp, she slipped away.

To the pleasant ripple of waves, the sound of
music and light voices, the yellow midsummer
moon again rose over Greyport. It looked upon
formless masses of rock and shrubbery, wide
spaces of lawn and beach, and a shimmering
expanse of water. It singled out particular objects, — a white sail in shore, a crystal globe upon
the lawn, and flashed upon something held between the teeth of a crouching figure scaling the
low wall of Cliffwood Lodge. Then, as a man
and woman passed out from under the shadows of
the foliage into the open moonlight of the garden
path, the figure leaped from the wall, and stood
erect and waiting in the shadow.

It was the figure of an old man, with rolling
eyes, his trembling hand grasping a long, keen
knife, — a figure more pitiable than pitiless, more
pathetic than terrible.   But the next moment the
knife was stricken from his hand, and he struggled in the firm grasp of another figure that apparently sprang from the wall beside him.

"D—n you, Masterman!" cried the old man,
hoarsely; "give me fair play, and I'll kill you
yet!"

"Which my name is Yuba Bill," said Bill,
quietly, "and it's time this d—n fooling was
stopped."

The old man glared in Bill's face savagely.   "I
know you. You're one of Masterman's friends, —
d—n you, — let me go till I cut his heart out, —
let me go!   Where is my Mary? — where is my
wife? — there she is!   there! — there! — there!
Mary!"   He would have screamed, but Bill
placed his powerful hand upon his mouth, as he
turned in the direction of the old man's glance.
Distinct in the moonlight the figures of Islington
and Blanche, arm in arm, stood out upon the garden path.

"Give me my wife!" muttered the old man
hoarsely, between Bill's fingers.   "Where is she?"

A sudden fury passed over Yuba Bill's face.
"Where is your wife?" he echoed, pressing the old
man back against the garden wall, and holding him

there as in a vice. "Where is your wife?" he repeated, thrusting his grim sardonic jaw and savage
eyes into the old man's frightened face. "Where
is Jack Adam's wife? Where is MY wife? Where
is the she-devil that drove one man mad, that sent
another to hell by his own hand, that eternally
broke and ruined me? Where! Where! Do you
ask where? In jail in Sacramento, — in jail, do you
hear? — in jail for murder, Johnson, — murder!"

The old man gasped, stiffened, and then, relaxing, suddenly slipped, a mere inanimate mass, at
Yuba Bill's feet. With a sudden revulsion of
feeling, Yuba Bill dropped at his side, and, lifting
him tenderly in his arms, whispered, "Look up, old
man, Johnson! look up, for God's sake! — it's me,
— Yuba Bill! and yonder is your daughter, and —
Tommy! — don't you know — Tommy, little Tommy Islington?"

Johnson's eyes slowly opened. He whispered,
"Tommy! yes, Tommy! Sit by me, Tommy. But
don't sit so near the bank. Don't you see
how the river is rising and beckoning to me, —
hissing, and boilin' over the rocks? It's gittin
higher! — hold me, Tommy, — hold me, and don't
let me go yet. We'll live to cut his heart out,
Tommy, — we'll live — we'll — " His head sank,
and the rushing river, invisible to all eyes save
his, leaped toward him out of the darkness, and
bore him away, no longer to the darkness, but
through it to the distant, peaceful, shining sea.

HOW SANTA CLAUS CAME TO SIMP-
SON'S BAR.

IT had been raining in the valley of the Sacramento. The North Fork had overflowed its
banks and Rattlesnake Creek was impassable. The
few boulders that had marked the summer ford at
Simpson's Crossing were obliterated by a vast
sheet of water stretching to the foothills. The up
stage was stopped at Grangers; the last mail had
been abandoned in the *tules*, the rider swimming
for his life. "An area," remarked the "Sierra
Avalanche," with pensive local pride, "as large as
the State of Massachusetts is now under water."

Nor was the weather any better in the foothills.
The mud lay deep on the mountain road ; wagons
that neither physical force nor moral objurgation
could move from the evil ways into which they
had fallen, encumbered the track, and the way to
Simpson's Bar was indicated by broken-down
teams and hard swearing. And farther on, cut off
and inaccessible, rained upon and bedraggled,
smitten by high winds and threatened by high
water, Simpson's Bar, on the eve of Christmas day,
1862, clung like a swallow's nest to the rocky

entablature and splintered capitals of Table Mountain, and shook in the blast.

As night shut down on the settlement, a few
lights gleamed through the mist from the windows
of cabins on either side of the highway now
crossed and gullied by lawless streams and swept
by marauding winds.   Happily most of the population were gathered at Thompson's store, clustered
around a red-hot stove, at which they silently spat
in some accepted sense of social communion that
perhaps rendered conversation unnecessary.   Indeed, most methods of diversion had long since
been exhausted on Simpson's Bar; high water
had suspended the regular occupations on gulch
and on river, and a consequent lack of money and
whiskey had taken the zest from most illegitimate
recreation.   Even Mr. Hamlin was fain to leave
the Bar with fifty dollars in his pocket, — the
only amount actually realized of the large sums
won by him in the successful exercise of his
arduous profession.   "Ef I was asked," he remarked somewhat later, — "ef I was asked to pint
out a purty little village where a retired sport as
did n't care for money could exercise hisself, frequent and lively, I 'd say Simpson's Bar; but for
a young man with a large family depending on
his exertions, it don't pay."   As Mr. Hamlin's
family consisted mainly of female adults, this
remark is quoted rather to show the breadth of

his humor than the exact extent of his responsibilities.

Howbeit, the unconscious objects of this satire sat that evening in the listless apathy begotten of idleness and lack of excitement. Even the sudden splashing of hoofs before the door did not arouse them. Dick Bullen alone paused in the act of scraping out his pipe, and lifted his head, but no other one of the group indicated any interest in, or recognition of, the man who entered.

It was a figure familiar enough to the company, and known in Simpson's Bar as "The Old Man." A man of perhaps fifty years; grizzled and scant of hair, but still fresh and youthful of complexion. A face full of ready, but not very powerful sympathy, with a chameleon-like aptitude for taking on the shade and color of contiguous moods and feelings. He had evidently just left some hilarious companions, and did not at first notice the gravity of the group, but clapped the shoulder of the nearest man jocularly, and threw himself into a vacant chair.

"Jest heard the best thing out, boys! Ye know Smiley, over yar, — Jim Smiley, — funniest man in the Bar? Well, Jim was jest telling the richest yarn about — "

"Smiley 's a —— fool," interrupted a gloomy voice.

"A particular —— skunk," added another in sepulchral accents.

A silence followed these positive statements. The Old Man glanced quickly around the group. Then his face slowly changed. "That's so," he said reflectively, after a pause, "certingly a sort of a skunk and suthin of a fool. In course." He was silent for a moment as in painful contemplation of the unsavoriness and folly of the unpopulaɪ Smiley. "Dismal weather, ain't it?" he added, now fully embarked on the current of prevailing sentiment. "Mighty rough papers on the boys, and no show for money this season. And to-morrow's Christmas."

There was a movement among the men at this announcement, but whether of satisfaction or disgust was not plain. "Yes," continued the Old Man in the lugubrious tone he had, within the last few moments, unconsciously adopted, — "yes, Christmas, and to-night's Christmas eve. Ye see, boys, I kinder thought — that is, I sorter had an idee, jest passin' like, you know — that may be ye'd all like to come over to my house to-night and have a sort of tear round. But I suppose, now, you wouldn't? Don't feel like it, may be?" he added with anxious sympathy, peering into the faces of his companions.

"Well, I don't know," responded Tom Flynn with some cheerfulness. "P'r'aps we may. But how about your wife, Old Man? What does *she* say to it?"

The Old Man hesitated. His conjugal experience had not been a happy one, and the fact was known to Simpson's Bar. His first wife, a delicate, pretty little woman, had suffered keenly and secretly from the jealous suspicions of her husband, until one day he invited the whole Bar to his house to expose her infidelity. On arriving, the party found the shy, *petite* creature quietly engaged in her household duties, and retired abashed and discomfited. But the sensitive woman did not easily recover from the shock of this extraordinary outrage. It was with difficulty she regained her equanimity sufficiently to release her lover from the closet in which he was concealed and escape with him. She left a boy of three years to comfort her bereaved husband. The Old Man's present wife had been his cook. She was large, loyal, and aggressive.

Before he could reply, Joe Dimmick suggested with great directness that it was the "Old Man's house," and that, invoking the Divine Power, if the case were his own, he would invite whom he pleased, even if in so doing he imperilled his salvation. The Powers of Evil, he further remarked, should contend against him vainly. All this delivered with a terseness and vigor lost in this necessary translation.

"In course. Certainly. Thet's it," said the Old Man with a sympathetic frown. "Thar's no

trouble about *thet*. It's my own house, built every
stick on it myself. Don't you be afeard o' her,
boys. She *may* cut up a trifle rough, — ez wimmin
do, — but she 'll come round." Secretly the Old
Man trusted to the exaltation of liquor and the
power of courageous example to sustain him in
such an emergency.

As yet, Dick Bullen, the oracle and leader of
Simpson's Bar, had not spoken. He now took his
pipe from his lips. " Old Man, how 's that yer
Johnny gettin' on ? Seems to me he did n't look
so peart last time I seed him on the bluff heavin'
rocks at Chinamen. Did n't seem to take much
interest in it. Thar was a gang of 'em by yar
yesterday, — drownded out up the river, — and I
kinder thought o' Johnny, and how he 'd miss 'em !
May be now, we 'd be in the way ef he wus sick ? "

The father, evidently touched not only by this
pathetic picture of Johnny's deprivation, but by
the considerate delicacy of the speaker, hastened
to assure him that Johnny was better and that
a " little fun might 'liven him up." Whereupon
Dick arose, shook himself, and saying, " I 'm ready.
Lead the way, Old Man : here goes," himself led
the way with a leap, a characteristic howl, and
darted out into the night. As he passed through
the outer room he caught up a blazing brand from
the hearth. The action was repeated by the rest
of the party, closely following and elbowing each

other, and before the astonished proprietor of
Thompson's grocery was aware of the intention of
his guests, the room was deserted.

The night was pitchy dark.   In the first gust of
wind their temporary torches were extinguished,
and only the red brands dancing and flitting in
the gloom like drunken will-o'-the-wisps indicated
their whereabouts.   Their way led up Pine-Tree
Cañon, at the head of which a broad, low, bark-
thatched cabin burrowed in the mountain-side.   It
was the home of the Old Man, and the entrance to
the tunnel in which he worked when he worked at
all.   Here the crowd paused for a moment, out of
delicate deference to their host, who came up panting in the rear.

" P'r'aps ye 'd better hold on a second out yer,
whilst I go in and see thet things is all right,"
said the Old Man, with an indifference he was far
from feeling.   The suggestion was graciously accepted, the door opened and closed on the host,
and the crowd, leaning their backs against the wall
and cowering under the eaves, waited and listened.

For a few moments there was no sound but the
dripping of water from the eaves, and the stir and
rustle of wrestling boughs above them.   Then the
men became uneasy, and whispered suggestion
and suspicion passed from the one to the other.
" Reckon she 's caved in his head the first lick ! "
" Decoyed him inter the tunnel and barred him

up, likely." "Got him down and sittin' on him."
"Prob'ly bilin suthin to heave on us : stand clear
the door, boys !" For just then the latch clicked,
the door slowly opened, and a voice said, "Come
in out o' the wet."

The voice was neither that of the Old Man nor
of his wife. It was the voice of a small boy, its
weak treble broken by that preternatural hoarse-
ness which only vagabondage and the habit of pre-
mature self-assertion can give. It was the face of
a small boy that looked up at theirs, — a face that
might have been pretty and even refined but that
it was darkened by evil knowledge from within,
and dirt and hard experience from without. He
had a blanket around his shoulders and had evidently just risen from his bed. "Come in," he repeated, "and don't make no noise. The Old Man's
in there talking to mar," he continued, pointing to
an adjacent room which seemed to be a kitchen,
from which the Old Man's voice came in deprecating accents. "Let me be," he added, querulously,
to Dick Bullen, who had caught him up, blanket
and all, and was affecting to toss him into the fire,
"let go o' me, you d—d old fool, d' ye hear ?"

Thus adjured, Dick Bullen lowered Johnny to
the ground with a smothered laugh, while the
men, entering quietly, ranged themselves around a
long table of rough boards which occupied the
centre of the room. Johnny then gravely pro-

ceeded to a cupboard and brought out several articles which he deposited on the table. "Thar's
whiskey. And crackers. And red herons. And
cheese." He took a bite of the latter on his way
to the table. "And sugar." He scooped up a
mouthful *en route* with a small and very dirty
hand. "And terbacker. Thar's dried appils too
on the shelf, but I don't admire 'em. Appils is
swellin'. Thar," he concluded, "now wade in,
and don't be afeard. *I* don't mind the old woman. She don't b'long to *me*. S'long."

He had stepped to the threshold of a small
room, scarcely larger than a closet, partitioned off
from the main apartment, and holding in its dim
recess a small bed. He stood there a moment
looking at the company, his bare feet peeping from
the blanket, and nodded.

"Hello, Johnny! You ain't goin' to turn in
agin, are ye?" said Dick.

"Yes, I are," responded Johnny, decidedly.

"Why, wot's up, old fellow?"

"I'm sick."

"How sick?"

"I've got a fevier. And childblains. And roo-
matiz," returned Johnny, and vanished within.
After a moment's pause, he added in the dark,
apparently from under the bedclothes, — "And
biles!"

There was an embarrassing silence. The men

looked at each other, and at the fire. Even with
the appetizing banquet before them, it seemed as
if they might again fall into the despondency of
Thompson's grocery, when the voice of the Old
Man, incautiously lifted, came deprecatingly from
the kitchen.

"Certainly ! Thet's so. In course they is. A
gang o' lazy drunken loafers, and that ar Dick
Bullen's the ornariest of all. Did n't hev no more
sabe than to come round yar with sickness in the
house and no provision. Thet's what I said :
'Bullen,' sez I, 'it's crazy drunk you are, or a
fool,' sez I, 'to think o' such a thing.' 'Staples,' I
sez, 'be you a man, Staples, and 'spect to raise
h—ll under my roof and invalids lyin' round ?'
But they would come, — they would. Thet's wot
you must 'spect o' such trash as lays round the
Bar."

A burst of laughter from the men followed this
unfortunate exposure. Whether it was overheard
in the kitchen, or whether the Old Man's irate
companion had just then exhausted all other modes
of expressing her contemptuous indignation, I cannot say, but a back door was suddenly slammed
with great violence. A moment later and the Old
Man reappeared, haply unconscious of the cause of
the late hilarious outburst, and smiled blandly.

"The old woman thought she'd jest run over to
Mrs. McFadden's for a sociable call," he explained,

with jaunty indifference, as he took a seat at the board.

Oddly enough it needed this untoward incident to relieve the embarrassment that was beginning to be felt by the party, and their natural audacity returned with their host. I do not propose to record the convivialities of that evening. The inquisitive reader will accept the statement that the conversation was characterized by the same intellectual exaltation, the same cautious reverence, the same fastidious delicacy, the same rhetorical precision, and the same logical and coherent discourse somewhat later in the evening, which distinguish similar gatherings of the masculine sex in more civilized localities and under more favorable auspices. No glasses were broken in the absence of any; no liquor was uselessly spilt on floor or table in the scarcity of that article.

It was nearly midnight when the festivities were interrupted. "Hush," said Dick Bullen, holding up his hand. It was the querulous voice of Johnny from his adjacent closet : "O dad ! "

The Old Man arose hurriedly and disappeared in the closet. Presently he reappeared. "His rheumatiz is coming on agin bad," he explained, " and he wants rubbin'." He lifted the demijohn of whiskey from the table and shook it. It was empty. Dick Bullen put down his tin cup with an embarrassed laugh. So did the others. The

Old Man examined their contents and said hope‑
fully, "I reckon that's enough; he don't need much.
You hold on all o' you for a spell, and I'll be
back"; and vanished in the closet with an old
flannel shirt and the whiskey. The door closed
but imperfectly, and the following dialogue was
distinctly audible: —

"Now, sonny, whar does she ache worst?"

"Sometimes over yar and sometimes under yer;
but it's most powerful from yer to yer. Rub yer,
dad."

A silence seemed to indicate a brisk rubbing.
Then Johnny:

"Hevin' a good time out yer, dad?"

"Yes, sonny."

"To-morrer's Chrismiss, — ain't it?"

"Yes, sonny. How does she feel now?"

"Better. Rub a little furder down. Wot's
Chrismiss, anyway? Wot's it all about?"

"O, it's a day."

This exhaustive definition was apparently satis‑
factory, for there was a silent interval of rubbing.
Presently Johnny again:

"Mar sez that everywhere else but yer every‑
body gives things to everybody Chrismiss, and
then she jist waded inter you. She sez thar's a
man they call Sandy Claws, not a white man, you
know, but a kind o' Chinemin, comes down the
chimbley night afore Chrismiss and gives things

to chillern, — boys like me.   Puts 'em in their
butes !   Thet's what she tried to play upon me.
Easy now, pop, whar are you rubbin' to, — thet's
a mile from the place.   She jest made that up,
did n't she, jest to aggrewate me and you ?   Don't
rub thar. . . . . Why, dad ! "

In the great quiet that seemed to have fallen
upon the house the sigh of the near pines and the
drip of leaves without was very distinct.   Johnny's voice, too, was lowered as he went on, " Don't
you take on now, fur I 'm gettin' all right fast.
Wot 's the boys doin' out thar ? "

The Old Man partly opened the door and peered
through.   His guests were sitting there sociably
enough, and there were a few silver coins and a
lean buckskin purse on the table.   " Bettin' on
suthin, — some little game or 'nother.   They 're
all right," he replied to Johnny, and recommenced
his rubbing.

" I 'd like to take a hand and win some money,"
said Johnny, reflectively, after a pause.

The Old Man glibly repeated what was evidently
a familiar formula, that if Johnny would wait until
he struck it rich in the tunnel he 'd have lots of
money, etc., etc.

" Yes," said Johnny, " but you don't.   And
whether you strike it or I win it, it 's about the
same.   It 's all luck.   But it 's mighty cur'o's
about Chrismiss, — ain't it ?   Why do they call
it Chrismiss ? "

Perhaps from some instinctive deference to the
overhearing of his guests, or from some vague
sense of incongruity, the Old Man's reply was so
low as to be inaudible beyond the room.

" Yes," said Johnny, with some slight abatement
of interest, " I 've heerd o' *him* before.   Thar, that
'll do, dad.   I don't ache near so bad as I did.
Now wrap me tight in this yer blanket.   So.
Now," he added in a muffled whisper, " sit down
yer by me till I go asleep."   To assure himself of
obedience, he disengaged one hand from the blanket and, grasping his father's sleeve, again composed himself to rest.

For some moments the Old Man waited patiently.   Then the unwonted stillness of the house
excited his curiosity, and without moving from
the bed, he cautiously opened the door with his
disengaged hand, and looked into the main room.
To his infinite surprise it was dark and deserted.
But even then a smouldering log on the hearth
broke, and by the upspringing blaze he saw the
figure of Dick Bullen sitting by the dying embers.

" Hello ! "

Dick started, rose, and came somewhat unsteadily toward him.

" Whar 's the boys ? " said the Old Man.

" Gone up the cañon on a little *pasear*.   They 're
coming back for me in a minit.   I 'm waitin'
round for 'em.   What are you starin' at, Old Man ? "

he added with a forced laugh ; " do you think I 'm drunk ? "

The Old Man might have been pardoned the supposition, for Dick's eyes were humid and his face flushed.   He loitered and lounged back to the chimney, yawned, shook himself, buttoned up his coat and laughed.   " Liquor ain't so plenty as that, Old Man.   Now don't you git up," he continued, as the Old Man made a movement to release his sleeve from Johnny's hand.   " Don't you mind manners.   Sit jest whar you be ; I 'm goin' in a jiffy.   Thar, that 's them now."

There was a low tap at the door.   Dick Bullen opened it quickly, nodded " Good night " to his host, and disappeared.   The Old Man would have followed him but for the hand that still unconsciously grasped his sleeve.   He could have easily disengaged it : it was small, weak, and emaciated. But perhaps because it *was* small, weak, and emaciated, he changed his mind, and, drawing his chair closer to the bed, rested his head upon it.   In this defenceless attitude the potency of his earlier potations surprised him.   The room flickered and faded before his eyes, reappeared, faded again, went out, and left him — asleep.

Meantime Dick Bullen, closing the door, confronted his companions.   "Are you ready ? " said Staples.   " Ready," said Dick ; " what 's the time ? " **" Past twelve,"** was the reply ; " can you make it ?

— it 's nigh on fifty miles, the round trip hither and yon." "I reckon," returned Dick, shortly. "Whar 's the mare ? " "Bill and Jack 's holdin' her at the crossin'." "Let 'em hold on a minit longer," said Dick.

He turned and re-entered the house softly. By the light of the guttering candle and dying fire he saw that the door of the little room was open. He stepped toward it on tiptoe and looked in. The Old Man had fallen back in his chair, snoring, his helpless feet thrust out in a line with his collapsed shoulders, and his hat pulled over his eyes. Beside him, on a narrow wooden bedstead, lay Johnny, muffled tightly in a blanket that hid all save a strip of forehead and a few curls damp with perspiration. Dick Bullen made a step forward, hesitated, and glanced over his shoulder into the deserted room. Everything was quiet. With a sudden resolution he parted his huge mustaches with both hands and stooped over the sleeping boy. But even as he did so a mischievous blast, lying in wait, swooped down the chimney, rekindled the hearth, and lit up the room with a shameless glow from which Dick fled in bashful terror.

His companions were already waiting for him at the crossing. Two of them were struggling in the darkness with some strange misshapen bulk, which as Dick came nearer took the semblance of a great yellow horse.

It was the mare. She was not a pretty picture. From her Roman nose to her rising haunches, from her arched spine hidden by the stiff *machillas* of a Mexican saddle, to her thick, straight, bony legs, there was not a line of equine grace. In her half-blind but wholly vicious white eyes, in her protruding under lip, in her monstrous color, there was nothing but ugliness and vice.

"Now then," said Staples, "stand cl'ar of her heels, boys, and up with you. Don't miss your first holt of her mane, and mind ye get your off stirrup *quick*. Ready!"

There was a leap, a scrambling struggle, a bound, a wild retreat of the crowd, a circle of flying hoofs, two springless leaps that jarred the earth, a rapid play and jingle of spurs, a plunge, and then the voice of Dick somewhere in the darkness, "All right!"

"Don't take the lower road back onless you're hard pushed for time! Don't hold her in down hill! We'll be at the ford at five. G'lang! Hoopa! Mula! GO!"

A splash, a spark struck from the ledge in the road, a clatter in the rocky cut beyond, and Dick was gone.

     .   .   .   .   .

Sing, O Muse, the ride of Richard Bullen! Sing, O Muse of chivalrous men! the sacred quest, the doughty deeds, the battery of low churls, the fear-

some ride and grewsome perils of the Flower of
Simpson's Bar!   Alack ! she is dainty, this Muse !
She will have none of this bucking brute and
swaggering, ragged rider, and I must fain follow
him in prose, afoot !

It was one o'clock, and yet he had only gained
Rattlesnake Hill.   For in that time Jovita had re-
hearsed to him all her imperfections and practised
all her vices.   Thrice had she stumbled.   Twice
had she thrown up her Roman nose in a straight
line with the reins, and, resisting bit and spur,
struck out madly across country.   Twice had she
reared, and, rearing, fallen backward ; and twice
had the agile Dick, unharmed, regained his seat
before she found her vicious legs again.   And a
mile beyond them, at the foot of a long hill, was
Rattlesnake Creek.   Dick knew that here was the
crucial test of his ability to perform his enterprise,
set his teeth grimly, put his knees well into her
flanks, and changed his defensive tactics to brisk
aggression.   Bullied and maddened, Jovita began
the descent of the hill.   Here the artful Richard
pretended to hold her in with ostentatious objurgation and well-feigned cries of alarm.   It is unnecessary to add that Jovita instantly ran away.
Nor need I state the time made in the descent ; it
is written in the chronicles of Simpson's Bar.
Enough that in another moment, as it seemed to
Dick, she was splashing on the overflowed banks

of Rattlesnake Creek.   As Dick expected, the
momentum she had acquired carried her beyond
the point of balking, and, holding her well together
for a mighty leap, they dashed into the middle of
the swiftly flowing current.   A few moments of
kicking, wading, and swimming, and Dick drew a
long breath on the opposite bank.

The road from Rattlesnake Creek to Red Mountain was tolerably level.   Either the plunge in
Rattlesnake Creek had dampened her baleful fire,
or the art which led to it had shown her the superior wickedness of her rider, for Jovita no longer
wasted her surplus energy in wanton conceits.
Once she bucked, but it was from force of habit ;
once she shied, but it was from a new freshly
painted meeting-house at the crossing of the county
road.   Hollows, ditches, gravelly deposits, patches
of freshly springing grasses, flew from beneath her
rattling hoofs.   She began to smell unpleasantly,
once or twice she coughed slightly, but there was
no abatement of her strength or speed.   By two
o'clock he had passed Red Mountain and begun
the descent to the plain.   Ten minutes later the
driver of the fast Pioneer coach was overtaken and
passed by a " man on a l'into hoss," — an event
sufficiently notable for remark.   At half past two
Dick rose in his stirrups with a great shout.
Stars were glittering through the rifted clouds, and
beyond him, out of the plain, rose two spires, a

flagstaff, and a straggling line of black objects.
Dick jingled his spurs and swung his *riata*, Jovita
bounded forward, and in another moment they
swept into Tuttleville and drew up before the
wooden piazza of " The Hotel of All Nations."

What transpired that night at Tuttleville is not
strictly a part of this record. Briefly I may state,
however, that after Jovita had been handed over
to a sleepy ostler, whom she at once kicked into
unpleasant consciousness, Dick sallied out with
the bar-keeper for a tour of the sleeping town.
Lights still gleamed from a few saloons and gam-
bling-houses ; but, avoiding these, they stopped
before several closed shops, and by persistent tap-
ping and judicious outcry roused the proprietors
from their beds, and made them unbar the doors
of their magazines and expose their wares. Sometimes they were met by curses, but oftener by interest and some concern in their needs, and the
interview was invariably concluded by a drink.
It was three o'clock before this pleasantry was
given over, and with a small waterproof bag of
india-rubber strapped on his shoulders Dick returned to the hotel. But here he was waylaid by
Beauty, — Beauty opulent in charms, affluent in
dress, persuasive in speech, and Spanish in accent !
In vain she repeated the invitation in " Excelsior,"
happily scorned by all Alpine-climbing youth, and
rejected by this child of the Sierras, — a rejection

softened in this instance by a laugh and his last
gold coin.   And then he sprang to the saddle and
dashed down the lonely street and out into the
lonelier plain, where presently the lights, the black
line of houses, the spires, and the flagstaff sank
into the earth behind him again and were lost in
the distance.

The storm had cleared away, the air was brisk
and cold, the outlines of adjacent landmarks were
distinct, but it was half past four before Dick
reached the meeting-house and the crossing of the
county road.   To avoid the rising grade he had
taken a longer and more circuitous road, in whose
viscid mud Jovita sank fetlock deep at every
bound.   It was a poor preparation for a steady
ascent of five miles more; but Jovita, gathering
her legs under her, took it with her usual blind,
unreasoning fury, and a half-hour later reached
the long level that led to Rattlesnake Creek.   Another half-hour would bring him to the creek.   He
threw the reins lightly upon the neck of the mare,
chirruped to her, and began to sing.

Suddenly Jovita shied with a bound that would
have unseated a less practised rider.   Hanging to
her rein was a figure that had leaped from the
bank, and at the same time from the road before
her arose a shadowy horse and rider.   "Throw up
your hands," commanded this second apparition,
with an oath.

Dick felt the mare tremble, quiver, and apparently sink under him. He knew what it meant and was prepared.

"Stand aside, Jack Simpson, I know you, you d—d thief. Let me pass or — "

He did not finish the sentence. Jovita rose straight in the air with a terrific bound, throwing the figure from her bit with a single shake of her vicious head, and charged with deadly malevolence down on the impediment before her. An oath, a pistol-shot, horse and highwayman rolled over in the road, and the next moment Jovita was a hundred yards away. But the good right arm of her rider, shattered by a bullet, dropped helplessly at his side.

Without slacking his speed he shifted the reins to his left hand. But a few moments later he was obliged to halt and tighten the saddle-girths that had slipped in the onset. This in his crippled condition took some time. He had no fear of pursuit, but looking up he saw that the eastern stars were already paling, and that the distant peaks had lost their ghostly whiteness, and now stood out blackly against a lighter sky. Day was upon him. Then completely absorbed in a single idea, he forgot the pain of his wound, and mounting again dashed on toward Rattlesnake Creek. But now Jovita's breath came broken by gasps, Dick reeled in his saddle, and brighter and brighter grew the sky.

Ride, Richard; run, Jovita; linger, O day!

For the last few rods there was a roaring in his ears. Was it exhaustion from loss of blood, or what? He was dazed and giddy as he swept down the hill, and did not recognize his surroundings. Had he taken the wrong road, or was this Rattlesnake Creek?

It was. But the brawling creek he had swam a few hours before had risen, more than doubled its volume, and now rolled a swift and resistless river between him and Rattlesnake Hill. For the first time that night Richard's heart sank within him. The river, the mountain, the quickening east, swam before his eyes. He shut them to recover his self-control. In that brief interval, by some fantastic mental process, the little room at Simpson's Bar and the figures of the sleeping father and son rose upon him. He opened his eyes wildly, cast off his coat, pistol, boots, and saddle, bound his precious pack tightly to his shoulders, grasped the bare flanks of Jovita with his bared knees, and with a shout dashed into the yellow water. A cry rose from the opposite bank as the head of a man and horse struggled for a few moments against the battling current, and then were swept away amidst uprooted trees and whirling drift-wood.

    .   .   .   .   .

The Old Man started and woke. The fire on

the hearth was dead, the candle in the outer room
flickering in its socket, and somebody was rapping
at the door. He opened it, but fell back with a
cry before the dripping, half-naked figure that
reeled against the doorpost.

"Dick?"

"Hush! Is he awake yet?"

"No, — but, Dick? — "

"Dry up, you old fool! Get me some whiskey
quick!" The Old Man flew and returned with —
an empty bottle! Dick would have sworn, but
his strength was not equal to the occasion. He
staggered, caught at the handle of the door, and
motioned to the Old Man.

"Thar's suthin' in my pack yer for Johnny.
Take it off. I can't."

The Old Man unstrapped the pack and laid it
before the exhausted man.

"Open it, quick!"

He did so with trembling fingers. It contained
only a few poor toys, — cheap and barbaric enough,
goodness knows, but bright with paint and tinsel.
One of them was broken; another, I fear, was
irretrievably ruined by water; and on the third —
ah me! there was a cruel spot.

"It don't look like much, that's a fact," said
Dick, ruefully. . . . . "But it's the best we could
do. . . . . Take 'em, Old Man, and put 'em in his
stocking, and tell him — tell him, you know —

hold me, Old Man — "   The Old Man caught at his sinking figure.   " Tell him," said Dick, with a weak little laugh, — " tell him Sandy Claus has come."

And even so, bedraggled, ragged, unshaven, and unshorn, with one arm hanging helplessly at his side, Santa Claus came to Simpson's Bar and fell fainting on the first threshold.   The Christmas dawn came slowly after, touching the remoter peaks with the rosy warmth of ineffable love. And it looked so tenderly on Simpson's Bar that the whole mountain, as if caught in a generous action, blushed to the skies.

THE PRINCESS BOB AND HER FRIENDS.

SHE was a Klamath Indian. Her title was, I think, a compromise between her claim as daughter of a chief, and gratitude to her earliest white protector, whose name, after the Indian fashion, she had adopted. "Bob" Walker had taken her from the breast of her dead mother at a time when the sincere volunteer soldiery of the California frontier were impressed with the belief that extermination was the manifest destiny of the Indian race. He had with difficulty restrained the noble zeal of his compatriots long enough to convince them that the exemption of one Indian baby would not invalidate this theory. And he took her to his home, — a pastoral clearing on the banks of the Salmon River, — where she was cared for after a frontier fashion.

Before she was nine years old, she had exhausted the scant kindliness of the thin, overworked Mrs. Walker. As a playfellow of the young Walkers she was unreliable ; as a nurse for the baby she was inefficient. She lost the former in the trackless depths of a redwood forest; she basely abandoned the latter in an extemporized cradle, hanging like a chrysalis to a convenient bough. She lied and she stole, — two unpardonable sins in a frontier community, where truth was a necessity and provisions were the only property. Worse than this, the outskirts of the clearing were sometimes haunted by blanketed tatterdemalions with whom she had mysterious confidences. Mr. Walker more than once regretted his indiscreet humanity; but she presently relieved him of responsibility, and possibly of bloodguiltiness, by disappearing entirely.

When she reappeared, it was at the adjacent village of Logport, in the capacity of housemaid to a trader's wife, who, joining some little culture to considerable conscientiousness, attempted to instruct her charge. But the Princess proved an unsatisfactory pupil to even so liberal a teacher. She accepted the alphabet with great good-humor, but always as a pleasing and recurring novelty, in which all interest expired at the completion of each lesson. She found a thousand uses for her books and writing materials other than those known to civilized children. She made a curious necklace of bits of slate-pencil, she constructed a miniature canoe from the pasteboard covers of her primer, she bent her pens into fish-hooks, and tattooed the faces of her younger companions with blue ink. Religious instruction she received as good-humoredly, and learned to pronounce the

name of the Deity with a cheerful familiarity that
shocked her preceptress. Nor could her reverence
be reached through analogy; she knew nothing of
the Great Spirit, and professed entire ignorance of
the Happy Hunting-Grounds. Yet she attended
divine service regularly, and as regularly asked
for a hymn-book; and it was only through the
discovery that she had collected twenty-five of
these volumes and had hidden them behind the
woodpile, that her connection with the First Baptist Church of Logport ceased. She would occasionally abandon these civilized and Christian
privileges, and disappear from her home, returning
after several days of absence with an odor of bark
and fish, and a peace-offering to her mistress in
the shape of venison or game.

To add to her troubles, she was now fourteen,
and, according to the laws of her race, a woman.
I do not think the most romantic fancy would
have called her pretty. Her complexion defied
most of those ambiguous similes through which
poets unconsciously apologize for any deviation
from the Caucasian standard. It was not wine
nor amber colored; if anything, it was smoky.
Her face was tattooed with red and white lines on
one cheek, as if a fine-toothed comb had been
drawn from cheek-bone to jaw, and, but for the
good-humor that beamed from her small berry-like
eyes and shone in her white teeth, would have

been repulsive. She was short and stout. In her scant drapery and unrestrained freedom she was hardly statuesque, and her more unstudied attitudes were marred by a simian habit of softly scratching her left ankle with the toes of her right foot, in moments of contemplation.

I think I have already shown enough to indicate the incongruity of her existence with even the low standard of civilization that obtained at Logport in the year 1860. It needed but one more fact to prove the far-sighted political sagacity and prophetic ethics of those sincere advocates of extermination, to whose virtues I have done but scant justice in the beginning of this article. This fact was presently furnished by the Princess. After one of her periodical disappearances, — this time unusually prolonged, — she astonished Logport by returning with a half-breed baby of a week old in her arms. That night a meeting of the hard-featured serious matrons of Logport was held at Mrs. Brown's. The immediate banishment of the Princess was demanded. Soft-hearted Mrs. Brown endeavored vainly to get a mitigation or suspension of the sentence. But, as on a former occasion, the Princess took matters into her own hands. A few mornings afterwards, a wicker cradle containing an Indian baby was found hanging on the handle of the door of the First Baptist Church. It was the Parthian arrow of the flying

Princess. From that day Logport knew her no more.

It had been a bright clear day on the upland, so clear that the ramparts of Fort Jackson and the flagstaff were plainly visible twelve miles away from the long curving peninsula that stretched a bared white arm around the peaceful waters of Logport Bay. It had been a clear day upon the sea-shore, albeit the air was filled with the flying spume and shifting sand of a straggling beach whose low dunes were dragged down by the long surges of the Pacific and thrown up again by the tumultuous trade-winds. But the sun had gone down in a bank of fleecy fog that was beginning to roll in upon the beach. Gradually the headland at the entrance of the harbor and the light-house disappeared, then the willow fringe that marked the line of Salmon River vanished, and the ocean was gone. A few sails still gleamed on the waters of the bay; but the advancing fog wiped them out one by one, crept across the steel-blue expanse, swallowed up the white mills and single spire of Logport, and, joining with reinforce-ments from the marshes, moved solemnly upon the hills. Ten minutes more and the landscape was utterly blotted out; simultaneously the wind died away, and a death-like silence stole over sea and shore. The faint clang, high overhead, of un-

seen brent, the nearer call of invisible plover, the
lap and wash of undistinguishable waters, and the
monotonous roll of the vanished ocean, were the
only sounds.   As night deepened, the far-off
booming of the fog-bell on the headland at intervals stirred the thick air.

Hard by the shore of the bay, and half hidden
by a drifting sand-hill, stood a low nondescript
structure, to whose composition sea and shore had
equally contributed.   It was built partly of logs
and partly of driftwood and tarred canvas.   Joined
to one end of the main building — the ordinary
log-cabin of the settler — was the half-round pilot-
house of some wrecked steamer, while the other
gable terminated in half of a broken whale-boat.
Nailed against the boat were the dried skins of
wild animals, and scattered about lay the flotsam
and jetsam of many years' gathering, — bamboo
crates, casks, hatches, blocks, oars, boxes, part of a
whale's vertebræ, and the blades of sword-fish.
Drawn up on the beach of a little cove before the
house lay a canoe.   As the night thickened and
the fog grew more dense, these details grew imperceptible, and only the windows of the pilot-house,
lit up by a roaring fire within the hut, gleamed
redly through the mist.

By this fire, beneath a ship's lamp that swung
from the roof, two figures were seated, a man and
a woman.   The man, broad-shouldered and heav-

ily bearded, stretched his listless powerful length
beyond a broken bamboo chair, with his eyes fixed
on the fire. The woman crouched cross-legged
upon the broad earthen hearth, with her eyes
blinkingly fixed on her companion. They were
small, black, round, berry-like eyes, and as the
firelight shone upon her smoky face, with its
one striped cheek of gorgeous brilliancy, it was
plainly the Princess Bob and no other.

Not a word was spoken. They had been sitting
thus for more than an hour, and there was about
their attitude a suggestion that silence was habitual. Once or twice the man rose and walked up
and down the narrow room, or gazed absently
from the windows of the pilot-house, but never
by look or sign betrayed the slightest consciousness of his companion. At such times the Princess from her nest by the fire followed him with
eyes of canine expectancy and wistfulness. But
he would as inevitably return to his contemplation
of the fire, and the Princess to her blinking watch-
fulness of his face.

They had sat there silent and undisturbed for
many an evening in fair weather and foul. They
had spent many a day in sunshine and storm,
gathering the unclaimed spoil of sea and shore.
They had kept these mute relations, varied only
by the incidents of the hunt or meagre household
duties, for three years, ever since the man, wan-

dering moodily over the lonely sands, had fallen
upon the half-starved woman lying in the little
hollow where she had crawled to die. It had
seemed as if they would never be disturbed,
until now, when the Princess started, and, with
the instinct of her race, bent her ear to the
ground.

The wind had risen and was rattling the tarred
canvas. But in another moment there plainly
came from without the hut the sound of voices.
Then followed a rap at the door; then another rap;
and then, before they could rise to their feet, the
door was flung briskly open.

" I beg your pardon," said a pleasant but somewhat decided contralto voice, " but I don't think
you heard me knock. Ah, I see you did not.
May I come in ? "

There was no reply. Had the battered figure-
head of the Goddess of Liberty, which lay deeply
embedded in the sand on the beach, suddenly
appeared at the door demanding admittance, the
occupants of the cabin could not have been more
speechlessly and hopelessly astonished than at the
form which stood in the open doorway.

It was that of a slim, shapely, elegantly dressed
young woman. A scarlet-lined silken hood was
half thrown back from the shining mass of the
black hair that covered her small head ; from her
pretty shoulders dropped a fur cloak, only re-

strained by a cord and tassel in her small gloved
hand. Around her full throat was a double necklace of large white beads, that by some cunning
feminine trick relieved with its infantile suggestion the strong decision of her lower face.

"Did you say yes? Ah, thank you. We may
come in, Barker." (Here a shadow in a blue
army overcoat followed her into the cabin, touched
its cap respectfully, and then stood silent and
erect against the wall.) "Don't disturb yourself
in the least, I beg. What a distressingly unpleasant night! Is this your usual climate?"

Half graciously, half absently overlooking the
still embarrassed silence of the group, she went
on: "We started from the fort over three hours
ago, — three hours ago, was n't it, Barker?" (the
erect Barker touched his cap,) — "to go to Captain Emmons's quarters on Indian Island, — I
think you call it Indian Island, don't you?" (she
was appealing to the awe-stricken Princess,) —
"and we got into the fog and lost our way; that
is, Barker lost his way," (Barker touched his cap
deprecatingly,) "and goodness knows where we
did n't wander to until we mistook your light for
the lighthouse and pulled up here. No, no, pray
keep your seat, do! Really I must insist."

Nothing could exceed the languid grace of the
latter part of this speech, — nothing except the
easy unconsciousness with which she glided by

the offered chair of her stammering, embarrassed host and stood beside the open hearth.

"Barker will tell you," she continued, warming her feet by the fire, "that I am Miss Portfire, daughter of Major Portfire, commanding the post. Ah, excuse me, child!" (She had accidentally trodden upon the bare yellow toes of the Princess.) "Really, I did not know you were there. I am very near-sighted." (In confirmation of her statement, she put to her eyes a dainty double eyeglass that dangled from her neck.) "It's a shocking thing to be near-sighted, is n't it?"

If the shamefaced uneasy man to whom this remark was addressed could have found words to utter the thought that even in his confusion struggled uppermost in his mind, he would, looking at the bold, dark eyes that questioned him, have denied the fact. But he only stammered, "Yes." The next moment, however, Miss Portfire had apparently forgotten him and was examining the Princess through her glass.

"And what is your name, child?"

The Princess, beatified by the eyes and eyeglass, showed all her white teeth at once, and softly scratched her leg.

"Bob."

"Bob? What a singular name!"

Miss Portfire's host here hastened to explain the origin of the Princess's title.

"Then *you* are Bob." (Eye-glass.)

"No, my name is Grey, — John Grey." And he actually achieved a bow where awkwardness was rather the air of imperfectly recalling a forgotten habit.

"Grey ? — ah, let me see. Yes, certainly. You are Mr. Grey the recluse, the hermit, the philosopher, and all that sort of thing. Why, certainly; Dr. Jones, our surgeon, has told me all about you. Dear me, how interesting a rencontre! Lived all alone here for seven — was it seven years ? — yes, I remember now. Existed quite *au naturel*, one might say. How odd! Not that I know anything about that sort of thing, you know. I 've lived always among people, and am really quite a stranger, I assure you. But honestly, Mr. — I beg your pardon — Mr. Grey, how do you like it ? "

She had quietly taken his chair and thrown her cloak and hood over its back, and was now thoughtfully removing her gloves. Whatever were the arguments, — and they were doubtless many and profound, — whatever the experience, — and it was doubtless hard and satisfying enough, — by which this unfortunate man had justified his life for the last seven years, somehow they suddenly became trivial and terribly ridiculous before this simple but practical question.

"Well, you shall tell me all about it after you

have given me something to eat. We will have time enough; Barker cannot find his way back in this fog to-night. Now don't put yourselves to any trouble on my account. Barker will assist."

Barker came forward. Glad to escape the scrutiny of his guest, the hermit gave a few rapid directions to the Princess in her native tongue, and disappeared in the shed. Left a moment alone, Miss Portfire took a quick, half-audible, feminine inventory of the cabin. "Books, guns, skins, *one* chair, *one* bed, no pictures, and no looking-glass!" She took a book from the swinging shelf and resumed her seat by the fire as the Princess re-entered with fresh fuel. But while kneeling on the hearth the Princess chanced to look up and met Miss Portfire's dark eyes over the edge of her book.

"Bob!"

The Princess showed her teeth.

"Listen. Would you like to have fine clothes, rings, and beads like these, to have your hair nicely combed and put up so? Would you?"

The Princess nodded violently.

"Would you like to live with me and have them? Answer quickly. Don't look round for *him*. Speak for yourself. Would you? Hush; never mind now."

The hermit re-entered, and the Princess, blinking, retreated into the shadow of the whale-boat shed, from which she did not emerge even when the homely repast of cold venison, ship biscuit, and tea was served. Miss Portfire noticed her absence: "You really must not let me interfere with your usual simple ways. Do you know this is exceedingly interesting to me, so pastoral and patriarchal and all that sort of thing. I must insist upon the Princess coming back; really, I must."

But the Princess was not to be found in the shed, and Miss Portfire, who the next minute seemed to have forgotten all about her, took her place in the single chair before an extemporized table. Barker stood behind her, and the hermit leaned against the fireplace. Miss Portfire's appetite did not come up to her protestations. For the first time in seven years it occurred to the hermit that his ordinary victual might be improved. He stammered out something to that effect.

"I have eaten better, and worse," said Miss Portfire, quietly.

"But I thought you — that is, you said — "

"I spent a year in the hospitals, when father was on the Potomac," returned Miss Portfire, composedly. After a pause she continued: "You remember after the second Bull Run — But, dear me! I beg your pardon; of course, you know nothing about the war and all that sort of thing, and don't care." (She put up her eye-glass and quietly surveyed his broad muscular figure against the chimney.) "Or, perhaps, your prejudices — But then, as a hermit you know you have no politics, of course. Please don't let me bore you."

To have been strictly consistent, the hermit should have exhibited no interest in this topic. Perhaps it was owing to some quality in the narrator, but he was constrained to beg her to continue in such phrases as his unfamiliar lips could command. So that, little by little, Miss Portfire yielded up incident and personal observation of the contest then raging; with the same half-abstracted, half-unconcerned air that seemed habitual to her, she told the stories of privation, of suffering, of endurance, and of sacrifice. With the same assumption of timid deference that concealed her great self-control, she talked of principles and rights. Apparently without enthusiasm and without effort, of which his morbid nature would have been suspicious, she sang the great American Iliad in a way that stirred the depths of her solitary auditor to its massive foundations. Then she stopped and asked quietly, "Where is Bob?"

The hermit started. He would look for her. But Bob, for some reason, was not forthcoming. Search was made within and without the hut, but in vain. For the first time that evening Miss

Portfire showed some anxiety. "Go," she said to Barker, "and find her. She *must* be found; stay, give me your overcoat, I 'll go myself." She threw the overcoat over her shoulders and stepped out into the night. In the thick veil of fog that seemed suddenly to inwrap her, she stood for a moment irresolute, and then walked toward the beach, guided by the low wash of waters on the sand. She had not taken many steps before she stumbled over some dark crouching object. Reaching down her hand she felt the coarse wiry mane of the Princess.

" Bob ! "

There was no reply.

" Bob   I 've been looking for you, come."

" Go 'way."

" Nonsense, Bob. I want you to stay with me to-night, come."

" Injin squaw no good for waugee woman. Go 'way."

" Listen, Bob. You are daughter of a chief : so am I. Your father had many warriors : so has mine. It is good that you stay with me. Come."

The Princess chuckled and suffered herself to be lifted up. A few moments later and they re-entered the hut, hand in hand.

With the first red streaks of dawn the next day the erect Barker touched his cap at the door of the hut. Beside him stood the hermit, also just

risen from his blanketed nest in the sand. Forth
from the hut, fresh as the morning air, stepped
Miss Portfire, leading the Princess by the hand.
Hand in hand also they walked to the shore, and
when the Princess had been safely bestowed in
the stern sheets, Miss Portfire turned and held out
her own to her late host.

"I shall take the best of care of her, of course.
You will come and see her often. I should ask
you to come and see me, but you are a hermit,
you know, and all that sort of thing. But if it's
the correct anchorite thing, and can be done, my
father will be glad to requite you for this night's
hospitality. But don't do anything on my account
that interferes with your simple habits. Good
by."

She handed him a card, which he took mechanically.

"Good by."

The sail was hoisted, and the boat shoved off.
As the fresh morning breeze caught the white canvas it seemed to bow a parting salutation. There
was a rosy flush of promise on the water, and as
the light craft darted forward toward the ascending sun, it seemed for a moment uplifted in its
glory.

Miss Portfire kept her word. If thoughtful
care and intelligent kindness could regenerate the

Princess, her future was secure. And it really
seemed as if she were for the first time inclined to
heed the lessons of civilization and profit by her
new condition. An agreeable change was first
noticed in her appearance. Her lawless hair was
caught in a net, and no longer strayed over her
low forehead. Her unstable bust was stayed and
upheld by French corsets; her plantigrade shuffle
was limited by heeled boots. Her dresses were
neat and clean, and she wore a double necklace of
glass beads. With this physical improvement
there also seemed some moral awakening. She no
longer stole nor lied. With the possession of personal property came a respect for that of others.
With increased dependence on the word of those
about her came a thoughtful consideration of her
own. Intellectually she was still feeble, although
she grappled sturdily with the simple lessons
which Miss Portfire set before her. But her zeal
and simple vanity outran her discretion, and she
would often sit for hours with an open book before her, which she could not read. She was a
favorite with the officers at the fort, from the Major, who shared his daughter's prejudices and often
yielded to her powerful self-will, to the subalterns,
who liked her none the less that their natural
enemies, the frontier volunteers, had declared war
against her helpless sisterhood. The only restraint put upon her was the limitation of her lib-

erty to the enclosure of the fort and parade; and only once did she break this parole, and was stopped by the sentry as she stepped into a boat at the landing.

The recluse did not avail himself of Miss Portfire's invitation. But after the departure of the Princess he spent less of his time in the hut, and was more frequently seen in the distant marshes of Eel River and on the upland hills. A feverish restlessness, quite opposed to his usual phlegm, led him into singular freaks strangely inconsistent with his usual habits and reputation. The purser of the occasional steamer which stopped at Logport with the mails reported to have been boarded, just inside the bar, by a strange bearded man, who asked for a newspaper containing the last war telegrams. He tore his red shirt into narrow strips, and spent two days with his needle over the pieces and the tattered remnant of his only white garment; and a few days afterward the fishermen on the bay were surprised to see what, on nearer approach, proved to be a rude imitation of the national flag floating from a spar above the hut.

One evening, as the fog began to drift over the sand-hills, the recluse sat alone in his hut. The fire was dying unheeded on the hearth, for he had been sitting there for a long time, completely absorbed in the blurred pages of an old newspaper.

v. 17—D

Presently he arose, and, refolding it, — an operation of great care and delicacy in its tattered condition, — placed it under the blankets of his bed. He resumed his seat by the fire, but soon began drumming with his fingers on the arm of his chair. Eventually this assumed the time and accent of some air. Then he began to whistle softly and hesitatingly, as if trying to recall a forgotten tune. Finally this took shape in a rude resemblance, not unlike that which his flag bore to the national standard, to Yankee Doodle. Suddenly he stopped.

There was an unmistakable rapping at the door. The blood which had at first rushed to his face now forsook it and settled slowly around his heart. He tried to rise, but could not. Then the door was flung open, and a figure with a scarlet-lined hood and fur mantle stood on the threshold. With a mighty effort he took one stride to the door. The next moment he saw the wide mouth and white teeth of the Princess, and was greeted by a kiss that felt like a baptism.

To tear the hood and mantle from her figure in the sudden fury that seized him, and to fiercely demand the reason of this masquerade, was his only return to her greeting. " Why are you here ? did you steal these garments ? " he again demanded in her guttural language, as he shook her roughly by the arm. The Princess hung her head. " Did you ?" he screamed, as he reached wildly for his rifle.

"I did."

His hold relaxed, and he staggered back against the wall. The Princess began to whimper. Between her sobs, she was trying to explain that the Major and his daughter were going away, and that they wanted to send her to the Reservation; but he cut her short. "Take off those things!" The Princess tremblingly obeyed. He rolled them up, placed them in the canoe she had just left, and then leaped into the frail craft. She would have followed, but with a great oath he threw her from him, and with one stroke of his paddle swept out into the fog, and was gone.

"Jessamy," said the Major, a few days after, as he sat at dinner with his daughter, "I think I can tell you something to match the mysterious disappearance and return of your wardrobe. Your crazy friend, the recluse, has enlisted this morning in the Fourth Artillery. He's a splendid-looking animal, and there's the right stuff for a soldier in him, if I'm not mistaken. He's in earnest too, for he enlists in the regiment ordered back to Washington. Bless me, child, another goblet broken; you'll ruin the mess in glassware, at this rate!"

"Have you heard anything more of the Princess, papa?"

"Nothing, but perhaps it's as well that she has gone. These cursed settlers are at their old complaints again about what they call 'Indian depredations,' and I have just received orders from head-quarters to keep the settlement clear of all vagabond aborigines. I am afraid, my dear, that a strict construction of the term would include your *protégée*."

The time for the departure of the Fourth Artillery had come. The night before was thick and foggy. At one o'clock, a shot on the ramparts called out the guard and roused the sleeping garrison. The new sentry, Private Grey, had challenged a dusky figure creeping on the glacis, and, receiving no answer, had fired. The guard sent out presently returned, bearing a lifeless figure in their arms. The new sentry's zeal, joined with an ex-frontiersman's aim, was fatal.

They laid the helpless, ragged form before the guard-house door, and then saw for the first time that it was the Princess. Presently she opened her eyes. They fell upon the agonized face of her innocent slayer, but haply without intelligence or reproach.

"Georgy!" she whispered.

"Bob!"

"All's same now. Me get plenty well soon. Me make no more fuss. Me go to Reservation."

Then she stopped, a tremor ran through her limbs, and she lay still. She had gone to the Reservation. Not that devised by the wisdom of man, but that one set apart from the foundation of the world for the wisest as well as the meanest of His creatures.

THE ILIAD OF SANDY BAR.

BEFORE nine o'clock it was pretty well known all along the river that the two partners of the "Amity Claim" had quarrelled and separated at daybreak. At that time the attention of their nearest neighbor had been attracted by the sounds of altercations and two consecutive pistol-shots. Running out, he had seen, dimly, in the gray mist that rose from the river, the tall form of Scott, one of the partners, descending the hill toward the *cañon*; a moment later, York, the other partner, had appeared from the cabin, and walked in an opposite direction toward the river, passing within a few feet of the curious watcher. Later it was discovered that a serious Chinaman, cutting wood before the cabin, had witnessed part of the quarrel. But John was stolid, indifferent, and reticent. "Me choppee wood, me no fightee," was his serene response to all anxious queries. "But what did they *say*, John?" John did not *sabe*. Colonel Starbottle deftly ran over the various popular epithets which a generous public sentiment might accept as reasonable provocation for an assault. But John did not recognize them. "And this yer's the cattle," said the Colonel, with some severity, "that some thinks oughter be allowed to testify ag'in' a White Man! Git — you heathen!"

Still the quarrel remained inexplicable. That two men, whose amiability and grave tact had earned for them the title of "The Peacemakers," in a community not greatly given to the passive virtues, — that these men, singularly devoted to each other, should suddenly and violently quarrel, might well excite the curiosity of the camp. A few of the more inquisitive visited the late scene of conflict, now deserted by its former occupants. There was no trace of disorder or confusion in the neat cabin. The rude table was arranged as if for breakfast; the pan of yellow biscuit still sat upon that hearth whose dead embers might have typified the evil passions that had raged there but an hour before. But Colonel Starbottle's eye — albeit somewhat bloodshot and rheumy — was more intent on practical details. On examination, a bullet-hole was found in the doorpost, and another, nearly opposite, in the casing of the window. The Colonel called attention to the fact that the one "agreed with" the bore of Scott's revolver, and the other with that of York's derringer. "They must hev stood about yer," said the Colonel, taking position; "not mor'n three feet apart, and — missed!" There was a fine touch of pathos in the falling inflection of the Colonel's voice, which was not without effect. A delicate perception of wasted opportunity thrilled his auditors.

But the Bar was destined to experience a greater disappointment. The two antagonists had not met since the quarrel, and it was vaguely rumored that, on the occasion of a second meeting, each had determined to kill the other "on sight." There was, consequently, some excitement — and, it is to be feared, no little gratification — when, at ten o'clock, York stepped from the Magnolia Saloon into the one long straggling street of the camp, at the same moment that Scott left the blacksmith's shop at the forks of the road. It was evident, at a glance, that a meeting could only be avoided by the actual retreat of one or the other.

In an instant the doors and windows of the adjacent saloons were filled with faces. Heads unaccountably appeared above the river-banks and from behind bowlders. An empty wagon at the cross-road was suddenly crowded with people, who seemed to have sprung from the earth. There was much running and confusion on the hillside. On the mountain-road, Mr. Jack Hamlin had reined up his horse, and was standing upright on the seat of his buggy. And the two objects of this absorbing attention approached each other.

"York's got the sun," "Scott'll line him on that

tree," "He's waitin' to draw his fire," came from
the cart; and then it was silent. But above
this human breathlessness the river rushed and
sang, and the wind rustled the tree-tops with an
indifference that seemed obtrusive. Colonel Starbottle felt it, and in a moment of sublime preoccu-
pation, without looking around, waved his cane
behind him, warningly to all nature, and said,
"Shu!"

The men were now within a few feet of each
other. A hen ran across the road before one of
them. A feathery seed-vessel, wafted from a wayside tree, fell at the feet of the other. And, unheeding this irony of nature, the two opponents
came nearer, erect and rigid, looked in each other's
eyes, and — passed!

Colonel Starbottle had to be lifted from the cart.
"This yer camp is played out," he said, gloomily,
as he affected to be supported into the Magnolia.
With what further expression he might have indicated his feelings it was impossible to say, for
at that moment Scott joined the group. "Did
you speak to me?" he asked of the Colonel, dropping his hand, as if with accidental familiarity, on
that gentleman's shoulder. The Colonel, recognizing some occult quality in the touch, and some
unknown quantity in the glance of his questioner,
contented himself by replying, "No, sir," with dignity. A few rods away, York's conduct was as

characteristic and peculiar. "You had a mighty
fine chance; why did n't you plump him?" said
Jack Hamlin, as York drew near the buggy.
"Because I hate him," was the reply, heard only
by Jack. Contrary to popular belief, this reply
was not hissed between the lips of the speaker, but
was said in an ordinary tone. But Jack Hamlin,
who was an observer of mankind, noticed that the
speaker's hands were cold, and his lips dry, as he
helped him into the buggy, and accepted the
seeming paradox with a smile.

When Sandy Bar became convinced that the
quarrel between York and Scott could not be
settled after the usual local methods, it gave no
further concern thereto. But presently it was
rumored that the "Amity Claim" was in litigation,
and that its possession would be expensively dis-
puted by each of the partners. As it was well
known that the claim in question was "worked
out" and worthless, and that the partners, whom
it had already enriched, had talked of abandoning
it but a day or two before the quarrel, this proceeding could only be accounted for as gratuitous
spite. Later, two San Francisco lawyers made
their appearance in this guileless Arcadia, and
were eventually taken into the saloons, and —
what was pretty much the same thing —the confidences of the inhabitants. The results of this

unhallowed intimacy were many subpœnas ; and,
indeed, when the "Amity Claim" came to trial,
all of Sandy Bar that was not in compulsory
attendance at the county seat came there from curiosity. The gulches and ditches for miles around
were deserted. I do not propose to describe that
already famous trial. Enough that, in the language
of the plaintiff's counsel, "it was one of no ordinary significance, involving the inherent rights of
that untiring industry which had developed the
Pactolian resources of this golden land"; and, in
the homelier phrase of Colonel Starbottle, "A fuss
that gentlemen might hev settled in ten minutes
over a social glass, ef they meant business ; or in
ten seconds with a revolver, ef they meant fun."
Scott got a verdict, from which York instantly appealed. It was said that he had sworn to spend
his last dollar in the struggle.

In this way Sandy Bar began to accept the
enmity of the former partners as a lifelong feud,
and the fact that they had ever been friends was
forgotten. The few who expected to learn from
the trial the origin of the quarrel were disappointed. Among the various conjectures, that which
ascribed some occult feminine influence as the
cause was naturally popular, in a camp given to
dubious compliment of the sex. "My word for
it, gentlemen," said Colonel Starbottle, who had
been known in Sacramento as a Gentleman of the

Old School, "there's some lovely creature at the
bottom of this." The gallant Colonel then proceeded to illustrate his theory, by divers sprightly
stories, such as Gentlemen of the Old School are
in the habit of repeating, but which, from deference to the prejudices of gentlemen of a more re-
cent school, I refrain from transcribing here. But
it would appear that even the Colonel's theory was
fallacious. The only woman who personally might
have exercised any influence over the partners
was the pretty daughter of "old man Folinsbee,"
of Poverty Flat, at whose hospitable house —
which exhibited some comforts and refinements
rare in that crude civilization — both York and
Scott were frequent visitors. Yet into this charming retreat York strode one evening, a month after
the quarrel, and, beholding Scott sitting there,
turned to the fair hostess with the abrupt query,
"Do you love this man?" The young woman
thus addressed returned that answer — at once
spirited and evasive — which would occur to most
of my fair readers in such an exigency. Without
another word, York left the house. "Miss Jo"
heaved the least possible sigh as the door closed
on York's curls and square shoulders, and then,
like a good girl, turned to her insulted guest.
"But would you believe it, dear?" she afterward
related to an intimate friend, "the other creature,
after glowering at me for a moment, got upon its

hind legs, took its hat, and left, too; and that's
the last I've seen of either."

The same hard disregard of all other interests or
feelings in the gratification of their blind rancor
characterized all their actions. When York purchased the land below Scott's new claim, and
obliged the latter, at a great expense, to make a
long détour to carry a " tail-race " around it, Scott
retaliated by building a dam that overflowed
York's claim on the river. It was Scott, who, in
conjunction with Colonel Starbottle, first organized
that active opposition to the Chinamen, which resulted in the driving off of York's Mongolian la-
borers ; it was York who built the wagon-road and
established the express which rendered Scott's
mules and pack-trains obsolete; it was Scott who
called into life the Vigilance Committee which ex-
patriated York's friend, Jack Hamlin; it was
York who created the " Sandy Bar Herald," which
characterized the act as "a lawless outrage," and
Scott as a " Border Ruffian "; it was Scott, at the
head of twenty masked men, who, one moonlight
night, threw the offending " forms " into the yellow river, and scattered the types in the dusty
road. These proceedings were received in the distant and more civilized outlying towns as vague
indications of progress and vitality. I have before me a copy of the " Poverty Flat Pioneer," for the
week ending August 12, 1856, in which the editor,

under the head of "County Improvements," says:
"The new Presbyterian Church on C Street, at
Sandy Bar, is completed. It stands upon the lot
formerly occupied by the Magnolia Saloon, which
was so mysteriously burnt last month. The
temple, which now rises like a Phœnix from the
ashes of the Magnolia, is virtually the free gift of
H. J. York, Esq., of Sandy Bar, who purchased
the lot and donated the lumber. Other buildings
are going up in the vicinity, but the most notice-
able is the 'Sunny South Saloon,' erected by Captain Mat. Scott, nearly opposite the church. Captain Scott has spared no expense in the furnishing
of this saloon, which promises to be one of the
most agreeable places of resort in old Tuolumne.
He has recently imported two new, first-class bil-
liard-tables, with cork cushions. Our old friend,
'Mountain Jimmy,' will dispense liquors at the
bar. We refer our readers to the advertisement
in another column. Visitors to Sandy Bar cannot do better than give 'Jimmy' a call." Among
the local items occurred the following: "H. J.
York, Esq., of Sandy Bar, has offered a reward of
$100 for the detection of the parties who hauled
away the steps of the new Presbyterian Church, C
Street, Sandy Bar, during divine service on Sabbath evening last. Captain Scott adds another
hundred for the capture of the miscreants who
broke the magnificent plate-glass windows of the

new saloon on the following evening.   There is
some talk of reorganizing the old Vigilance Committee at Sandy Bar."

When, for many months of cloudless weather,
the hard, unwinking sun of Sandy Bar had regularly gone down on the unpacified wrath of these
men, there was some talk of mediation.   In particular, the pastor of the church to which I have
just referred — a sincere, fearless, but perhaps not
fully enlightened man — seized gladly upon the
occasion of York's liberality to attempt to reunite
the former partners.   He preached an earnest sermon on the abstract sinfulness of discord and rancor.   But the excellent sermons of the Rev. Mr.
Daws were directed to an ideal congregation that
did not exist at Sandy Bar, — a congregation of
beings of unmixed vices and virtues, of single im-
pulses, and perfectly logical motives, of preternatural simplicity, of childlike faith, and grown-up
responsibilities.   As, unfortunately, the people who
actually attended Mr. Daws's church were mainly
very human, somewhat artful, more self-excusing
than self-accusing, rather good-natured, and decidedly weak, they quietly shed that portion of the
sermon which referred to themselves, and, accepting York and Scott — who were both in defiant
attendance — as curious examples of those ideal
beings above referred to, felt a certain satisfaction
— which, I fear, was not altogether Christian-like

— in their " raking-down." If Mr. Daws expected
York and Scott to shake hands after the sermon,
he was disappointed. But he did not relax his
purpose. With that quiet fearlessness and deter-
mination which had won for him the respect of
men who were too apt to regard piety as synony-
mous with effeminacy, he attacked Scott in his
own house. What he said has not been recorded,
but it is to be feared that it was part of his sermon. When he had concluded, Scott looked at
him, not unkindly, over the glasses of his bar, and
said, less irreverently than the words might con-
vey, "Young man, I rather like your style ; but
when you know York and me as well as you do
God Almighty, it 'll be time to talk."

And so the feud progressed ; and so, as in more
illustrious examples, the private and personal enmity of two representative men led gradually to
the evolution of some crude, half-expressed principle or belief. It was not long before it was
made evident that those beliefs were identical with
certain broad principles laid down by the founders
of the American Constitution, as expounded by
the statesmanlike A. ; or were the fatal quicksands,
on which the ship of state might be wrecked,
warningly pointed out by the eloquent B. The
practical result of all which was the nomination of
York and Scott to represent the opposite factions
of Sandy Bar in legislative councils.

For some weeks past, the voters of Sandy Bar and the adjacent camps had been called upon, in large type, to "RALLY!" In vain the great pines at the cross-roads — whose trunks were compelled to bear this and other legends — moaned and pro‧ tested from their windy watch-towers. But one day, with fife and drum, and flaming transparency, a procession filed into the triangular grove at the head of the gulch. The meeting was called to order by Colonel Starbottle, who, having once enjoyed legislative functions, and being vaguely known as a "war-horse," was considered to be a valuable partisan of York. He concluded an appeal for his friend, with an enunciation of prin-ciples, interspersed with one or two anecdotes so gratuitously coarse that the very pines might have been moved to pelt him with their cast-off cones, as he stood there. But he created a laugh, on which his candidate rode into popular notice; and when York rose to speak, he was greeted with cheers. But, to the general astonishment, the new speaker at once launched into bitter denunciation of his rival. He not only dwelt upon Scott's deeds and example, as known to Sandy Bar, but spoke of facts connected with his previous career, hitherto unknown to his auditors. To great precision of epithet and directness of statement, the speaker added the fascination of revelation and exposure. The crowd cheered, yelled, and were delighted, but when this astounding philippic was concluded, there was a unanimous call for "Scott!" Colonel Starbottle would have resisted this manifest impropriety, but in vain. Partly from a crude sense of justice, partly from a meaner craving for excitement, the assemblage was inflexible; and Scott was dragged, pushed, and pulled upon the platform.

As his frowsy head and unkempt beard appeared above the railing, it was evident that he was drunk. But it was also evident, before he opened his lips, that the orator of Sandy Bar — the one man who could touch their vagabond sympathies (perhaps because he was not above appealing to them) — stood before them. A consciousness of this power lent a certain dignity to his figure, and I am not sure but that his very physical condition impressed them as a kind of regal unbending and large condescension. Howbeit, when this unexpected Hector arose from the ditch, York's myrmidons trembled.

"There's naught, gentlemen," said Scott, leaning forward on the railing, — "there's naught as that man hez said as is n't true. I was run outer Cairo; I did belong to the Regulators; I did desert from the army; I did leave a wife in Kansas. But thar's one thing he did n't charge me with, and, maybe, he's forgotten. For three years, gentlemen, I was that man's pardner! —" Whether he intended to say more, I cannot tell; a burst of applause artistically rounded and enforced the climax, and virtually elected the speaker. That fall he went to Sacramento, York went abroad; and for the first time in many years, distance and a new atmosphere isolated the old antagonists.

With little of change in the green wood, gray rock, and yellow river, but with much shifting of human landmarks, and new faces in its habitations, three years passed over Sandy Bar. The two men, once so identified with its character, seemed to have been quite forgotten. "You will never return to Sandy Bar," said Miss Folinsbee, the "Lily of Poverty Flat," on meeting York in Paris, "for Sandy Bar is no more. They call it Riverside now; and the new town is built higher up on the river-bank. By the by, 'Jo' says that Scott has won his suit about the 'Amity Claim,' and that he lives in the old cabin, and is drunk half his time. O, I beg your pardon," added the lively lady, as a flush crossed York's sallow cheek; "but, bless me, I really thought that old grudge was made up. I'm sure it ought to be."

It was three months after this conversation, and a pleasant summer evening, that the Poverty Flat coach drew up before the veranda of the Union Hotel at Sandy Bar. Among its passengers was one, apparently a stranger, in the local distinction

of well-fitting clothes and closely shaven face, who
demanded a private room and retired early to rest.
But before sunrise next morning he arose, and,
drawing some clothes from his carpet-bag, proceeded to array himself in a pair of white duck
trousers, a white duck overshirt, and straw hat.
When his toilet was completed, he tied a red ban-
danna handkerchief in a loop and threw it loosely
over his shoulders. The transformation was complete. As he crept softly down the stairs and
stepped into the road, no one would have detected
in him the elegant stranger of the previous night,
and but few have recognized the face and figure of
Henry York of Sandy Bar.

In the uncertain light of that early hour, and in
the change that had come over the settlement, he
had to pause for a moment to recall where he
stood. The Sandy Bar of his recollection lay below him, nearer the river; the buildings around
him were of later date and newer fashion. As he
strode toward the river, he noticed here a school-
house and there a church. A little farther on,
"The Sunny South" came in view, transformed
into a restaurant, its gilding faded and its paint
rubbed off. He now knew where he was; and,
running briskly down a declivity, crossed a ditch,
and stood upon the lower boundary of the Amity
Claim.

The gray mist was rising slowly from the river,

clinging to the tree-tops and drifting up the mountain-side, until it was caught among those rocky
altars, and held a sacrifice to the ascending sun.
At his feet the earth, cruelly gashed and scarred
by his forgotten engines, had, since the old days,
put on a show of greenness here and there, and
now smiled forgivingly up at him, as if things
were not so bad after all. A few birds were bath-
ing in the ditch with a pleasant suggestion of its
being a new and special provision of nature, and
a hare ran into an inverted sluice-box, as he approached, as if it were put there for that purpose.

He had not yet dared to look in a certain direction. But the sun was now high enough to paint
the little eminence on which the cabin stood. In
spite of his self-control, his heart beat faster as he
raised his eyes toward it. Its window and door
were closed, no smoke came from its *adobe* chimney, but it was else unchanged. When within a
few yards of it, he picked up a broken shovel, and,
shouldering it with a smile, strode toward the door
and knocked. There was no sound from within.
The smile died upon his lips as he nervously
pushed the door open.

A figure started up angrily and came toward
him, — a figure whose bloodshot eyes suddenly
fixed into a vacant stare, whose arms were at first
outstretched and then thrown up in warning ges-

ticulation, — a figure that suddenly gasped, choked, and then fell forward in a fit.

But before he touched the ground, York had him out into the open air and sunshine. In the struggle, both fell and rolled over on the ground. But the next moment York was sitting up, holding the convulsed frame of his former partner on his knee, and wiping the foam from his inarticulate lips. Gradually the tremor became less frequent, and then ceased; and the strong man lay unconscious in his arms.

For some moments York held him quietly thus, looking in his face. Afar, the stroke of a woodman's axe — a mere phantom of sound — was all that broke the stillness. High up the mountain, a wheeling hawk hung breathlessly above them. And then came voices, and two men joined them.

"A fight?" No, a fit; and would they help him bring the sick man to the hotel?

And there, for a week, the stricken partner lay, unconscious of aught but the visions wrought by disease and fear. On the eighth day, at sunrise, he rallied, and, opening his eyes, looked upon York, and pressed his hand; then he spoke: —

"And it's you. I thought it was only whiskey."

York replied by taking both of his hands, boyishly working them backward and forward, as his elbow rested on the bed, with a pleasant smile.

"And you 've been abroad.   How did you like
Paris ? "

" So, so.   How did *you* like Sacramento ? "

" Bully."

And that was all they could think to say.
Presently Scott opened his eyes again.

" I 'm mighty weak."

" You 'll get better soon."

"Not much."

A long silence followed, in which they could
hear the sounds of wood-chopping, and that Sandy
Bar was already astir for the coming day.   Then
Scott slowly and with difficulty turned his face to
York, and said, —

" I might hev killed you once."

"I wish you had."

They pressed each other's hands again, but
Scott's grasp was evidently failing.   He seemed to
summon his energies for a special effort.

" Old man ! "

" Old chap."

" Closer ! "

York bent his head toward the slowly fading
face.

" Do ye mind that morning ? "

" Yes."

A gleam of fun slid into the corner of Scott's
blue eye, as he whispered, —

" Old man, thar *was* too much saleratus in that
bread."

It is said that these were his last words. For when the sun, which had so often gone down upon the idle wrath of these foolish men, looked again upon them reunited, it saw the hand of Scott fall cold and irresponsive from the yearning clasp of his former partner, and it knew that the feud of Sandy Bar was at an end.

MR. THOMPSON'S PRODIGAL

WE all knew that Mr. Thompson was looking for his son, and a pretty bad one at that. That he was coming to California for this sole object was no secret to his fellow-passengers ; and the physical peculiarities, as well as the moral weaknesses, of the missing prodigal were made equally plain to us through the frank volubility of the parent. "You was speaking of a young man which was hung at Red Dog for sluice-robbing," said Mr. Thompson to a steerage passenger, one day ; "be you aware of the color of his eyes ? " "Black," responded the passenger. "Ah," said Mr. Thompson, referring to some mental memoranda, " Char-les's eyes was blue." He then walked away. Perhaps it was from this unsympathetic mode of inquiry, perhaps it was from that Western predilection to take a humorous view of any principle or sentiment persistently brought before them, that Mr. Thompson's quest was the subject of some satire among the passengers. A gratuitous advertisement of the missing Charles, addressed to " Jailers and Guardians," circulated privately among them ; everybody remembered to have met

Charles under distressing circumstances. Yet it is but due to my countrymen to state that when it was known that Thompson had embarked some wealth in this visionary project, but little of this satire found its way to his ears, and nothing was uttered in his hearing that might bring a pang to a father's heart, or imperil a possible pecuniary advantage of the satirist. Indeed, Mr. Bracy Tibbets's jocular proposition to form a joint-stock company to "prospect" for the missing youth received at one time quite serious entertainment.

Perhaps to superficial criticism Mr. Thompson's nature was not picturesque nor lovable. His history, as imparted at dinner, one day, by himself, was practical even in its singularity. After a hard and wilful youth and maturity, — in which he had buried a broken-spirited wife, and driven his son to sea, — he suddenly experienced religion. "I got it in New Orleans in '59," said Mr. Thompson, with the general suggestion of referring to an epidemic. "Enter ye the narrer gate. Parse me the beans." Perhaps this practical quality upheld him in his apparently hopeless search. He had no clew to the whereabouts of his runaway son; indeed, scarcely a proof of his present existence. From his indifferent recollection of the boy of twelve, he now expected to identify the man of twenty-five.

It would seem that he was successful. How he

succeeded was one of the few things he did not
tell. There are, I believe, two versions of the
story. One, that Mr. Thompson, visiting a hospital, discovered his son by reason of a peculiar
hymn, chanted by the sufferer, in a delirious dream
of his boyhood. This version, giving as it did
wide range to the finer feelings of the heart, was
quite popular; and as told by the Rev. Mr. Gush-
ington, on his return from his California tour,
never failed to satisfy an audience. The other was
less simple, and, as I shall adopt it here, deserves
more elaboration.

It was after Mr. Thompson had given up searching for his son among the living, and had taken
to the examination of cemeteries, and a careful inspection of the " cold *hic jacets* of the dead." At
this time he was a frequent visitor of " Lone
Mountain," — a dreary hill-top, bleak enough in
its original isolation, and bleaker for the white-
faced marbles by which San Francisco anchored
her departed citizens, and kept them down in a
shifting sand that refused to cover them, and
against a fierce and persistent wind that strove to
blow them utterly away. Against this wind the
old man opposed a will quite as persistent, — a
grizzled, hard face, and a tall, crape-bound hat
drawn tightly over his eyes, — and so spent days
in reading the mortuary inscriptions audibly to
himself. The frequency of Scriptural quotation

pleased him, and he was fond of corroborating
them by a pocket Bible. "That's from Psalms,"
he said, one day, to an adjacent grave-digger. The
man made no reply. Not at all rebuffed, Mr.
Thompson at once slid down into the open grave,
with a more practical inquiry, "Did you ever, in
your profession, come across Char-les Thompson?"
"Thompson be d—d!" said the grave-digger, with
great directness. "Which, if he had n't religion, I
think he is," responded the old man, as he clambered out of the grave.

It was, perhaps, on this occasion that Mr.
Thompson stayed later than usual. As he turned
his face toward the city, lights were beginning to
twinkle ahead, and a fierce wind, made visible by
fog, drove him forward, or, lying in wait, charged
him angrily from the corners of deserted suburban
streets. It was on one of these corners that something else, quite as indistinct and malevolent,
leaped upon him with an oath, a presented pistol,
and a demand for money. But it was met by a
will of iron and a grip of steel. The assailant and
assailed rolled together on the ground. But the
next moment the old man was erect; one hand
grasping the captured pistol, the other clutching
at arm's length the throat of a figure, surly, youthful, and savage.

"Young man," said Mr. Thompson, setting his
thin lips together, "what might be your name?"

"Thompson!"

The old man's hand slid from the throat to the arm of his prisoner, without relaxing its firmness.

"Char-les Thompson, come with me," he said, presently, and marched his captive to the hotel. What took place there has not transpired, but it was known the next morning that Mr. Thompson had found his son.

It is proper to add to the above improbable story, that there was nothing in the young man's appearance or manners to justify it. Grave, reticent, and handsome, devoted to his newly found parent, he assumed the emoluments and responsibilities of his new condition with a certain serious ease that more nearly approached that which San Francisco society lacked, and — rejected. Some chose to despise this quality as a tendency to "psalm singing"; others saw in it the inherited qualities of the parent, and were ready to prophesy for the son the same hard old age. But all agreed that it was not inconsistent with the habits of money-getting, for which father and son were respected.

And yet, the old man did not seem to be happy. Perhaps it was that the consummation of his wishes left him without a practical mission; perhaps — and it is the more probable — he had little love for the son he had regained. The obedience

he exacted was freely given, the reform he had set
his heart upon was complete; and yet, somehow, it
did not seem to please him.   In reclaiming his
son, he had fulfilled all the requirements that his
religious duty required of him, and yet the act
seemed to lack sanctification.   In this perplexity,
he read again the parable of the Prodigal Son, —
which he had long ago adopted for his guidance, —
and found that he had omitted the final feast of
reconciliation.   This seemed to offer the proper
quality of ceremoniousness in the sacrament between himself and his son; and so, a year after
the appearance of Charles, he set about giving him
a party.   " Invite everybody, Char-les," he said,
dryly ; " everybody who knows that I brought
you out of the wine-husks of iniquity, and the
company of harlots ; and bid them eat, drink, and
be merry."

Perhaps the old man had another reason, not
yet clearly analyzed.   The fine house he had built
on the sand-hills sometimes seemed lonely and
bare.   He often found himself trying to recon-
struct, from the grave features of Charles, the little
boy whom he but dimly remembered in the past,
and of whom lately he had been thinking a great
deal.   He believed this to be a sign of impending
old age and childishness ; but coming, one day, in
his formal drawing-room, upon a child of one of
the servants, who had strayed therein, he would

have taken him in his arms, but the child fled from before his grizzled face. So that it seemed eminently proper to invite a number of people to his house, and, from the array of San Francisco maidenhood, to select a daughter-in-law. And then there would be a child — a boy, whom he could " rare up " from the beginning, and — love — as he did not love Charles.

We were all at the party. The Smiths, Joneses, Browns, and Robinsons also came, in that fine flow of animal spirits, unchecked by any respect for the entertainer, which most of us are apt to find so fascinating. The proceedings would have been somewhat riotous, but for the social position of the actors. In fact, Mr. Bracy Tibbets, having naturally a fine appreciation of a humorous situation, but further impelled by the bright eyes of the Jones girls, conducted himself so remarkably as to attract the serious regard of Mr. Charles Thompson, who approached him, saying quietly : " You look ill, Mr. Tibbets ; let me conduct you to your carriage. Resist, you hound, and I 'll throw you through that window. This way, please ; the room is close and distressing." It is hardly necessary to say that but a part of this speech was audible to the company, and that the rest was not divulged by Mr. Tibbets, who afterward regretted the sudden illness which kept him from witnessing a certain amusing incident, which the fastest Miss Jones characterized as the " richest part of the blow-out," and which I hasten to record.

It was at supper. It was evident that Mr. Thompson had overlooked much lawlessness in the conduct of the younger people, in his abstract contemplation of some impending event. When the cloth was removed, he rose to his feet, and grimly tapped upon the table. A titter, that broke out among the Jones girls, became epidemic on one side of the board. Charles Thompson, from the foot of the table, looked up in tender perplexity. " He's going to sing a Doxology," " He's going to pray," " Silence for a speech," ran round the room.

" It's one year to-day, Christian brothers and sisters," said Mr. Thompson, with grim deliberation, — " one year to-day since my son came home from eating of wine-husks and spending of his substance on harlots." (The tittering suddenly ceased.) " Look at him now. Char-les Thompson, stand up." (Charles Thompson stood up.) " One year ago to-day, — and look at him now."

He was certainly a handsome prodigal, standing there in his cheerful evening-dress, — a repentant prodigal, with sad, obedient eyes turned upon the harsh and unsympathetic glance of his father. The youngest Miss Smith, from the pure depths of her foolish little heart, moved unconsciously toward him.

"It's fifteen years ago since he left my house,"
said Mr. Thompson, "a rovier and a prodigal. I
was myself a man of sin, O Christian friends, — a
man of wrath and bitterness" ("Amen," from
the eldest Miss Smith), — "but praise be God, I've
fled the wrath to come. It's five years ago since
I got the peace that passeth understanding. Have
you got it, friends?" (A general sub-chorus of
"No, no," from the girls, and, "Pass the word for
it," from Midshipman Coxe, of the U. S. sloop
Wethersfield.) "Knock, and it shall be opened to
you.

"And when I found the error of my ways, and
the preciousness of grace," continued Mr. Thompson, "I came to give it to my son. By sea and
land I sought him far, and fainted not. I did not
wait for him to come to me, which the same I
might have done, and justified myself by the Book
of books, but I sought him out among his husks,
and — " (the rest of the sentence was lost in the
rustling withdrawal of the ladies). "Works,
Christian friends, is my motto. By their works
shall ye know them, and there is mine."

The particular and accepted work to which Mr.
Thompson was alluding had turned quite pale, and
was looking fixedly toward an open door leading
to the veranda, lately filled by gaping servants,
and now the scene of some vague tumult. As the
noise continued, a man, shabbily dressed, and evi-

dently in liquor, broke through the opposing guardians, and staggered into the room. The transition from the fog and darkness without to the glare and heat within ev'dently dazzled and stupefied him. He removed his battered hat, and passed it once or twice before his eyes, as he steadied himself, but unsuccessfully, by the back of a chair. Suddenly, his wandering glance fell upon the pale face of Charles Thompson; and with a gleam of childlike recognition, and a weak, falsetto laugh, he darted forward, caught at the table, upset the glasses, and literally fell upon the prodigal's breast.

"Sha'ly! yo' d—d ol' scoun'rel, hoo rar ye!"

"Hush!— sit down!— hush!" said Charles Thompson, hurriedly endeavoring to extricate himself from the embrace of his unexpected guest.

"Look at 'm!" continued the stranger, unheeding the admonition, but suddenly holding the unfortunate Charles at arm's length, in loving and undisguised admiration of his festive appearance. "Look at 'm! Ain't he nasty? Sha'ls, I'm prow of yer!"

"Leave the house!" said Mr. Thompson, rising, with a dangerous look in his cold, gray eye. " Char-les, how dare you?"

"Simmer down, ole man! Sha'ls, who's th' ol' bloat? Eh?"

"Hush, man; here, take this!" With nervous

hands, Charles Thompson filled a glass with liquor. "Drink it and go — until to-morrow — any time, but — leave us! — go now!" But even then, ere the miserable wretch could drink, the old man, pale with passion, was upon him. Half carrying him in his powerful arms, half dragging him through the circling crowd of frightened guests, he had reached the door, swung open by the waiting servants, when Charles Thompson started from a seeming stupor, crying, —

"Stop!"

The old man stopped. Through the open door the fog and wind drove chilly. "What does this mean?" he asked, turning a baleful face on Charles.

"Nothing — but stop — for God's sake. Wait till to-morrow, but not to-night. Do not — I implore you — do this thing."

There was something in the tone of the young man's voice, something, perhaps, in the contact of the struggling wretch he held in his powerful arms; but a dim, indefinite fear took possession of the old man's heart. "Who," he whispered, hoarsely, "is this man?"

Charles did not answer.

"Stand back, there, all of you," thundered Mr. Thompson, to the crowding guests around him. "Char-les — come here! I command you — I — I — I — beg you — tell me *who* is this man?"

Only two persons heard the answer that came
faintly from the lips of Charles Thompson, —

"YOUR SON."

When day broke over the bleak sand-hills, the
guests had departed from Mr. Thompson's ban-
quet-halls. The lights still burned dimly and
coldly in the deserted rooms, — deserted by all
but three figures, that huddled together in the
chill drawing-room, as if for warmth. One lay in
drunken slumber on a couch ; at his feet sat he
who had been known as Charles Thompson ; and
beside them, haggard and shrunken to half his
size, bowed the figure of Mr. Thompson, his gray
eye fixed, his elbows upon his knees, and his hands
clasped over his ears, as if to shut out the sad, en-
treating voice that seemed to fill the room.

"God knows I did not set about to wilfully
deceive. The name I gave that night was the
first that came into my thought, — the name of one
whom I thought dead, — the dissolute companion
of my shame. And when you questioned further,
I used the knowledge that I gained from him to
touch your heart to set me free ; only, I swear,
for that ! But when you told me who you were,
and I first saw the opening of another life before
me — then — then —   O, sir, if I was hungry,
homeless, and reckless, when I would have robbed
you of your gold, I was heart-sick, helpless, and

desperate, when I would have robbed you of your love ! "

The old man stirred not. From his luxurious couch the newly found prodigal snored peacefully.

" I had no father I could claim. I never knew a home but this. I was tempted. I have been happy, — very happy."

He rose and stood before the old man.

" Do not fear that I shall come between your son and his inheritance. To-day I leave this place, never to return. The world is large, sir, and, thanks to your kindness, I now see the way by which an honest livelihood is gained. Good by. You will not take my hand ? Well, well. Good by."

He turned to go. But when he had reached the door he suddenly came back, and, raising with both hands the grizzled head, he kissed it once and twice.

" Char-les."

There was no reply.

" Char-les ! "

The old man rose with a frightened air, and tottered feebly to the door. It was open. There came to him the awakened tumult of a great city, in which the prodigal's footsteps were lost forever.

THE ROMANCE OF MADROÑO HOLLOW.

THE latch on the garden gate of the Folinsbee Ranch clicked twice. The gate itself was so much in shadow that lovely night, that "old man Folinsbee," sitting on his porch, could distinguish nothing but a tall white hat and beside it a few fluttering ribbons, under the pines that marked the entrance. Whether because of this fact, or that he considered a sufficient time had elapsed since the clicking of the latch for more positive disclosure, I do not know; but after a few moments' hesitation he quietly laid aside his pipe and walked slowly down the winding path toward the gate. At the Ceanothus hedge he stopped and listened.

There was not much to hear. The hat was saying to the ribbons that it was a fine night, and remarking generally upon the clear outline of the Sierras against the blue-black sky. The ribbons, it so appeared, had admired this all the way home, and asked the hat if it had ever seen anything half so lovely as the moonlight on the summit. The hat never had; it recalled some lovely nights in the South in Alabama ("in the South in Ahlabahm" was the way the old man heard it), but then there were other things that made this night seem so pleasant. The ribbons could not possibly conceive what the hat could be thinking about. At this point there was a pause, of which Mr. Folinsbee availed himself to walk very grimly and craunchingly down the gravel-walk toward the gate. Then the hat was lifted, and disappeared in the shadow, and Mr. Folinsbee confronted only the half-foolish, half-mischievous, but wholly pretty face of his daughter.

It was afterward known to Madroño Hollow that sharp words passed between "Miss Jo" and the old man, and that the latter coupled the names of one Culpepper Starbottle and his uncle, Colonel Starbottle, with certain uncomplimentary epithets, and that Miss Jo retaliated sharply. "Her father's blood before her father's face boiled up and proved her truly of his race," quoted the blacksmith, who leaned toward the noble verse of Byron. "She saw the old man's bluff and raised him," was the directer comment of the college-bred Masters.

Meanwhile the subject of these animadversions proceeded slowly along the road to a point where the Folinsbee mansion came in view, — a long, narrow, white building, unpretentious, yet superior to its neighbors, and bearing some evidences of taste and refinement in the vines that clambered over its porch, in its French windows, and the

white muslin curtains that kept out the fierce California sun by day, and were now touched with silver in the gracious moonlight.   Culpepper leaned
against the low fence, and gazed long and earnestly
at the building.   Then the moonlight vanished ghost-
like from one of the windows, a material glow took
its place, and a girlish figure, holding a candle, drew
the white curtains together.   To Culpepper it was
a vestal virgin standing before a hallowed shrine ;
to the prosaic observer I fear it was only a fair-
haired young woman, whose wicked black eyes still
shone with unfilial warmth.   Howbeit, when the
figure had disappeared he stepped out briskly into
the moonlight of the high-road.   Here he took off
his distinguishing hat to wipe his forehead, and and
the moon shone full upon his face.

It was not an unprepossessing one, albeit a trifle
too thin and lank and bilious to be altogether
pleasant.   The cheek-bones were prominent, and
the black eyes sunken in their orbits.   Straight
black hair fell slantwise off a high but narrow
forehead, and swept part of a hollow cheek.   A
long black mustache followed the perpendicular
curves of his mouth.   It was on the whole a serious, even Quixotic face, but at times it was relieved
by a rare smile of such tender and even pathetic
sweetness, that Miss Jo is reported to have said
that, if it would only last through the ceremony,
she would have married its possessor on the spot.

"I once told him so," added that shameless young woman ; "but the man instantly fell into a settled melancholy, and has n't smiled since."

A half-mile below the Folinsbee Ranch the white road dipped and was crossed by a trail that ran through Madroño Hollow. Perhaps because it was a near cut-off to the settlement, perhaps from some less practical reason, Culpepper took this trail, and in a few moments stood among the rarely beautiful trees that gave their name to the valley. Even in that uncertain light the weird beauty of these harlequin masqueraders was apparent ; their red trunks — a blush in the moonlight, a deep blood-stain in the shadow — stood out against the silvery green foliage. It was as if Nature in some gracious moment had here caught and crystallized the gypsy memories of the transplanted Spaniard, to cheer him in his lonely exile.

As Culpepper entered the grove he heard loud voices. As he turned toward a clump of trees, a figure so *bizarre* and characteristic that it might have been a resident Daphne — a figure over-dressed in crimson silk and lace, with bare brown arms and shoulders, and a wreath of honeysuckle — stepped out of the shadow. It was followed by a man. Culpepper started. To come to the point briefly, he recognized in the man the features of his respected uncle, Colonel Starbottle ; in the female, a lady who may be briefly described as one

possessing absolutely no claim to an introduction
to the polite reader. To hurry over equally unpleasant details, both were evidently under the
influence of liquor.

From the excited conversation that ensued, Culpepper gathered that some insult had been put
upon the lady at a public ball which she had attended that evening; that the Colonel, her escort,
had failed to resent it with the sanguinary completeness that she desired. I regret that, even in
a liberal age, I may not record the exact and even
picturesque language in which this was conveyed
to her hearers. Enough that at the close of a fiery
peroration, with feminine inconsistency she flew at
the gallant Colonel, and would have visited her
delayed vengeance upon his luckless head, but for
the prompt interference of Culpepper. Thwarted
in this, she threw herself upon the ground, and
then into unpicturesque hysterics. There was a
fine moral lesson, not only in this grotesque performance of a sex which cannot afford to be grotesque, but in the ludicrous concern with which
it inspired the two men. Culpepper, to whom
woman was more or less angelic, was pained and
sympathetic; the Colonel, to whom she was more or
less improper, was exceedingly terrified and embarrassed. Howbeit the storm was soon over, and
after Mistress Dolores had returned a little dagger
to its sheath (her garter), she quietly took herself

out of Madroño Hollow, and happily out of these
pages forever. The two men, left to themselves,
conversed in low tones. Dawn stole upon them
before they separated: the Colonel quite sobered
and in full possession of his usual jaunty self-
assertion; Culpepper with a baleful glow in his
hollow cheek, and in his dark eyes a rising fire.

The next morning the general ear of Madroño
Hollow was filled with rumors of the Colonel's
mishap. It was asserted that he had been invited
to withdraw his female companion from the floor
of the Assembly Ball at the Independence Hotel,
and that, failing to do this, both were expelled. It
is to be regretted that in 1854 public opinion was
divided in regard to the propriety of this step, and
that there was some discussion as to the comparative virtue of the ladies who were not expelled;
but it was generally conceded that the real *casus
belli* was political. "Is this a dashed Puritan
meeting?" had asked the Colonel, savagely. "It's
no Pike County shindig," had responded the floor-
manager, cheerfully. "You're a Yank!" had
screamed the Colonel, profanely qualifying the
noun. "Get! you border ruffian," was the reply.
Such at least was the substance of the reports.
As, at that sincere epoch, expressions like the
above were usually followed by prompt action, a
fracas was confidently looked for.

Nothing, however, occurred. Colonel Starbottle
made his appearance next day upon the streets
with somewhat of his usual pomposity, a little
restrained by the presence of his nephew, who
accompanied him, and who, as a universal favorite,
also exercised some restraint upon the curious and
impertinent. But Culpepper's face wore a look of
anxiety quite at variance with his usual grave repose. "The Don don't seem to take the old man's
set-back kindly," observed the sympathizing blacksmith. "P'r'aps he was sweet on Dolores himself," suggested the sceptical expressman.

It was a bright morning, a week after this occurrence, that Miss Jo Folinsbee stepped from her
garden into the road. This time the latch did not
click as she cautiously closed the gate behind her.
After a moment's irresolution, which would have
been awkward but that it was charmingly em-
ployed, after the manner of her sex, in adjusting a
bow under a dimpled but rather prominent chin,
and in pulling down the fingers of a neatly fitting
glove, she tripped toward the settlement. Small
wonder that a passing teamster drove his six
mules into the wayside ditch and imperilled his
load, to keep the dust from her spotless garments ;
small wonder that the "Lightning Express" withheld its speed and flash to let her pass, and that
the expressman, who had never been known to
exchange more than rapid monosyllables with his

fellow-man, gazed after her with breathless admiration. For she was certainly attractive. In a country where the ornamental sex followed the example of youthful Nature, and were prone to overdress and glaring efflorescence, Miss Jo's simple and tasteful raiment added much to the physical charm of, if it did not actually suggest a sentiment to, her presence. It is said that Euchre-deck Billy, working in the gulch at the crossing, never saw Miss Folinsbee pass but that he always remarked apologetically to his partner, that "he believed he *must* write a letter home." Even Bill Masters, who saw her in Paris presented to the favorable criticism of that most fastidious man, the late Emperor, said that she was stunning, but a big discount on what she was at Madroño Hollow.

It was still early morning, but the sun, with California extravagance, had already begun to beat hotly on the little chip hat and blue ribbons, and Miss Jo was obliged to seek the shade of a by-path. Here she received the timid advances of a vagabond yellow dog graciously, until, emboldened by his success, he insisted upon accompanying her, and, becoming slobberingly demonstrative, threatened her spotless skirt with his dusty paws, when she drove him from her with some slight acerbity, and a stone which haply fell within fifty feet of its destined mark. Having thus proved her

ability to defend herself, with characteristic inconsistency she took a small panic, and, gathering her
white skirts in one hand, and holding the brim of
her hat over her eyes with the other, she ran
swiftly at least a hundred yards before she stopped.
Then she began picking some ferns and a few
wild-flowers still spared to the withered fields, and
then a sudden distrust of her small ankles seized
her, and she inspected them narrowly for those
burrs and bugs and snakes which are supposed to
lie in wait for helpless womanhood. Then she
plucked some golden heads of wild oats, and with
a sudden inspiration placed them in her black
hair, and then came quite unconsciously upon the
trail leading to Madroño Hollow.

Here she hesitated. Before her ran the little
trail, vanishing at last into the bosky depths below. The sun was very hot. She must be very
far from home. Why should she not rest awhile
under the shade of a madroño ?

She answered these questions by going there at
once. After thoroughly exploring the grove, and
satisfying herself that it contained no other living
human creature, she sat down under one of the
largest trees, with a satisfactory little sigh. Miss
Jo loved the madroño. It was a cleanly tree ; no
dust ever lay upon its varnished leaves ; its im-
maculate shade never was known to harbor grub
or insect.

She looked up at the rosy arms interlocked and arched above her head. She looked down at the delicate ferns and cryptogams at her feet. Something glittered at the root of the tree. She picked it up; it was a bracelet. She examined it carefully for cipher or inscription; there was none. She could not resist a natural desire to clasp it on her arm, and to survey it from that advantageous view-point. This absorbed her attention for some moments; and when she looked up again she beheld at a little distance Culpepper Starbottle.

He was standing where he had halted, with instinctive delicacy, on first discovering her. Indeed, he had even deliberated whether he ought not to go away without disturbing her. But some fascination held him to the spot. Wonderful power of humanity! Far beyond jutted an outlying spur of the Sierra, vast, compact, and silent. Scarcely a hundred yards away, a league-long chasm dropped its sheer walls of granite a thousand feet. On every side rose up the serried ranks of pine-trees, in whose close-set files centuries of storm and change had wrought no breach. Yet all this seemed to Culpepper to have been planned by an all-wise Providence as the natural background to the figure of a pretty girl in a yellow dress.

Although Miss Jo had confidently expected to meet Culpepper somewhere in her ramble, now

that he came upon her suddenly, she felt disappointed and embarrassed. His manner, too, was
more than usually grave and serious, and more
than ever seemed to jar upon that audacious levity
which was this giddy girl's power and security in
a society where all feeling was dangerous. As he
approached her she rose to her feet, but almost before she knew it he had taken her hand and drawn
her to a seat beside him. This was not what Miss
Jo had expected, but nothing is so difficult to pred-
icate as the exact preliminaries of a declaration
of love.

What did Culpepper say ? Nothing, I fear, that
will add anything to the wisdom of the reader;
nothing, I fear, that Miss Jo had not heard sub-
stantially from other lips before. But there was a
certain conviction, fire-speed, and fury in the manner that was deliciously novel to the young lady.
It was certainly something to be courted in the
nineteenth century with all the passion and extravagance of the sixteenth ; it was something to
hear, amid the slang of a frontier society, the language of knight-errantry poured into her ear by
this lantern-jawed, dark-browed descendant of the
Cavaliers.

I do not know that there was anything more in
it. The facts, however, go to show that at a certain point Miss Jo dropped her glove, and that in
recovering it Culpepper possessed himself first of

her hand and then her lips.   When they stood up
to go Culpepper had his arm around her waist, and
her black hair, with its sheaf of golden oats, rested
against the breast pocket of his coat.   But even
then I do not think her fancy was entirely captive.
She took a certain satisfaction in this demonstra-
tion of Culpepper's splendid height, and mentally
compared it with a former flame, one Lieutenant
McMirk, an active, but under-sized Hector, who
subsequently fell a victim to the incautiously composed and monotonous beverages of a frontier garrison.   Nor was she so much preoccupied but that
her quick eyes, even while absorbing Culpepper's
glances, were yet able to detect, at a distance, the
figure of a man approaching.   In an instant she
slipped out of Culpepper's arm, and, whipping
her hands behind her, said, "There's that horrid
man !"

Culpepper looked up and beheld his respected
uncle panting and blowing over the hill.   His
brow contracted as he turned to Miss Jo : "You
don't like my uncle !"

"I hate him !"   Miss Jo was recovering her
ready tongue.

Culpepper blushed.   He would have liked to
enter upon some details of the Colonel's pedigree
and exploits, but there was not time.   He only
smiled sadly.   The smile melted Miss Jo.   She
held out her hand quickly, and said with even

more than her usual effrontery, " Don't let that man get you into any trouble. Take care of yourself, dear, and don't let anything happen to you."

Miss Jo intended this speech to be pathetic; the tenure of life among her lovers had hitherto been very uncertain. Culpepper turned toward her, but she had already vanished in the thicket.

The Colonel came up panting. " I 've looked all over town for you, and be dashed to you, sir. Who was that with you ? "

" A lady."   (Culpepper never lied, but he was discreet.)

" D—m 'em all ! Look yar, Culp, I 've spotted the man who gave the order to put me off the floor " (" flo" was what the Colonel said) " the other night ! "

" Who was it ? " asked Culpepper, listlessly.

" Jack Folinsbee."

" Who ? "

" Why, the son of that dashed nigger-worshipping psalm-singing Puritan Yankee. What 's the matter, now ? Look yar, Culp, you ain't goin' back on your blood, ar' ye ? You ain't goin' back on your word ? Ye ain't going down at the feet of this trash, like a whipped hound ? "

Culpepper was silent. He was very white. Presently he looked up and said quietly, " No."

Culpepper Starbottle had challenged Jack Fol-

insbee, and the challenge was accepted. The cause
alleged was the expelling of Culpepper's uncle from
the floor of the Assembly Ball by the order of
Folinsbee. This much Madroño Hollow knew and
could swear to; but there were other strange rumors afloat, of which the blacksmith was an able
expounder. "You see, gentlemen," he said to the
crowd gathered around his anvil, "I ain't got no
theory of this affair, I only give a few facts as have
come to my knowledge. Culpepper and Jack
meets quite accidental like in Bob's saloon. Jack
goes up to Culpepper and says, 'A word with you.'
Culpepper bows and steps aside in this way, Jack
standing about *here*." (The blacksmith demon-
strates the position of the parties with two old
horseshoes on the anvil.) "Jack pulls a bracelet
from his pocket and says, 'Do you know that
bracelet?' Culpepper says, 'I do not,' quite cool-
like and easy. Jack says, 'You gave it to my sister.' Culpepper says, still cool as you please, 'I did
not.' Jack says, 'You lie, G—d d—mn you,' and
draws his derringer. Culpepper jumps forward
about here" (reference is made to the diagram)
"and Jack fires. Nobody hit. It's a mighty cu-
r'o's thing, gentlemen," continued the blacksmith,
dropping suddenly into the abstract, and leaning
meditatively on his anvil, — "it's a mighty cur'o's
thing that nobody gets hit so often. You and me
empties our revolvers sociably at each other over a

little game, and the room full and nobody gets hit! That 's what gets me."

" Never mind, Thompson," chimed in Bill Masters, " there 's another and a better world where we shall know all that and — become better shots. Go on with your story."

" Well, some grabs Culpepper and some grabs Jack, and so separates them. Then Jack tells 'em as how he had seen his sister wear a bracelet which he knew was one that had been given to Dolores by Colonel Starbottle. That Miss Jo would n't say where she got it, but owned up to having seen Culpepper that day. Then the most cur'o's thing of it yet, what does Culpepper do but rise up and takes all back that he said, and allows that he *did* give her the bracelet. Now my opinion, gentlemen, is that he lied ; it ain't like that man to give a gal that he respects anything off of that piece, Dolores. But it 's all the same now, and there 's but one thing to be done."

The way this one thing was done belongs to the record of Madroño Hollow. The morning was bright and clear ; the air was slightly chill, but that was from the mist which arose along the banks of the river. As early as six o'clock the designated ground — a little opening in the madroño grove — was occupied by Culpepper Starbottle, Colonel Starbottle, his second, and the surgeon. The Colonel was exalted and excited, albeit in a

rather imposing, dignified way, and pointed out to
the surgeon the excellence of the ground, which at
that hour was wholly shaded from the sun, whose
steady stare is more or less discomposing to your
duellist.   The surgeon threw himself on the grass
and smoked his cigar.   Culpepper, quiet and
thoughtful, leaned against a tree and gazed up the
river.   There was a strange suggestion of a picnic
about the group, which was heightened when the
Colonel drew a bottle from his coat-tails, and, taking a preliminary draught, offered it to the others.
"Cocktails, sir," he explained with dignified precision.   "A gentleman, sir, should never go out
without 'em.   Keeps off the morning chill.   I remember going out in '53 with Hank Boompirater.
Good ged, sir, the man had to put on his overcoat,
and was shot in it.   Fact."

But the noise of wheels drowned the Colonel's
reminiscences, and a rapidly driven buggy, containing Jack Folinsbee, Calhoun Bungstarter, his second, and Bill Masters, drew up on the ground.
Jack Folinsbee leaped out gayly.   "I had the jol-
liest work to get away without the governor's
hearing," he began, addressing the group before him
with the greatest volubility.   Calhoun Bungstarter
touched his arm, and the young man blushed.   It
was his first duel.

"If you are ready, gentlemen," said Mr. Bungstarter, "we had better proceed to business.   I

believe it is understood that no apology will be
offered or accepted. We may as well settle preliminaries at once, or I fear we shall be interrupted.
There is a rumor in town that the Vigilance Committee are seeking our friends the Starbottles, and
I believe, as their fellow-countryman, I have the
honor to be included in their warrant."

At this probability of interruption, that gravity
which had hitherto been wanting fell upon the
group. The preliminaries were soon arranged and
the principals placed in position. Then there was
a silence.

To a spectator from the hill, impressed with the
picnic suggestion, what might have been the pop-
ping of two champagne corks broke the stillness.

Culpepper had fired in the air. Colonel Starbottle uttered a low curse. Jack Folinsbee sulkily
demanded another shot.

Again the parties stood opposed to each other.
Again the word was given, and what seemed to be
the simultaneous report of both pistols rose upon
the air. But after an interval of a few seconds all
were surprised to see Culpepper slowly raise his
unexploded weapon and fire it harmlessly above
his head. Then, throwing the pistol upon the
ground, he walked to a tree and leaned silently
against it.

Jack Folinsbee flew into a paroxysm of fury.
Colonel Starbottle raved and swore. Mr. Bung-

starter was properly shocked at their conduct.
"Really, gentlemen, if Mr. Culpepper Starbottle
declines another shot, I do not see how we can
proceed."

But the Colonel's blood was up, and Jack Folinsbee was equally implacable. A hurried consul-
tation ensued, which ended by Colonel Starbottle
taking his nephew's place as principal, Bill Masters
acting as second, *vice* Mr. Bungstarter, who de-
clined all further connection with the affair.

Two distinct reports rang through the Hollow.
Jack Folinsbee dropped his smoking pistol, took a
step forward, and then dropped heavily upon his
face.

In a moment the surgeon was at his side. The
confusion was heightened by the trampling of
hoofs, and the voice of the blacksmith bidding
them flee for their lives before the coming storm.
A moment more and the ground was cleared, and
the surgeon, looking up, beheld only the white face
of Culpepper bending over him.

" Can you save him ? "

" I cannot say. Hold up his head a moment,
while I run to the buggy."

Culpepper passed his arm tenderly around the
neck of the insensible man. Presently the surgeon returned with some stimulants.

" There, that will do, Mr. Starbottle, thank you.
Now my advice is to get away from here while

you can. I 'll look after Folinsbee. Do you hear ? "

Culpepper's arm was still round the neck of his late foe, but his head had drooped and fallen on the wounded man's shoulder. The surgeon looked down, and, catching sight of his face, stooped and lifted him gently in his arms. He opened his coat and waistcoat. There was blood upon his shirt, and a bullet-hole in his breast. He had been shot unto death at the first fire.

THE POET OF SIERRA FLAT.

AS the enterprising editor of the "Sierra Flat
Record" stood at his case setting type for
his next week's paper, he could not help hearing
the woodpeckers who were busy on the roof above
his head. It occurred to him that possibly the
birds had not yet learned to recognize in the rude
structure any improvement on nature, and this idea
pleased him so much that he incorporated it in the
editorial article which he was then doubly compos-
ing. For the editor was also printer of the "Record"; and although that remarkable journal was
reputed to exert a power felt through all Calaveras and a greater part of Tuolumne County, strict
economy was one of the conditions of its beneficent
existence.

Thus preoccupied, he was startled by the sudden
irruption of a small roll of manuscript, which was
thrown through the open door and fell at his feet.
He walked quickly to the threshold and looked
down the tangled trail which led to the high-road.
But there was nothing to suggest the presence of
his mysterious contributor. A hare limped slowly
away, a green-and-gold lizard paused upon a pine

stump, the woodpeckers ceased their work. So
complete had been his sylvan seclusion, that he
found it difficult to connect any human agency
with the act; rather the hare seemed to have an
inexpressibly guilty look, the woodpeckers to main-
tain a significant silence, and the lizard to be con-
science-stricken into stone.

An examination of the manuscript, however,
corrected this injustice to defenceless nature. It
was evidently of human origin, — being verse, and
of exceeding bad quality. The editor laid it
aside. As he did so he thought he saw a face at
the window. Sallying out in some indignation, he
penetrated the surrounding thicket in every direction, but his search was as fruitless as before. The
poet, if it were he, was gone.

A few days after this the editorial seclusion was
invaded by voices of alternate expostulation and
entreaty. Stepping to the door, the editor was
amazed at beholding Mr. Morgan McCorkle, a well-
known citizen of Angelo, and a subscriber to the
" Record," in the act of urging, partly by force and
partly by argument, an awkward young man toward
the building. When he had finally effected his
object, and, as it were, safely landed his prize in a
chair, Mr. McCorkle took off his hat, carefully
wiped the narrow isthmus of forehead which divided his black brows from his stubby hair, and
with an explanatory wave of his hand toward his

reluctant companion, said, "A borned poet, and the cussedest fool you ever seed !"

Accepting the editor's smile as a recognition of the introduction, Mr. McCorkle panted and went on : "Did n't want to come ! 'Mister Editor don't want to see me, Morg,' sez he. 'Milt,' sez I, 'he do ; a borned poet like you and a gifted genius like he oughter come together sociable !' And I fetched him. Ah, will yer ? " The born poet had, after exhibiting signs of great distress, started to run. But Mr. McCorkle was down upon him instantly, seizing him by his long linen coat, and settled him back in his chair. " 'T ain't no use stampeding. Yer ye are and yer ye stays. For yer a borned poet, — ef ye are as shy as a jackass rabbit. Look at 'im now ! "

He certainly was not an attractive picture. There was hardly a notable feature in his weak face, except his eyes, which were moist and shy and not unlike the animal to which Mr. McCorkle had compared him. It was the face that the editor had seen at the window.

"Knowed him for fower year, — since he war a boy," continued Mr. McCorkle in a loud whisper. "Allers the same, bless you ! Can jerk a rhyme as easy as turnin' jack. Never had any eddication ; lived out in Missooray all his life. But he 's chock full o' poetry. On'y this mornin' sez I to him, — he camps along o' me, — ' Milt !' sez I, ' are break-

fast ready?' and he up and answers back quite
peart and chipper, 'The breakfast it is ready, and
the birds is singing free, and it's risin' in the dawn-
in' light is happiness to me!' When a man," said
Mr. McCorkle, dropping his voice with deep solemnity, "gets off things like them, without any
call to do it, and handlin' flapjacks over a cook-
stove at the same time, — that man's a borned
poet."

There was an awkward pause. Mr. McCorkle
beamed patronizingly on his *protégé*. The born
poet looked as if he were meditating another flight,
— not a metaphorical one. The editor asked if he
could do anything for them.

"In course you can," responded Mr. McCorkle,
" that's jest it. Milt, where's that poetry?"

The editor's countenance fell as the poet produced from his pocket a roll of manuscript. He
however, took it mechanically and glanced over it.
It was evidently a duplicate of the former mysterious contribution.

The editor then spoke briefly but earnestly. I
regret that I cannot recall his exact words, but it
appeared that never before, in the history of the
" Record," had the pressure been so great upon its
columns. Matters of paramount importance, deeply affecting the material progress of Sierra, questions touching the absolute integrity of Calaveras
and Tuolumne as social communities, were even

now waiting expression. Weeks, nay, months, must elapse before that pressure would be removed, and the " Record " could grapple with any but the sternest of topics. Again, the editor had noticed with pain the absolute decline of poetry in the foot-hills of the Sierras. Even the works of Byron and Moore attracted no attention in Dutch Flat, and a prejudice seemed to exist against Tennyson in Grass Valley. But the editor was not without hope for the future. In the course of four or five years, when the country was settled, —

"What would be the cost to print this yer?" interrupted Mr. McCorkle, quietly.

"About fifty dollars, as an advertisement," responded the editor with cheerful alacrity.

Mr. McCorkle placed the sum in the editor's hand. " Yer see thet 's what I sez to Milt, ' Milt,' sez I, ' pay as you go, for you are a borned poet. Hevin no call to write, but doin' it free and spontaneous like, in course you pays. Thet 's why Mr. Editor never printed your poetry.' "

"What name shall I put to it?" asked the editor.

" Milton."

It was the first word that the born poet had spoken during the interview, and his voice was so very sweet and musical that the editor looked at him curiously, and wondered if he had a sister.

"Milton ; is that all ? "

"Thet 's his furst name," exclaimed Mr. Mc-
Corkle.

The editor here suggested that as there had been
another poet of that name —

"Milt might be took for him! Thet 's bad,"
reflected Mr. McCorkle with simple gravity.
"Well, put down his hull name, — Milton Chubbuck."

The editor made a note of the fact. "I 'll set it
up now," he said. This was also a hint that the
interview was ended. The poet and patron, arm
in arm, drew towards the door. "In next week's
paper," said the editor, smilingly, in answer to the
childlike look of inquiry in the eyes of the poet,
and in another moment they were gone.

The editor was as good as his word. He straightway betook himself to his case, and, unrolling the
manuscript, began his task. The woodpeckers on
the roof recommenced theirs, and in a few moments
the former sylvan seclusion was restored. There
was no sound in the barren, barn-like room but the
birds above, and below the click of the composing-
rule as the editor marshalled the types into lines
in his stick, and arrayed them in solid column on
the galley. Whatever might have been his opinion
of the copy before him, there was no indication of
it in his face, which wore the stolid indifference of
his craft. Perhaps this was unfortunate, for as the
day wore on and the level rays of the sun began

to pierce the adjacent thicket, they sought out and
discovered an anxious ambushed figure drawn up
beside the editor's window, — a figure that had sat
there motionless for hours.   Within, the editor
worked on as steadily and impassively as Fate.
And without, the born poet of Sierra Flat sat and
watched him as waiting its decree.

The effect of the poem on Sierra Flat was remarkable and unprecedented.   The absolute vile-
ness of its doggerel, the gratuitous imbecility of
its thought, and above all the crowning audacity
of the fact that it was the work of a citizen and
published in the county paper, brought it instantly
into popularity.   For many months Calaveras had
languished for a sensation ; since the last vigilance
committee nothing had transpired to dispel the
listless *ennui* begotten of stagnant business and
growing civilization.   In more prosperous moments the office of the " Record " would have been
simply gutted and the editor deported ; at present
the paper was in such demand that the edition
was speedily exhausted.   In brief, the poem of
Mr. Milton Chubbuck came like a special providence to Sierra Flat.   It was read by camp-fires,
in lonely cabins, in flaring bar-rooms and noisy
saloons, and declaimed from the boxes of stage-
coaches.   It was sung in Poker Flat with the addition of a local chorus, and danced as an unhal-

lowed rhythmic dance by the Pyrrhic phalanx of
One Horse Gulch, known as "The Festive Stags
of Calaveras." Some unhappy ambiguities of expression gave rise to many new readings, notes,
and commentaries, which, I regret to state, were
more often marked by ingenuity than delicacy of
thought or expression.

Never before did poet acquire such sudden local
reputation. From the seclusion of McCorkle's
cabin and the obscurity of culinary labors, he was
haled forth into the glowing sunshine of Fame.
The name of Chubbuck was written in letters of
chalk on unpainted walls, and carved with a pick
on the sides of tunnels. A drink known variously
as "The Chubbuck Tranquillizer," or "The Chubbuck Exalter," was dispensed at the bars. For
some weeks a rude design for a Chubbuck statue,
made up of illustrations from circus and melodeon
posters, representing the genius of Calaveras in
brief skirts on a flying steed in the act of crowning the poet Chubbuck, was visible at Keeler's
Ferry. The poet himself was overborne with invitations to drink and extravagant congratulations.
The meeting between Colonel Starbottle of Siskyion and Chubbuck, as previously arranged by our
"Boston," late of Roaring Camp, is said to have
been indescribably affecting. The Colonel embraced him unsteadily. "I could not return to
my constituents at Siskyion, sir, if this hand,

which has grasped that of the gifted Prentice and the lamented Poe, should not have been honored by the touch of the godlike Chubbuck. Gentlemen, American literature is looking up. Thank you, I will take sugar in mine." It was "Boston" who indited letters of congratulations from H. W. Longfellow, Tennyson, and Browning, to Mr. Chubbuck, deposited them in the Sierra Flat post-office, and obligingly consented to dictate the replies.

The simple faith and unaffected delight with which these manifestations were received by the poet and his patron might have touched the hearts of these grim masters of irony, but for the sudden and equal development in both of the variety of weak natures. Mr. McCorkle basked in the popularity of his *protégé*, and became alternately supercilious or patronizing toward the dwellers of Sierra Flat; while the poet, with hair carefully oiled and curled, and bedecked with cheap jewelry and flaunting neck-handkerchief, paraded himself before the single hotel. As may be imagined, this new disclosure of weakness afforded intense satisfaction to Sierra Flat, gave another lease of popularity to the poet, and suggested another idea to the facetious "Boston."

At that time a young lady popularly and professionally known as the "California Pet" was performing to enthusiastic audiences in the interior. Her specialty lay in the personation of youthful masculine character; as a *gamin* of the street she was irresistible, as a negro-dancer she carried the honest miner's heart by storm. A saucy, pretty brunette, she had preserved a wonderful moral reputation even under the Jove-like advances of showers of gold that greeted her appearance on the stage at Sierra Flat. A prominent and delighted member of that audience was Milton Chubbuck. He attended every night. Every day he lingered at the door of the Union Hotel for a glimpse of the "California Pet." It was not long before he received a note from her, — in " Boston's " most popular and approved female hand, — acknowledging his admiration. It was not long before " Boston " was called upon to indite a suitable reply. At last, in furtherance of his facetious design, it became necessary for " Boston " to call upon the young actress herself and secure her personal participation To her he unfolded a plan, the successful carrying out of which he felt would secure his fame to posterity as a practical humorist. The " California Pet's " black eyes sparkled approvingly and mischievously. She only stipulated that she should see the man first, — a concession to her feminine weakness which years of dancing Juba and wearing trousers and boots had not wholly eradicated from her wilful breast. By all means, it should be done. And the interview was arranged for the next week.

It must not be supposed that during this interval of popularity Mr. Chubbuck had been unmindful of his poetic qualities. A certain portion of each day he was absent from town, — "a communin' with natur'," as Mr. McCorkle expressed it, — and actually wandering in the mountain trails, or lying on his back under the trees, or gathering fragrant herbs and the bright-colored berries of the Marzanita. These and his company he generally brought to the editor's office, late in the afternoon, often to that enterprising journalist's infinite weariness. Quiet and uncommunicative, he would sit there patiently watching him at his work until the hour for closing the office arrived, when he would as quietly depart. There was something so humble and unobtrusive in these visits, that the editor could not find it in his heart to deny them, and accepting them, like the woodpeckers, as a part of his sylvan surroundings, often forgot even his presence. Once or twice, moved by some beauty of expression in the moist, shy eyes, he felt like seriously admonishing his visitor of his idle folly ; but his glance falling upon the oiled hair and the gorgeous necktie, he invariably thought better of it. The case was evidently hopeless.

The interview between Mr. Chubbuck and the " California Pet " took place in a private room of the Union Hotel ; propriety being respected by the presence of that arch-humorist, "Boston." To this gentleman we are indebted for the only true account of the meeting. However reticent Mr. Chubbuck might have been in the presence of his own sex, toward the fairer portion of humanity he was, like most poets, exceedingly voluble. Accustomed as the "California Pet" had been to excessive compliment, she was fairly embarrassed by the extravagant praises of her visitor. Her personation of boy characters, her dancing of the "champion jig," were particularly dwelt upon with fervid but unmistakable admiration. At last, recovering her audacity and emboldened by the presence of "Boston," the "California Pet" electrified her hearers by demanding, half jestingly, half viciously, if it were as a boy or a girl that she was the subject of his flattering admiration.

"That knocked him out o' time," said the delighted "Boston," in his subsequent account of the interview. "But do you believe the d—d fool actually asked her to take him with her; wanted to engage in the company."

The plan, as briefly unfolded by "Boston," was to prevail upon Mr. Chubbuck to make his appearance in costume (already designed and prepared by the inventor) before a Sierra Flat audience, and recite an original poem at the Hall immediately on the conclusion of the "California Pet's" performance. At a given signal the audience were to rise and deliver a volley of unsavory articles (previously provided by the originator of the scheme); then a select few were to rush on the stage, seize the poet, and, after marching him in triumphal procession through town, were to deposit him beyond its uttermost limits, with strict injunctions never to enter it again. To the first part of the plan the poet was committed, for the latter portion it was easy enough to find participants.

The eventful night came, and with it an audience that packed the long narrow room with one dense mass of human beings. The "California Pet" never had been so joyous, so reckless, so fascinating and audacious before. But the applause was tame and weak compared to the ironical outburst that greeted the second rising of the curtain and the entrance of the born poet of Sierra Flat. Then there was a hush of expectancy, and the poet stepped to the foot-lights and stood with his manuscript in his hand.

His face was deadly pale. Either there was some suggestion of his fate in the faces of his audience, or some mysterious instinct told him of his danger. He attempted to speak, but faltered, tottered, and staggered to the wings.

Fearful of losing his prey, "Boston" gave the signal and leaped upon the stage. But at the same moment a light figure darted from behind the scenes, and delivering a kick that sent the discomfited humorist back among the musicians, cut a pigeon-wing, executed a double-shuffle, and then advancing to the foot-lights with that inimitable look, that audacious swagger and utter *abandon* which had so thrilled and fascinated them a moment before, uttered the characteristic speech: " Wot are you goin' to hit a man fur, when he 's down, s-a-a-y ? "

The look, the drawl, the action, the readiness, and above all the downright courage of the little woman, had its effect. A roar of sympathetic applause followed the act. " Cut and run while you can," she whispered hurriedly over her one shoulder, without altering the other's attitude of pert and saucy defiance toward the audience. But even as she spoke the poet tottered and sank fainting upon the stage. Then she threw a despairing whisper behind the scenes, " Ring down the curtain."

There was a slight movement of opposition in the audience, but among them rose the burly shoulders of Yuba Bill, the tall, erect figure of Henry York of Sandy Bar, and the colorless, determined face of John Oakhurst. The curtain came down.

Behind it knelt the " California Pet " beside the prostrate poet. " Bring me some water. Run for a doctor. Stop !! CLEAR OUT, ALL OF YOU ! "

She had unloosed the gaudy cravat and opened

the shirt-collar of the insensible figure before her. Then she burst into an hysterical laugh.

" Manuela ! "

Her tiring-woman, a Mexican half-breed, came toward her.

" Help me with him to my dressing-room, quick; then stand outside and wait. If any one questions you, tell them he 's gone. Do you hear? HE 's gone."

The old woman did as she was bade. In a few moments the audience had departed. Before morning so also had the " California Pet," Manuela, and — the poet of Sierra Flat.

But, alas ! with them also had departed the fair fame of the " California Pet." Only a few, and these it is to be feared of not the best moral character themselves, still had faith in the stainless honor of their favorite actress. " It was a mighty foolish thing to do, but it 'll all come out right yet." On the other hand, a majority gave her full credit and approbation for her undoubted pluck and gallantry, but deplored that she should have thrown it away upon a worthless object. To elect for a lover the despised and ridiculed vagrant of Sierra Flat, who had not even the manliness to stand up in his own defence, was not only evidence of inherent moral depravity, but was an insult to the community. Colonel Starbottle saw in it only another instance of the extreme frailty of the sex;

he had known similar cases ; and remembered distinctly, sir, how a well-known Philadelphia heiress,
one of the finest women that ever rode in her ker-
ridge, that, gad, sir ! had thrown over a Southern
member of Congress to consort with a d—d nigger.
The Colonel had also noticed a singular look in the
dog's eye which he did not entirely fancy. He
would not say anything against the lady, sir, but
he had noticed — And here haply the Colonel
became so mysterious and darkly confidential
as to be unintelligible and inaudible to the bystanders.

A few days after the disappearance of Mr. Chubbuck a singular report reached Sierra Flat, and it
was noticed that " Boston," who since the failure
of his elaborate joke had been even more depressed
in spirits than is habitual with great humorists,
suddenly found that his presence was required in
San Francisco.   But as yet nothing but the vaguest
surmises were afloat, and nothing definite was
known.

It was a pleasant afternoon when the editor of
the " Sierra Flat Record " looked up from his case
and beheld the figure of Mr. Morgan McCorkle
standing in the doorway.   There was a distressed
look on the face of that worthy gentleman that at
once enlisted the editor's sympathizing attention.
He held an open letter in his hand, as he advanced
toward the middle of the room.

"As a man as has allers borne a fair reputation," began Mr. McCorkle slowly, " I should like, if so be as I could, Mister Editor, to make a correction in the columns of your valooable paper."

Mr. Editor begged him to proceed.

" Ye may not disremember that about a month ago I fetched here what so be as we 'll call a young man whose name might be as it were Milton — Milton Chubbuck."

Mr. Editor remembered perfectly.

" Thet same party I 'd knowed better nor fower year, two on 'em campin' out together. Not that I 'd known him all the time, fur he war shy and strange at spells and had odd ways that I took war nat'ral to a borned poet. Ye may remember that I said he was a borned poet ? "

The editor distinctly did.

" I picked this same party up in St. Jo, takin' a fancy to his face, and kinder calklating he 'd runn'd away from home, — for I 'm a married man, Mr. Editor, and hev children of my own, — and thinkin' belike he was a borned poet."

"Well ? " said the editor.

" And as I said before, I should like now to make a correction in the columns of your valooable paper."

" What correction ? " asked the editor.

" I said, ef you remember my words, as how he was a borned poet."

" Yes."

" From statements in this yer letter it seems as how I war wrong."

" Well ? "

" She war a woman."

THE CHRISTMAS GIFT THAT CAME TO RUPERT.

A STORY FOR LITTLE SOLDIERS.

IT was the Christmas season in California, — a season of falling rain and springing grasses. There were intervals when, through driving clouds and flying scud, the sun visited the haggard hills with a miracle, and death and resurrection were as one, and out of the very throes of decay a joyous life struggled outward and upward. Even the storms that swept down the dead leaves nurtured the tender buds that took their places. There were no episodes of snowy silence; over the quickening fields the farmer's ploughshare hard followed the furrows left by the latest rains. Perhaps it was for this reason that the Christmas evergreens which decorated the drawing-room took upon themselves a foreign aspect, and offered a weird contrast to the roses, seen dimly through the windows, as the southwest wind beat their soft faces against the panes.

"Now," said the Doctor, drawing his chair closer to the fire, and looking mildly but firmly at the semicircle of flaxen heads around him, "I want it distinctly understood before I begin my story, that I am not to be interrupted by any ridiculous questions. At the first one I shall stop. At the second, I shall feel it my duty to administer a dose of castor-oil, all around. The boy that moves his legs or arms will be understood to invite amputation. I have brought my instruments with me, and never allow pleasure to interfere with my business. Do you promise?"

"Yes, sir," said six small voices, simultaneously. The volley was, however, followed by half a dozen dropping questions.

"Silence! Bob, put your feet down, and stop rattling that sword. Flora shall sit by my side, like a little lady, and be an example to the rest. Fung Tang shall stay, too, if he likes. Now, turn down the gas a little; there, that will do, — just enough to make the fire look brighter, and to show off the Christmas candles. Silence, everybody! The boy who cracks an almond, or breathes too loud over his raisins, will be put out of the room."

There was a profound silence. Bob laid his sword tenderly aside, and nursed his leg thoughtfully. Flora, after coquettishly adjusting the pocket of her little apron, put her arm upon the Doctor's shoulder, and permitted herself to be drawn beside him. Fung Tang, the little heathen page, who was permitted, on this rare occasion, to share the Christian revels in the drawing-room, surveyed the group with a smile that was at once sweet and philosophical. The light ticking of a French clock on the mantel, supported by a young shepherdess of bronze complexion and great symmetry of limb, was the only sound that disturbed the Christmas-like peace of the apartment, — a peace which held the odors of evergreens, new toys, cedar-boxes, glue, and varnish in an harmonious combination that passed all understanding.

"About four years ago at this time," began the Doctor, "I attended a course of lectures in a certain city. One of the professors, who was a sociable, kindly man, — though somewhat practical and hard-headed, — invited me to his house on Christmas night. I was very glad to go, as I was anxious to see one of his sons, who, though only twelve years old, was said to be very clever. I dare not tell you how many Latin verses this little fellow could recite, or how many English ones he had composed. In the first place, you'd want me to repeat them; secondly, I'm not a judge of poetry, Latin or English. But there were judges who said they were wonderful for a boy, and everybody predicted a splendid future for him. Everybody but his father. He shook his head doubtingly, whenever it was mentioned, for, as I have told you, he was a practical, matter-of-fact man.

"There was a pleasant party at the Professor's that night. All the children of the neighborhood were there, and among them the Professor's clever son, Rupert, as they called him, — a thin little chap, about as tall as Bobby there, and as fair and delicate as Flora by my side. His health was feeble, his father said; he seldom ran about and played with other boys, preferring to stay at home and brood over his books, and compose what he called his verses.

"Well, we had a Christmas-tree just like this, and we had been laughing and talking, calling off the names of the children who had presents on the tree, and everybody was very happy and joyous, when one of the children suddenly uttered a cry of mingled surprise and hilarity, and said, 'Here's something for Rupert; and what do you think it is?'

"We all guessed. 'A desk'; 'A copy of Milton'; 'A gold pen'; 'A rhyming dictionary.' 'No? what then?'

"'A drum!'

"'A what?' asked everybody.

"'A drum! with Rupert's name on it.'

"Sure enough there it was. A good-sized, bright, new, brass-bound drum, with a slip of paper on it, with the inscription, 'FOR RUPERT.'

"Of course we all laughed, and thought it a good joke. 'You see you're to make a noise in the world, Rupert!' said one. 'Here's parchment for the poet,' said another. 'Rupert's last work in sheepskin covers,' said a third. 'Give us a classical tune, Rupert,' said a fourth; and so on. But Rupert seemed too mortified to speak; he changed color, bit his lips, and finally burst into a passionate fit of crying, and left the room. Then those who had joked him felt ashamed, and everybody began to ask who had put the drum there. But no one knew, or if they did, the unexpected sympathy awakened for the sensitive boy kept them silent. Even the servants were called up and questioned, but no one could give any idea where it came from. And, what was still more singular, everybody declared that up to the moment it was produced, no one had seen it hanging on the tree. What do I think? Well, I have my own opinion. But no questions! Enough for you to know that Rupert did not come down stairs again that night, and the party soon after broke up.

"I had almost forgotten those things, for the war of the Rebellion broke out the next spring, and I was appointed surgeon in one of the new regiments, and was on my way to the seat of war. But I had to pass through the city where the Professor lived, and there I met him. My first question was about Rupert. The Professor shook his head sadly. 'He's not so well,' he said; 'he has been declining since last Christmas, when you saw him. A very strange case,' he added, giving it a long Latin name, — 'a very singular case. But go and see him yourself,' he urged; 'it may distract his mind and do him good.'

"I went accordingly to the Professor's house, and found Rupert lying on a sofa, propped up with pillows. Around him were scattered his books, and, what seemed in singular contrast, that drum I told you about was hanging on a nail, just above his head. His face was thin and wasted; there was a red spot on either cheek, and his eyes were very bright and widely opened. He was glad to see me, and when I told him where I was going, he asked a thousand questions about the war. I thought I had thoroughly diverted his mind from its sick and languid fancies, when he suddenly grasped my hand and drew me toward him.

"'Doctor,' said he, in a low whisper, 'you won't laugh at me if I tell you something?'

"'No, certainly not,' I said.

"'You remember that drum?' he said, pointing to the glittering toy that hung against the wall. 'You know, too, how it came to me. A few weeks after Christmas, I was lying half asleep here, and the drum was hanging on the wall, when suddenly I heard it beaten; at first, low and slowly, then faster and louder, until its rolling filled the house. In the middle of the night, I heard it again. I did not dare to tell anybody about it, but I have heard it every night ever since.'

" He paused and looked anxiously in my face. Sometimes,' he continued, 'it is played softly, sometimes loudly, but always quickening to a long-roll, so loud and alarming that I have looked to see people coming into my room to ask what was the matter. But I think, Doctor, — I think,' he repeated slowly, looking up with painful interest into my face, 'that no one hears it but myself.'

" I thought so, too, but I asked him if he had heard it at any other time.

" 'Once or twice in the daytime,' he replied, 'when I have been reading or writing ; then very loudly, as though it were angry, and tried in that way to attract my attention away from my books.'

" I looked into his face, and placed my hand upon his pulse. His eyes were very bright, and his pulse a little flurried and quick. I then tried to explain to him that he was very weak, and that his senses were very acute, as most weak people's are ; and how that when he read, or grew interested and excited, or when he was tired at night, the throbbing of a big artery made the beating sound he heard. He listened to me with a sad smile of unbelief, but thanked me, and in a little while I went away. But as I was going down stairs, I met the Professor. I gave him my opinion of the case, — well, no matter what it was.

" ' He wants fresh air and exercise,' said the Professor, ' and some practical experience of life, sir.' The Professor was not a bad man, but he was a little worried and impatient, and thought — as clever people are apt to think — that things which he did n't understand were either silly or improper.

" I left the city that very day, and in the excitement of battle-fields and hospitals, I forgot all about little Rupert, nor did I hear of him again, until one day, meeting an old classmate in the army, who had known the Professor, he told me that Rupert had become quite insane, and that in one of his paroxysms he had escaped from the house, and as he had never been found, it was feared that he had fallen in the river and was drowned. I was terribly shocked for the moment, as you may imagine ; but, dear me, I was living just then among scenes as terrible and shocking, and I had little time to spare to mourn over poor Rupert.

" It was not long after receiving this intelligence that we had a terrible battle, in which a portion of our army was surprised and driven back with great slaughter. I was detached from my brigade to ride over to the battle-field and assist the surgeons of the beaten division, who had more on their hands than they could attend to. When I reached the barn that served for a temporary hospital, I went at once to work. Ah, Bob," said the Doctor, thoughtfully taking the bright sword from the hands of the half-frightened Bob, and holding it gravely before him, "these pretty playthings are symbols of cruel, ugly realities.

"I turned to a tall, stout Vermonter," he continued very slowly, tracing a pattern on the rug with the point of the scabbard, "who was badly wounded in both thighs, but he held up his hands and begged me to help others first who needed it more than he. I did not at first heed his request, for this kind of unselfishness was very common in the army; but he went on, 'For God's sake, Doctor, leave me here; there is a drummer-boy of our regiment — a mere child — dying, if he is n't dead now. Go, and see him first. He lies over there. He saved more than one life. He was at his post in the panic this morning, and saved the honor of the regiment.' I was so much more impressed by the man's manner than by the substance of his speech, which was, however, corroborated by the other poor fellows stretched around me, that I passed over to where the drummer lay, with his drum beside him. I gave one glance at his face —and — yes, Bob — yes, my children — it *was* Rupert.

"Well! well! it needed not the chalked cross which my brother-surgeons had left upon the rough board whereon he lay to show how urgent was the relief he sought; it needed not the prophetic words

of the Vermonter, nor the damp that mingled with
the brown curls that clung to his pale forehead, to
show how hopeless it was now. I called him by
name. He opened his eyes — larger, I thought, in
the new vision that was beginning to dawn upon
him — and recognized me. He whispered, 'I'm
glad you are come, but I don't think you can do
me any good.'

"I could not tell him a lie. I could not say
anything. I only pressed his hand in mine, as he
went on.

"'But you will see father, and ask him to forgive me. Nobody is to blame but myself. It was
a long time before I understood why the drum
came to me that Christmas night, and why it kept
calling to me every night, and what it said. I
know it now. The work is done, and I am content.
Tell father it is better as it is. I should have
lived only to worry and perplex him, and something in me tells me this is right.'

"He lay still for a moment, and then, grasping
my hand, said, —

"'Hark!'

"I listened, but heard nothing but the sup-
pressed moans of the wounded men around me.
'The drum,' he said faintly; 'don't you hear it?
The drum is calling me.'

"He reached out his arm to where it lay, as
though he would embrace it.

" ' Listen,' he went on, ' it 's the reveille. There are the ranks drawn up in review. Don't you see the sunlight flash down the long line of bayonets ? Their faces are shining, — they present arms, — there comes the General ; but his face I cannot look at, for the glory round his head. He sees me ; he smiles, it is — ' And with a name upon his lips that he had learned long ago, he stretched himself wearily upon the planks, and lay quite still.

" That 's all. No questions now ; never mind what became of the drum. Who 's that snivelling ? Bless my soul, where 's my pill-box ? "

URBAN SKETCHES.

A VENERABLE IMPOSTOR.

AS I glance across my table, I am somewhat
distracted by the spectacle of a venerable
head whose crown occasionally appears beyond, at
about its level. The apparition of a very small
hand — whose fingers are bunchy and have the
appearance of being slightly webbed — which is
frequently lifted above the table in a vain and
impotent attempt to reach the inkstand, always
affects me as a novelty at each recurrence of the
phenomenon. Yet both the venerable head and
bunchy fingers belong to an individual with whom
I am familiar, and to whom, for certain reasons
hereafter described, I choose to apply the epithet
written above this article.

His advent in the family was attended with
peculiar circumstances. He was received with
some concern — the number of retainers having
been increased by one in honor of his arrival.
He appeared to be weary, — his pretence was that
he had come from a long journey, — so that for
days, weeks, and even months, he did not leave
his bed except when he was carried. But it was
remarkable that his appetite was invariably regu-

lar and healthy, and that his meals, which he
required should be brought to him, were seldom
rejected. During this time he had little conversation with the family, his knowledge of our vernacular being limited, but occasionally spoke to
himself in his own language, — a foreign tongue.
The difficulties attending this eccentricity were
obviated by the young woman who had from the
first taken him under her protection, — being, like
the rest of her sex, peculiarly open to impositions,
— and who at once disorganized her own tongue
to suit his. This was affected by the contraction
of the syllables of some words, the addition of
syllables to others, and an ingenious disregard
for tenses and the governing powers of the verb.
The same singular law which impels people in
conversation with foreigners to imitate their
broken English governed the family in their
communications with him. He received these
evidences of his power with an indifference not
wholly free from scorn. The expression of his eye
would occasionally denote that his higher nature
revolted from them. I have no doubt myself that
his wants were frequently misinterpreted; that the
stretching forth of his hands toward the moon and
stars might have been the performance of some religious rite peculiar to his own country, which was
in ours misconstrued into a desire for physical
nourishment. His repetition of the word "goo-

goo," — which was subject to a variety of opposite interpretations, — when taken in conjunction with his size, in my mind seemed to indicate his aboriginal or Aztec origin.

I incline to this belief, as it sustains the impression I have already hinted at, that his extreme youth is a simulation and deceit ; that he is really older and has lived before at some remote period, and that his conduct fully justifies his title as A Venerable Impostor. A variety of circumstances corroborate this impression : His tottering walk, which is a senile as well as a juvenile condition; his venerable head, thatched with such imperceptible hair that, at a distance, it looks like a mild aureola, and his imperfect dental exhibition. But beside these physical peculiarities may be observed certain moral symptoms, which go to disprove his assumed youth. He is in the habit of falling into reveries, caused, I have no doubt, by some circumstance which suggests a comparison with his experience in his remoter boyhood, or by some serious retrospection of the past years. He has been detected lying awake, at times when he should have been asleep, engaged in curiously comparing the bed-clothes, walls, and furniture with some recollection of his youth. At such moments he has been heard to sing softly to himself fragments of some unintelligible composition, which probably still linger in his memory as the echoes of a music

he has long outgrown. He has the habit of receiving strangers with the familiarity of one who had
met them before, and to whom their antecedents
and peculiarities were matters of old acquaintance,
and so unerring is his judgment of their previous
character that when he withholds his confidence I
am apt to withhold mine. It is somewhat remarkable that while the maturity of his years and the
respect due to them is denied by man, his superiority and venerable age is never questioned by the
brute creation. The dog treats him with a respect
and consideration accorded to none others, and the
cat permits a familiarity which I should shudder
to attempt. It may be considered an evidence of
some Pantheistic quality in his previous education,
that he seems to recognize a fellowship even in inarticulate objects ; he has been known to verbally
address plants, flowers, and fruit, and to extend his
confidence to such inanimate objects as chairs and
tables. There can be little doubt that, in the remote period of his youth, these objects were en-
dowed with not only sentient natures, but moral
capabilities, and he is still in the habit of beating them when they collide with him, and of
pardoning them with a kiss.

As he has grown older — rather let me say, as
we have approximated to his years — he has, in
spite of the apparent paradox, lost much of his
senile gravity. It must be confessed that some of

his actions of late appear to our imperfect com-
prehension inconsistent with his extreme age. A
habit of marching up and down with a string tied
to a soda-water bottle, a disposition to ride anything that could by any exercise of the liveliest
fancy be made to assume equine proportions, a
propensity to blacken his venerable white hair
with ink and coal dust, and an omnivorous appetite
which did not stop at chalk, clay, or cinders, were
peculiarities not calculated to excite respect. In
fact, he would seem to have become demoralized,
and when, after a prolonged absence the other day,
he was finally discovered standing upon the front
steps addressing a group of delighted children out
of his limited vocabulary, the circumstance could
only be accounted for as the garrulity of age.

But I lay aside my pen amidst an ominous silence and the disappearance of the venerable head
from my plane of vision. As I step to the other
side of the table, I find that sleep has overtaken
him in an overt act of hoary wickedness. The
very pages I have devoted to an exposition of his
deceit he has quietly abstracted, and I find them
covered with cabalistic figures and wild-looking
hieroglyphs traced with his forefinger dipped in
ink, which doubtless in his own language conveys
a scathing commentary on my composition. But
he sleeps peacefully, and there is something in his
face which tells me that he has already wandered

away to that dim region of his youth where I cannot follow him.   And as there comes a strange
stirring at my heart when I contemplate the immeasurable gulf which lies between us, and how
slight and feeble as yet is his grasp on this world
and its strange realities, I find, too late, that I also
am a willing victim of the Venerable Impostor.

FROM A BALCONY.

THE little stone balcony, which, by a popular fallacy, is supposed to be a necessary appurtenance of my window, has long been to me a source of curious interest. The fact that the asperities of our summer weather will not permit me to use it but once or twice in six months does not alter my concern for this incongruous ornament. It affects me as I suppose the conscious possession of a linen coat or a nankeen trousers might affect a sojourner here who has not entirely outgrown his memory of Eastern summer heat and its glorious compensations,— a luxurious providence against a possible but by no means probable contingency. I do no longer wonder at the persistency with which San Franciscans adhere to this architectural superfluity in the face of climatical impossibilities. The balconies in which no one sits, the piazzas on which no one lounges, are timid advances made to a climate whose churlishness we are trying to temper by an ostentation of confidence. Ridiculous as this spectacle is at all seasons, it is never more so than in that bleak interval between sunset and dark, when the shrill scream

of the factory whistle seems to have concentrated
all the hard, unsympathetic quality of the climate
into one vocal expression. Add to this the appearance of one or two pedestrians, manifestly too late
for their dinners, and tasting in the shrewish air a
bitter premonition of the welcome that awaits them
at home, and you have one of those ordinary views
from my balcony which makes the balcony itself
ridiculous.

But as I lean over its balustrade to-night — a
night rare in its kindness and beauty — and watch
the fiery ashes of my cigar drop into the abysmal
darkness below, I am inclined to take back the
whole of that preceding paragraph, although it
cost me some labor to elaborate its polite malevolence. I can even recognize some melody in the
music which comes irregularly and fitfully from
the balcony of the Museum on Market Street, although it may be broadly stated that, as a general
thing, the music of all museums, menageries, and
circuses becomes greatly demoralized, — possibly
through associations with the beasts. So soft and
courteous is this atmosphere that I have detected
the flutter of one or two light dresses on the adjacent balconies and piazzas, and the front parlor
windows of a certain aristocratic mansion in the
vicinity, which have always maintained a studious
reserve in regard to the interior, to-night are suddenly thrown into the attitude of familiar dis-

closure. A few young people are strolling up the
street with a lounging step which is quite a relief
to that usual brisk, business-like pace which the
chilly nights impose upon even the most senti-
mental lovers. The genial influences of the air
are not restricted to the opening of shutters and
front doors; other and more gentle disclosures
are made, no doubt, beneath this moonlight. The
bonnet and hat which passed beneath my balcony
a few moments ago were suspiciously close together. I argued from this that my friend the
editor will probably receive any quantity of verses
for his next issue, containing allusions to "Luna,"
in which the original epithet of "silver" will be
applied to this planet, and that a "boon" will be
asked for the evident purpose of rhyming with
"moon," and for no other. Should neither of the
parties be equal to this expression, the pent-up
feelings of the heart will probably find vent later
in the evening over the piano, in "I wandered by
the Brookside," or "When the Moon on the Lake is
Beaming." But it has been permitted me to hear
the fulfilment of my prophecy even as it was uttered. From the window of number Twelve Hundred and Seven gushes upon the slumberous misty
air the maddening ballad, "Ever of Thee," while
at Twelve Hundred and Eleven the "Star of the
Evening" rises with a chorus. I am inclined to
think that there is something in the utter vacuity

v. 17—G

of the refrain in this song which especially commends itself to the young. The simple statement, " Star of the evening," is again and again repeated with an imbecile relish ; while the adjective " beautiful " recurs with a steady persistency, too exasperating to dwell upon here. At occasional intervals, a base voice enunciates " Star-r ! Star-r ! " as a solitary and independent effort. Sitting here in my balcony, I picture the possessor of that voice as a small, stout young man, standing a little apart from the other singers, with his hands behind him, under his coat-tail, and a severe expression of countenance. He sometimes leans forward, with a futile attempt to read the music over somebody else's shoulder, but always resumes his old severity of attitude before singing his part. Meanwhile the celestial subjects of this choral adoration look down upon the scene with a tranquillity and patience which can only result from the security with which their immeasurable remoteness invests them. I would remark that the stars are not the only topics subject to this "damnable iteration." A certain popular song, which contains the statement, " I will not forget you, mother," apparently reposes all its popularity on the constant and dreary repetition of this unimportant information, which at least produces the desired result among the audience. If the best operatic choruses are not above this weakness, the unfamiliar language in which they are sung offers less violation to common sense.

It may be parenthetically stated here that the songs alluded to above may be found in sheet music on the top of the piano of any young lady who has just come from boarding-school. "The Old Arm-Chair," or "Woodman, spare that Tree," will be also found in easy juxtaposition. The latter songs are usually brought into service at the instance of an uncle or bachelor brother, whose request is generally prefaced by a remark deprecatory of the opera, and the gratuitous observation that "we are retrograding, sir, — retrograding," and that "there is no music like the old songs." He sometimes condescends to accompany "Marie" in a tremulous barytone, and is particularly forcible in those passages where the word "repeat" is written, for reasons stated above. When the song is over, to the success of which he feels he has materially contributed, he will inform you that you may talk of your "arias," and your "romanzas," "but for music, sir, — music —" at which point he becomes incoherent and unintelligible. It is this gentleman who suggests "China," or "Brattle Street," as a suitable and cheerful exercise for the social circle. There are certain amatory songs, of an arch and coquettish character, familiar to these localities, which the young lady, being called upon to sing, declines with a bashful and tantalizing hesitation. Prominent among these may be mentioned an erotic effusion entitled "I'm

talking in my Sleep," which, when sung by a
young person vivaciously and with appropriate
glances, can be made to drive languishing swains
to the verge of madness. Ballads of this quality
afford splendid opportunities for bold young men,
who, by ejaculating " Oh!" and "Ah!" at the
affecting passages, frequently gain a fascinating
reputation for wildness and scepticism.

But the music which called up these paren-
thetical reflections has died away, and with it the
slight animosities it inspired. The last song has
been sung, the piano closed, the lights are withdrawn from the windows, and the white skirts
flutter away from stoops and balconies. The silence is broken only by the rattle and rumble of
carriages coming from theatre and opera. I fancy
that this sound — which, seeming to be more distinct at this hour than at any other time, might be
called one of the civic voices of the night — has
certain urbane suggestions, not unpleasant to those
born and bred in large cities. The moon, round
and full, gradually usurps the twinkling lights of
the city, that one by one seem to fade away and
be absorbed in her superior lustre. The distant
Mission hills are outlined against the sky, but
through one gap the outlying fog which has stealth-
ily invested us seems to have effected a breach,
and only waits the co-operation of the laggard sea-
breezes to sweep down and take the beleaguered

city by assault. An ineffable calm sinks over the
landscape. In the magical moonlight the shot-
tower loses its angular outline and practical relations, and becomes a minaret from whose balcony
an invisible muezzin calls the Faithful to prayer.
"Prayer is better than sleep." But what is this?
A shuffle of feet on the pavement, a low hum of
voices, a twang of some diabolical instrument, a
preliminary hem and cough. Heavens! it cannot
be! Ah, yes — it is — it is — SERENADERS!

Anathema Maranatha! May purgatorial pains
seize you, William, Count of Poitou, Girard de
Boreuil, Arnaud de Marveil, Bertrand de Born, mischievous progenitors of *jongleurs,* troubadours, pro-
vençals, minnesingers, minstrels, and singers of
cansos and love chants! Confusion overtake and
confound your modern descendants, the "metre
ballad-mongers," who carry the shamelessness of
the Middle Ages into the nineteenth century, and
awake a sleeping neighborhood to the brazen
knowledge of their loves and wanton fancies!
Destruction and demoralization pursue these pitiable imitators of a barbarous age, when ladies'
names and charms were shouted through the land,
and modest maiden never lent presence to tilt or
tourney without hearing a chronicle of her virtues
go round the lists, shouted by wheezy heralds and
taken up by roaring swashbucklers! Perdition
overpower such ostentatious wooers! Marry! shall

I shoot the amorous feline who nightly iterates
his love songs on my roof, and yet withhold my
trigger finger from yonder pranksome gallant?
Go to! Here is an orange left of last week's repast. Decay hath overtaken it, — it possesseth neither savor nor cleanliness. Ha! cleverly thrown!
A hit — a palpable hit! Peradventure I have
still a boot that hath done me service, and, barring
a looseness of the heel, an ominous yawning at
the side, 't is in good case! Na'theless, 't will
serve. So! so! What! dispersed! Nay, then, I
too will retire.

MELONS.

A S I do not suppose the most gentle of readers
will believe that anybody's sponsors in baptism ever wilfully assumed the responsibility of
such a name, I may as well state that I have reason to infer that Melons was simply the nickname
of a small boy I once knew. If he had any other,
I never knew it.

Various theories were often projected by me to
account for this strange cognomen. His head,
which was covered with a transparent down, like
that which clothes very small chickens, plainly
permitting the scalp to show through, to an im-
aginative mind might have suggested that succu-
lent vegetable. That his parents, recognizing some
poetical significance in the fruits of the season,
might have given this name to an August child, was
an Oriental explanation. That from his infancy,
he was fond of indulging in melons, seemed on the
whole the most likely, particularly as Fancy was not
bred in McGinnis's Court. He dawned upon me
as Melons. His proximity was indicated by shrill,
youthful voices, as " Ah, Melons ! " or playfully,
" Hi, Melons ! " or authoritatively, " You, Melons !"

McGinnis's Court was a democratic expression of some obstinate and radical property-holder. Occupying a limited space between two fashionable thoroughfares, it refused to conform to circumstances, but sturdily paraded its unkempt glories, and frequently asserted itself in ungrammatical language. My window — a rear room on the ground floor — in this way derived blended light and shadow from the court. So low was the window-sill, that had I been the least predisposed to somnambulism, it would have broken out under such favorable auspices, and I should have haunted McGinnis's Court. My speculations as to the origin of the court were not altogether gratuitous, for by means of this window I once saw the Past, as through a glass darkly. It was a Celtic shadow that early one morning obstructed my ancient lights. It seemed to belong to an individual with a pea-coat, a stubby pipe, and bristling beard. He was gazing intently at the court, resting on a heavy cane, somewhat in the way that heroes dramatically visit the scenes of their boyhood. As there was little of architectural beauty in the court, I came to the conclusion that it was McGinnis looking after his property. The fact that he carefully kicked a broken bottle out of the road somewhat strengthened me in the opinion. But he presently walked away, and the court knew him no more. He probably collected his rents by proxy — if he collected them at all.

Beyond Melons, of whom all this is purely in-
troductory, there was little to interest the most
sanguine and hopeful nature. In common with
all such localities, a great deal of washing was
done, in comparison with the visible results. There
was always something whisking on the line, and
always something whisking through the court, that
looked as if it ought to be there. A fish-geranium
— of all plants kept for the recreation of mankind,
certainly the greatest illusion — straggled under
the window. Through its dusty leaves I caught
the first glance of Melons.

His age was about seven. He looked older,
from the venerable whiteness of his head, and it
was impossible to conjecture his size, as he always
wore clothes apparently belonging to some shapely
youth of nineteen. A pair of pantaloons, that,
when sustained by a single suspender, completely
equipped him, formed his every-day suit. How,
with this lavish superfluity of clothing, he managed to perform the surprising gymnastic feats it
has been my privilege to witness, I have never
been able to tell. His "turning the crab," and
other minor dislocations, were always attended
with success. It was not an unusual sight at any
hour of the day to find Melons suspended on a
line, or to see his venerable head appearing above
the roofs of the outhouses. Melons knew the
exact height of every fence in the vicinity, its

facilities for scaling, and the possibility of seizure on the other side. His more peaceful and quieter amusements consisted in dragging a disused boiler by a large string, with hideous outcries, to imaginary fires.

Melons was not gregarious in his habits. A few youth of his own age sometimes called upon him, but they eventually became abusive, and their visits were more strictly predatory incursions for old bottles and junk which formed the staple of McGinnis's Court. Overcome by loneliness one day, Melons inveigled a blind harper into the court. For two hours did that wretched man prosecute his unhallowed calling, unrecompensed, and going round and round the court, apparently under the impression that it was some other place, while Melons surveyed him from an adjoining fence with calm satisfaction. It was this absence of conscientious motives that brought Melons into disrepute with his aristocratic neighbors. Orders were issued that no child of wealthy and pious parentage should play with him. This mandate, as a matter of course, invested Melons with a fascinating interest to them. Admiring glances were cast at Melons from nursery windows. Baby fingers beckoned to him. Invitations to tea (on wood and pewter) were lisped to him from aristocratic back-yards. It was evident he was looked upon as a pure and noble being, untrammelled by the conventionalities of parentage, and physically as well as mentally exalted above them. One afternoon an unusual commotion prevailed in the vicinity of McGinnis's Court. Looking from my window I saw Melons perched on the roof of a stable, pulling up a rope by which one "Tommy," an infant scion of an adjacent and wealthy house, was suspended in mid-air. In vain the female relatives of Tommy congregated in the back-yard, expostulated with Melons; in vain the unhappy father shook his fist at him. Secure in his position, Melons redoubled his exertions and at last landed Tommy on the roof. Then it was that the humiliating fact was disclosed that Tommy had been acting in collusion with Melons. He grinned delightedly back at his parents, as if "by merit raised to that bad eminence." Long before the ladder arrived that was to succor him, he became the sworn ally of Melons, and, I regret to say, incited by the same audacious boy, " chaffed " his own flesh and blood below him. He was eventually taken, though, of course, Melons escaped. But Tommy was restricted to the window after that, and the companionship was limited to " Hi, Melons !" and "You, Tommy !" and Melons, to all practical purposes, lost him forever. I looked afterward to see some signs of sorrow on Melons's part, but in vain; he buried his grief, if he had any, somewhere in his one voluminous garment.

At about this time my opportunities of knowing
Melons became more extended. I was engaged in
filling a void in the Literature of the Pacific Coast.
As this void was a pretty large one, and as I was
informed that the Pacific Coast languished under
it, I set apart two hours each day to this work of
filling in. It was necessary that I should adopt a
methodical system, so I retired from the world and
locked myself in my room at a certain hour each
day, after coming from my office. I then carefully
drew out my portfolio and read what I had written
the day before. This would suggest some altera-
tion, and I would carefully rewrite it. During
this operation I would turn to consult a book of
reference, which invariably proved extremely interesting and attractive. It would generally suggest another and better method of "filling in."
Turning this method over reflectively in my mind,
I would finally commence the new method which
I eventually abandoned for the original plan. At
this time I would become convinced that my exhausted faculties demanded a cigar. The operation
of lighting a cigar usually suggested that a little
quiet reflection and meditation would be of service
to me, and I always allowed myself to be guided
by prudential instincts. Eventually, seated by my
window, as before stated, Melons asserted himself,
Though our conversation rarely went further than
" Hello, Mister!" and " Ah, Melons!" a vagabond

instinct we felt in common implied a communion deeper than words. In this spiritual commingling the time passed, often beguiled by gymnastics on the fence or line (always with an eye to my window) until dinner was announced and I found a more practical void required my attention. An unlooked for incident drew us in closer relation.

A sea-faring friend just from a tropical voyage had presented me with a bunch of bananas. They were not quite ripe, and I hung them before my window to mature in the sun of McGinnis's Court, whose forcing qualities were remarkable. In the mysteriously mingled odors of ship and shore which they diffused throughout my room, there was a lingering reminiscence of low latitudes. But even that joy was fleeting and evanescent: they never reached maturity.

Coming home one day, as I turned the corner of that fashionable thoroughfare before alluded to, I met a small boy eating a banana. There was nothing remarkable in that, but as I neared McGinnis's Court I presently met another small boy, also eating a banana. A third small boy engaged in a like occupation obtruded a painful coincidence upon my mind. I leave the psychological reader to determine the exact co-relation between this circumstance and the sickening sense of loss that overcame me on witnessing it. I reached my room — and found the bunch of bananas was gone.

There was but one who knew of their existence, but one who frequented my window, but one capable of the gymnastic effort to procure them, and that was — I blush to say it — Melons. Melons the depredator — Melons, despoiled by larger boys of his ill-gotten booty, or reckless and indiscreetly liberal; Melons — now a fugitive on some neighboring house-top. I lit a cigar, and, drawing my chair to the window, sought surcease of sorrow in the contemplation of the fish-geranium. In a few moments something white passed my window at about the level of the edge. There was no mistaking that hoary head, which now represented to me only aged iniquity. It was Melons, that venerable, juvenile hypocrite.

He affected not to observe me, and would have withdrawn quietly, but that horrible fascination which causes the murderer to revisit the scene of his crime, impelled him toward my window. I smoked calmly and gazed at him without speaking. He walked several times up and down the court with a half-rigid, half-belligerent expression of eye and shoulder, intended to represent the carelessness of innocence.

Once or twice he stopped, and putting his arms their whole length into his capacious trousers, gazed with some interest at the additional width they thus acquired. Then he whistled. The singular conflicting conditions of John Brown's body

and soul were at that time beginning to attract the
attention of youth, and Melons's performance of
that melody was always remarkable. But to-day
he whistled falsely and shrilly between his teeth.
At last he met my eye. He winced slightly, but
recovered himself, and going to the fence, stood for
a few moments on his hands, with his bare feet
quivering in the air. Then he turned toward me
and threw out a conversational preliminary.

"They is a cirkis" — said Melons gravely, hanging with his back to the fence and his arms twisted
around the palings — "a cirkis over yonder!" —
indicating the locality with his foot — "with hosses,
and hossback riders. They is a man wot rides six
hosses to onct — six hosses to onct — and nary
saddle" — and he paused in expectation.

Even this equestrian novelty did not affect me.
I still kept a fixed gaze on Melons's eye, and he
began to tremble and visibly shrink in his capacious garment. Some other desperate means —
conversation with Melons was always a desperate means — must be resorted to. He recommenced more artfully.

"Do you know Carrots?"

I had a faint remembrance of a boy of that
euphonious name, with scarlet hair, who was a
playmate and persecutor of Melons. But I said
nothing.

"Carrots is a bad boy. Killed a policeman onct.

Wears a dirk knife in his boots, saw him to-day looking in your windy."

I felt that this must end here. I rose sternly and addressed Melons.

" Melons, this is all irrelevant and impertinent to the case. *You* took those bananas. Your proposition regarding Carrots, even if I were inclined to accept it as credible information, does not alter the material issue. You took those bananas. The offence under the statutes of California is felony. How far Carrots may have been accessory to the fact either before or after, is not my intention at present to discuss. The act is complete. Your present conduct shows the *animo furandi* to have been equally clear."

By the time I had finished this exordium, Melons had disappeared, as I fully expected.

He never reappeared. The remorse that I have experienced for the part I had taken in what I fear may have resulted in his utter and complete extermination, alas, he may not know, except through these pages. For I have never seen him since. Whether he ran away and went to sea to reappear at some future day as the most ancient of mariners, or whether he buried himself completely in his trousers, I never shall know. I have read the papers anxiously for accounts of him. I have gone to the Police Office in the vain attempt of identifying him as a lost child. But I never saw

him or heard of him since. Strange fears have
sometimes crossed my mind that his venerable
appearance may have been actually the result of
senility, and that he may have been gathered peacefully to his fathers in a green old age. I have
even had doubts of his existence, and have sometimes thought that he was providentially and mysteriously offered to fill the void I have before
alluded to. In that hope I have written these
pages.

SURPRISING ADVENTURES OF MASTER CHARLES SUMMERTON.

AT exactly half past nine o'clock on the morning of Saturday, August 26, 1865, Master Charles Summerton, aged five years, disappeared mysteriously from his paternal residence on Folsom Street, San Francisco. At twenty-five minutes past nine he had been observed, by the butcher, amusing himself by going through that popular youthful exercise known as " turning the crab," a feat in which he was singularly proficient. At a court of inquiry summarily held in the back parlor at 10.15, Bridget, cook, deposed to have detected him at twenty minutes past nine, in the felonious abstraction of sugar from the pantry, which, by the same token, had she known what was a-comin', she 'd have never previnted. Patsey, a shrill-voiced youth from a neighboring alley, testified to have seen " Chowley " at half past nine, in front of the butcher's shop round the corner, but as this young gentleman chose to throw out the gratuitous belief that the missing child had been converted into sausages by the butcher, his testimony was received with some caution by the female portion of

the court, and with downright scorn and contume-
ly by its masculine members. But whatever might
have been the hour of his departure, it was certain
that from half past ten A. M. until nine P. M., when
he was brought home by a policeman, Charles Summerton was missing. Being naturally of a reticent
disposition, he has since resisted, with but one ex-
ception, any attempt to wrest from him a statement
of his whereabouts during that period. That ex-
ception has been myself. He has related to me
the following in the strictest confidence.

His intention on leaving the door-steps of his
dwelling was to proceed without delay to Van Dieman's Land, by way of Second and Market streets.
This project was subsequently modified so far as to
permit a visit to Otaheite, where Captain Cook was
killed. The outfit for his voyage consisted of two
car-tickets, five cents in silver, a fishing-line, the
brass capping of a spool of cotton, which, in his
eyes, bore some resemblance to metallic currency,
and a Sunday-school library ticket. His garments,
admirably adapted to the exigencies of any climate,
were severally a straw hat with a pink ribbon, a
striped shirt, over which a pair of trousers, uncom-
monly wide in comparison to their length, were
buttoned, striped balmoral stockings, which gave
his youthful legs something of the appearance of
wintergreen candy, and copper-toed shoes with
iron heels, capable of striking fire from any flag-

stone. This latter quality, Master Charley could
not help feeling, would be of infinite service to him
in the wilds of Van Dieman's Land, which, as pic-
torially represented in his geography, seemed to be
deficient in corner groceries and matches.

Exactly as the clock struck the half-hour, the
short legs and straw hat of Master Charles Summerton disappeared around the corner. He ran
rapidly, partly by way of inuring himself to the
fatigues of the journey before him, and partly by
way of testing his speed with that of a North Beach
car which was proceeding in his direction. The
conductor, not being aware of this generous and
lofty emulation, and being somewhat concerned at
the spectacle of a pair of very short, twinkling legs
so far in the rear, stopped his car and generously
assisted the youthful Summerton upon the platform. From this point a hiatus of several hours'
duration occurs in Charles's narrative. He is under
the impression that he "rode out" not only his two
tickets, but that he became subsequently indebted
to the company for several trips to and from the
opposite termini, and that at last, resolutely refus-
ing to give any explanation of his conduct, he was
finally ejected, much to his relief, on a street corner. Although, as he informs us, he felt perfectly
satisfied with this arrangement, he was impelled
under the circumstances to hurl after the conductor
an opprobrious appellation which he had ascertained

from Patsey was the correct thing in such emergencies, and possessed peculiarly exasperating properties.

We now approach a thrilling part of the narrative, before which most of the adventures of the "Boys' Own Book" pale into insignificance. There are times when the recollection of this adventure causes Master Charles to break out in a cold sweat, and he has several times since its occurrence been awakened by lamentations and outcries in the night season by merely dreaming of it. On the corner of the street lay several large empty sugar hogsheads. A few young gentlemen disported themselves therein, armed with sticks, with which they removed the sugar which still adhered to the joints of the staves, and conveyed it to their mouths. Finding a cask not yet preëmpted, Master Charles set to work, and for a few moments revelled in a wild saccharine dream, whence he was finally roused by an angry voice and the rapidly retreating footsteps of his comrades. An ominous sound smote his ear, and the next moment he felt the cask wherein he lay uplifted and set upright against the wall. He was a prisoner, but as yet undiscovered. Being satisfied in his mind that hanging was the systematic and legalized penalty for the outrage he had committed, he kept down manfully the cry that rose to his lips.

In a few moments he felt the cask again lifted

by a powerful hand, which appeared above him at the edge of his prison, and which he concluded belonged to the ferocious giant Blunderbore, whose features and limbs he had frequently met in colored pictures. Before he could recover from his astonishment, his cask was placed with several others on a cart, and rapidly driven away. The ride which ensued he describes as being fearful in the extreme. Rolled around like a pill in a box, the agonies which he suffered may be hinted at, not spoken. Evidences of that protracted struggle were visible in his garments, which were of the consistency of syrup, and his hair, which for several hours, under the treatment of hot water, yielded a thin treacle. At length the cart stopped on one of the wharves, and the cartman began to unload. As he tilted over the cask in which Charles lay, an exclamation broke from his lips, and the edge of the cask fell from his hands, sliding its late occupant upon the wharf. To regain his short legs, and to put the greatest possible distance between himself and the cartman, were his first movements on regaining his liberty. He did not stop until he reached the corner of Front Street.

Another blank succeeds in this veracious history. He cannot remember how or when he found himself in front of the circus tent. He has an indistinct recollection of having passed through a long street of stores which were all closed, and which made him fear that it was Sunday, and that he had spent a miserable night in the sugar cask. But he remembers hearing the sound of music within the tent, and of creeping on his hands and knees, when no one was looking, until he passed under the canvas. His description of the wonders contained within that circle; of the terrific feats which were performed by a man on a pole, since practised by him in the back yard; of the horses, one of which was spotted and resembled an animal in his Noah's Ark, hitherto unrecognized and undefined; of the female equestrians, whose dresses could only be equalled in magnificence by the frocks of his sister's doll; of the painted clown, whose jokes excited a merriment, somewhat tinged by an undefined fear, was an effort of language which this pen could but weakly transcribe, and which no quantity of exclamation points could sufficiently illustrate. He is not quite certain what followed. He remembers that almost immediately on leaving the circus it became dark, and that he fell asleep, waking up at intervals on the corners of the streets, on front steps, in somebody's arms, and finally in his own bed. He was not aware of experiencing any regret for his conduct; he does not recall feeling at any time a disposition to go home; he remembers distinctly that he felt hungry.

He has made this disclosure in confidence. He wishes it to be respected. He wants to know if you have five cents about you.

SIDEWALKINGS.

THE time occupied in walking to and from my business I have always found to yield me a certain mental enjoyment which no other part of the twenty-four hours could give. Perhaps the physical exercise may have acted as a gentle stimulant of the brain, but more probably the comfortable consciousness that I could not reasonably be expected to be doing anything else — to be studying or improving my mind, for instance — always gave a joyous liberty to my fancy. I once thought it necessary to employ this interval in doing sums in arithmetic, — in which useful study I was and still am lamentably deficient, — but after one or two attempts at peripatetic computation, I gave it up. I am satisfied that much enjoyment is lost to the world by this nervous anxiety to improve our leisure moments, which, like the "shining hours" of Dr. Watts, unfortunately offer the greatest facilities for idle pleasure. I feel a profound pity for those misguided beings who are still impelled to carry text-books with them in cars, omnibuses, and ferryboats, and who generally manage to defraud themselves of those intervals of rest they most require.

Nature must have her fallow moments, when she covers her exhausted fields with flowers instead of grain. Deny her this, and the next crop suffers for it. I offer this axiom as some apology for obtruding upon the reader a few of the speculations which have engaged my mind during these daily perambulations.

Few Californians know how to lounge gracefully. Business habits, and a deference to the custom, even with those who have no business, give an air of restless anxiety to every pedestrian. The exceptions to this rule are apt to go to the other extreme, and wear a defiant, obtrusive kind of indolence which suggests quite as much inward disquiet and unrest. The shiftless lassitude of a gambler can never be mistaken for the lounge of a gentleman. Even the brokers who loiter upon Montgomery Street at high noon are not loungers. Look at them closely and you will see a feverishness and anxiety under the mask of listlessness. They do not lounge — they lie in wait. No surer sign, I imagine, of our peculiar civilization can be found than this lack of repose in its constituent elements. You cannot keep Californians quiet even in their amusements. They dodge in and out of the theatre, opera, and lecture-room ; they prefer the street cars to walking because they think they get along faster. The difference of locomotion between Broadway, New York, and Montgomery Street, San Francisco, is a comparative view of Eastern and Western civilization.

There is a habit peculiar to many walkers, which Punch, some years ago, touched upon satirically, but which seems to have survived the jester's ridicule. It is that custom of stopping friends in the street, to whom we have nothing whatever to communicate, but whom we embarrass for no other purpose than simply to show our friendship. Jones meets his friend Smith, whom he has met in nearly the same locality but a few hours before. During that interval, it is highly probable that no event of any importance to Smith, nor indeed to Jones, which by a friendly construction Jones could imagine Smith to be interested in, has occurred, or is likely to occur. Yet both gentlemen stop and shake hands earnestly. " Well, how goes it ? " remarks Smith with a vague hope that something may have happened. " So so," replies the eloquent Jones, feeling intuitively the deep vacuity of his friend answering to his own. A pause ensues, in which both gentlemen regard each other with an imbecile smile and a fervent pressure of the hand. Smith draws a long breath and looks up the street ; Jones sighs heavily and gazes down the street. Another pause, in which both gentlemen disengage their respective hands and glance anxiously around for some conventional avenue of escape. Finally, Smith (with a sudden assumption of having forgotten an important engagement) ejaculates, "Well, I must be off," — a remark instantly echoed by the voluble Jones, and these gentlemen separate, only to repeat their miserable formula the next day. In the above example I have compassionately shortened the usual leave-taking, which, in skilful hands, may be protracted to a length which I shudder to recall. I have sometimes, when an active participant in these atrocious transactions, lingered in the hope of saying something natural to my friend (feeling that he, too, was groping in the mazy labyrinths of his mind for a like expression), until I have felt that we ought to have been separated by a policeman. It is astonishing how far the most wretched joke will go in these emergencies, and how it will, as it were, convulsively detach the two cohering particles. I have laughed (albeit hysterically) at some witticism under cover of which I escaped, that five minutes afterward I could not perceive possessed a grain of humor. I would advise any person who may fall into this pitiable strait, that, next to getting in the way of a passing dray and being forcibly disconnected, a joke is the most efficacious. A foreign phrase often may be tried with success ; I have sometimes known *Au revoir* pronounced "O-reveer," to have the effect (as it ought) of severing friends.

But this is a harmless habit compared to a certain reprehensible practice in which sundry feeble-

minded young men indulge.   I have been stopped
in the street and enthusiastically accosted by some
fashionable young man, who has engaged me in
animated conversation, until (quite accidentally) a
certain young belle would pass, whom my friend, of
course, saluted.   As, by a strange coincidence, this
occurred several times in the course of the week,
and as my young friend's conversational powers
invariably flagged after the lady had passed, I am
forced to believe that the deceitful young wretch
actually used me as a conventional background to
display the graces of his figure to the passing fair.
When I detected the trick, of course I made a point
of keeping my friend, by strategic movements,
with his back toward the young lady, while I bowed
to her myself.   Since then, I understand that it is
a regular custom of these callow youths to encounter
each other, with simulated cordiality, some paces
in front of the young lady they wish to recognize,
so that she cannot possibly cut them.   The corner of California and Montgomery streets is their
favorite haunt.   They may be easily detected by
their furtive expression of eye, which betrays
them even in the height of their apparent enthusiasm.

Speaking of eyes, you can generally settle the
average gentility and good breeding of the people
you meet in the street by the manner in which
they return or evade your glance.   "A gentleman,"

as the Autocrat has wisely said, is always " calm-
eyed." There is just enough abstraction in his
look to denote his individual power and the capacity for self-contemplation, while he is, nevertheless, quietly and unobtrusively observant. He does
not seek, neither does he evade your observation.
Snobs and prigs do the first ; bashful and mean
people do the second. There are some men who,
on meeting your eye, immediately assume an expression quite different from the one which they
previously wore, which, whether an improvement
or not, suggests a disagreeable self-consciousness.
Perhaps they fancy they are betraying something.
There are others who return your look with
unnecessary defiance, which suggests a like concealment. The symptoms of the eye are generally
borne out in the figure. A man is very apt to
betray his character by the manner in which he
appropriates his part of the sidewalk. The man
who resolutely keeps the middle of the pavement,
and deliberately brushes against you, you may be
certain would take the last piece of pie at the
hotel table, and empty the cream-jug on its way to
your cup. The man who sidles by you, keeping
close to the houses, and selecting the easiest planks,
manages to slip through life in some such way, and
to evade its sternest duties. The awkward man,
who gets in your way, and throws you back upon
the man behind you, and so manages to derange the

harmonious procession of an entire block, is very apt to do the same thing in political and social economy. The inquisitive man, who deliberately shortens his pace, so that he may participate in the confidence you impart to your companion, has an eye not unfamiliar to keyholes, and probably opens his wife's letters. The loud man, who talks with the intention of being overheard, is the same egotist elsewhere. If there was any justice in Iago's sneer, that there were some " so weak of soul that in their sleep they mutter their affairs," what shall be said of the walking revery-babblers ? I have met men who were evidently rolling over, "like a sweet morsel under the tongue," some speech they were about to make, and others who were framing curses. I remember once that, while walking behind an apparently respectable old gentleman, he suddenly uttered the exclamation, "Well, I'm d—d!" and then quietly resumed his usual manner. Whether he had at that moment become impressed with a truly orthodox disbelief in his ultimate salvation, or whether he was simply indignant, I never could tell.

I have been hesitating for some time to speak — or if indeed to speak at all—of that lovely and critic-defying sex, whose bright eyes and voluble prattle have not been without effect in tempering the austerities of my peripatetic musing. I have been humbly thankful that I have been permitted to

view their bright dresses and those charming bonnets which seem to have brought the birds and flowers of spring within the dreary limits of the town, and — I trust I shall not be deemed unkind in saying . it — my pleasure was not lessened by the reflection that the display, to me at least, was inexpensive. I have walked in — and I fear occasionally on — the train of the loveliest of her sex who has preceded me. If I have sometimes wondered why two young ladies always began to talk vivaciously on the approach of any good-looking fellow; if I have wondered whether the mirror-like qualities of all large show-windows at all influenced their curiosity regarding silks and calicoes; if I have ever entertained the same ungentlemanly thought concerning daguerreotype show-cases; if I have ever misinterpreted the eye-shot which has passed between two pretty women — more searching, exhaustive and sincere than any of our feeble ogles; if I have ever committed these or any other impertinences, it was only to retire beaten and discomfited, and to confess that masculine philosophy, while it soars beyond Sirius and the ring of Saturn, stops short at the steel periphery which encompasses the simplest school-girl.

A BOYS' DOG.

AS I lift my eyes from the paper, I observe a
dog lying on the steps of the opposite house.
His attitude might induce passers-by and casual
observers to believe him to belong to the people who live there, and to accord to him a certain
standing position. I have seen visitors pat him,
under the impression that they were doing an act
of courtesy to his master, he lending himself to
the fraud by hypocritical contortions of the body.
But his attitude is one of deceit and simulation.
He has neither master nor habitation. He is a
very Pariah and outcast ; in brief, " A Boys' Dog."

There is a degree of hopeless and irreclaimable
vagabondage expressed in this epithet, which may
not be generally understood. Only those who are
familiar with the roving nature and predatory
instincts of boys in large cities will appreciate its
strength. It is the lowest step in the social scale
to which a respectable canine can descend. A
blind man's dog, or the companion of a knife-
grinder, is comparatively elevated. He at least
owes allegiance to but one master. But the Boys'
Dog is the thrall of an entire juvenile community,

obedient to the beck and call of the smallest imp
in the neighborhood, attached to and serving not
the individual boy so much as the boy element
and principle. In their active sports, in small
thefts, raids into back-yards, window-breaking, and
other minor juvenile recreations, he is a full participant. In this way he is the reflection of the
wickedness of many masters, without possessing
the virtues or peculiarities of any particular one.

If leading a "dog's life" be considered a peculiar phase of human misery, the life of a Boys'
Dog is still more infelicitous. He is associated in
all schemes of wrong-doing, and unless he be a dog
of experience is always the scapegoat. He never
shares the booty of his associates. In absence
of legitimate amusement, he is considered fair
game for his companions; and I have seen him
reduced to the ignominy of having a tin kettle
tied to his tail. His ears and tail have generally
been docked to suit the caprice of the unholy band
of which he is a member; and if he has any spunk,
he is invariably pitted against larger dogs in mortal
combat. He is poorly fed and hourly abused; the
reputation of his associates debars him from outside sympathies; and once a Boys' Dog, he cannot
change his condition. He is not unfrequently sold
into slavery by his inhuman companions. I remember once to have been accosted on my own
doorsteps by a couple of precocious youths, who

offered to sell me a dog which they were then
leading by a rope. The price was extremely moderate, being, if I remember rightly, but fifty cents.
Imagining the unfortunate animal to have lately
fallen into their wicked hands, and anxious to
reclaim him from the degradation of becoming a
Boys' Dog, I was about to conclude the bargain,
when I saw a look of intelligence pass between
the dog and his two masters. I promptly stopped
all negotiation, and drove the youthful swindlers
and their four-footed accomplice from my presence.
The whole thing was perfectly plain. The dog
was an old, experienced, and hardened Boys' Dog,
and I was perfectly satisfied that he would run
away and rejoin his old companions at the first
opportunity. This I afterwards learned he did, on
the occasion of a kind-hearted but unsophisticated
neighbor buying him; and a few days ago I saw
him exposed for sale by those two Arcadians, in
another neighborhood, having been bought and
paid for half a dozen times in this.

But, it will be asked, if the life of a Boys' Dog
is so unhappy, why do they enter upon such an un-
enviable situation, and why do they not dissolve the
partnership when it becomes unpleasant? I will
confess that I have been often puzzled by this
question. For some time I could not make up my
mind whether their unholy alliance was the result
of the influence of the dog on the boy, or *vice versa*,

and which was the weakest and most impressible nature. I am satisfied now that, at first, the dog is undoubtedly influenced by the boy, and, as it were, is led, while yet a puppy, from the paths of canine rectitude by artful and designing boys. As he grows older and more experienced in the ways of his Bohemian friends, he becomes a willing decoy, and takes delight in leading boyish innocence astray, in beguiling children to play truant, and thus revenges his own degradation on the boy nature generally. It is in this relation, and in regard to certain unhallowed practices I have detected him in, that I deem it proper to expose to parents and guardians the danger to which their offspring is exposed by the Boys' Dog.

The Boys' Dog lays his plans artfully. He begins to influence the youthful mind by suggestions of unrestrained freedom and frolic which he offers in his own person. He will lie in wait at the garden gate for a very small boy, and endeavor to lure him outside its sacred precincts, by gambolling and jumping a little beyond the inclosure. He will set off on an imaginary chase and run around the block in a perfectly frantic manner, and then return, breathless, to his former position, with a look as of one who would say, "There, you see how perfectly easy it's done!" Should the unhappy infant find it difficult to resist the effect which this glimpse of the area of freedom pro-

duces, and step beyond the gate, from that moment
he is utterly demoralized. The Boys' Dog owns
him body and soul. Straightway he is led by the
deceitful brute into the unhallowed circle of his
Bohemian masters. Sometimes the unfortunate
boy, if he be very small, turns up eventually at
the station-house as a lost child. Whenever I
meet a stray boy in the street looking utterly bewildered and astonished, I generally find a Boys'
Dog lurking on the corner. When I read the advertisements of lost children, I always add mentally to the description, "was last seen in company
with a Boys' Dog." Nor is his influence wholly
confined to small boys. I have seen him waiting
patiently for larger boys on the way to school, and
by artful and sophistical practices inducing them
to play truant. I have seen him lying at the
school-house door, with the intention of enticing
the children on their way home to distant and remote localities. He has led many an unsuspecting
boy to the wharves and quays by assuming the
character of a water-dog, which he was not, and
again has induced others to go with him on a gun-
ning excursion by pretending to be a sporting dog,
in which quality he was knowingly deficient. Un-
scrupulous, hypocritical, and deceitful, he has won
many children's hearts by answering to any name
they might call him, attaching himself to their
persons until they got into trouble, and deserting

them at the very moment they most needed his
assistance. I have seen him rob small school-boys
of their dinners by pretending to knock them
down by accident; and have seen larger boys in
turn dispossess him of his ill-gotten booty for
their own private gratification. From being a tool,
he has grown to be an accomplice; through much
imposition, he has learned to impose on others; in
his best character, he is simply a vagabond's vagabond.

I could find it in my heart to pity him, as he
lies there through the long summer afternoon, en-
joying brief intervals of tranquillity and rest which
he surreptitiously snatches from a stranger's door-
step. For a shrill whistle is heard in the streets,
the boys are coming home from school, and he is
startled from his dreams by a deftly thrown potato,
which hits him on the head, and awakens him to
the stern reality that he is now and forever — a
Boys' Dog.

CHARITABLE REMINISCENCES.

A S the new Benevolent Association has had the effect of withdrawing beggars from the streets, and as Professional Mendicancy bids fair to be presently ranked with the Lost Arts, to preserve some records of this noble branch of industry, I have endeavored to recall certain traits and peculiarities of individual members of the order whom I have known, and whose forms I now miss from their accustomed haunts. In so doing, I confess to feeling a certain regret at this decay of Professional Begging, for I hold the theory that mankind are bettered by the occasional spectacle of misery, whether simulated or not, on the same principle that our sympathies are enlarged by the fictitious woes of the Drama, though we know that the actors are insincere. Perhaps I am indiscreet in saying that I have rewarded the artfully dressed and well-acted performance of the begging impostor through the same impulse that impelled me to expend a dollar in witnessing the counterfeited sorrows of poor "Triplet," as represented by Charles Wheatleigh. I did not quarrel with deceit in either case. My coin was given in recognition of the sentiment;

the moral responsibility rested with the per-
former.

The principal figure that I now mourn over as
lost forever is one that may have been familiar to
many of my readers.   It was that of a dark-com-
plexioned, black-eyed, foreign-looking woman, who
supported in her arms a sickly baby.   As a patho-
logical phenomenon the baby was especially interesting, having presented the Hippocratic face and
other symptoms of immediate dissolution, without
change, for the past three years.   The woman
never verbally solicited alms.   Her appearance
was always mute, mysterious, and sudden.   She
made no other appeal than that which the dramatic
tableau of herself and baby suggested, with an outstretched hand and deprecating eye sometimes
superadded.   She usually stood in my doorway,
silent and patient, intimating her presence, if my
attention were preoccupied, by a slight cough from
her baby, whom I shall always believe had its part
to play in this little pantomime, and generally
obeyed a secret signal from the maternal hand.   It
was useless for me to refuse alms, to plead business,
or affect inattention.   She never moved ; her position
was always taken with an appearance of latent
capabilities of endurance and experience in waiting
which never failed to impress me with awe and the
futility of any hope of escape.   There was also something in the reproachful expression of her eye which

plainly said to me, as I bent over my paper, "Go on with your mock sentimentalities and simulated pathos; portray the imaginary sufferings of your bodiless creations, spread your thin web of philosophy, but look you, sir, here is real misery! Here is genuine suffering!" I confess that this artful suggestion usually brought me down. In three minutes after she had thus invested the citadel I usually surrendered at discretion, without a gun having been fired on either side. She received my offering and retired as mutely and mysteriously as she had appeared. Perhaps it was well for me that she did not know her strength. I might have been forced, had this terrible woman been conscious of her real power, to have borrowed money which I could not pay, or have forged a check to purchase immunity from her awful presence. I hardly know if I make myself understood, and yet I am unable to define my meaning more clearly when I say that there was something in her glance which suggested to the person appealed to, when in the presence of others, a certain idea of some individual responsibility for her sufferings, which, while it never failed to affect him with a mingled sense of ludicrousness and terror, always made an impression of unqualified gravity on the minds of the bystanders. As she has disappeared within the last month, I imagine that she has found a home at the San Francisco Benevolent Association,

— at least, I cannot conceive of any charity, however guarded by wholesome checks or sharp-eyed almoners, that could resist that mute apparition. I should like to go there and inquire about her, and also learn if the baby was convalescent or dead, but I am satisfied that she would rise up, a mute and reproachful appeal, so personal in its artful suggestions, that it would end in the Association instantly transferring her to my hands.

My next familiar mendicant was a vender of printed ballads. These effusions were so stale, atrocious, and unsalable in their character, that it was easy to detect that hypocrisy, which — in imitation of more ambitious beggary — veiled the real eleemosynary appeal under the thin pretext of offering an equivalent. This beggar — an aged female in a rusty bonnet — I unconsciously precipitated upon myself in an evil moment. On our first meeting, while distractedly turning over the ballads, I came upon a certain production entitled, I think, "The Fire Zouave," and was struck with the truly patriotic and American manner in which " Zouave " was made to rhyme in different stanzas with "grave, brave, save, and glaive." As I purchased it at once, with a gratified expression of countenance, it soon became evident that the act was misconstrued by my poor friend, who from that moment never ceased to haunt me. Perhaps in the whole course of her precarious existence

she had never before sold a ballad. My solitary
purchase evidently made me, in her eyes, a cus-
tomer, and in a measure exalted her vocation ; so
thereafter she regularly used to look in at my
door, with a chirping, confident air, and the question, " Any more songs to-day ? " as though it were
some necessary article of daily consumption. I
never took any more of her songs, although that
circumstance did not shake her faith in my literary
taste ; my abstinence from this exciting mental
pabulum being probably ascribed to charitable
motives. She was finally absorbed by the S. F.
B. A., who have probably made a proper disposition of her effects. She was a little old woman,
of Celtic origin, predisposed to melancholy, and
looking as if she had read most of her ballads.

My next reminiscence takes the shape of a very
seedy individual, who had, for three or four years,
been vainly attempting to get back to his relatives
in Illinois, where sympathizing friends and a comfortable almshouse awaited him. Only a few dollars, he informed me, — the uncontributed remain-
der of the amount necessary to purchase a steerage
ticket, — stood in his way. These last few dollars
seem to have been most difficult to get, and he
had wandered about, a sort of antithetical Flying
Dutchman, forever putting to sea, yet never getting
away from shore. He was a " 49-er," and had recently been blown up in a tunnel, or had fallen

down a shaft, I forget which.   This sad accident
obliged him to use large quantities of whiskey as
a liniment, which, he informed me, occasioned
the mild fragrance which his garments exhaled.
Though belonging to the same class, he was not to
be confounded with the unfortunate miner who
could not get back to his claim without pecuniary
assistance, or the desolate Italian, who hopelessly
handed you a document in a foreign language, very
much bethumbed and illegible, — which, in your
ignorance of the tongue, you could n't help suspiciously feeling might have been a price current,
but which you could see was proffered as an excuse
for alms.   Indeed, whenever any stranger handed
me, without speaking, an open document, which
bore the marks of having been carried in the greasy
lining of a hat, I always felt safe in giving him a
quarter and dismissing him without further questioning.   I always noticed that these circular letters,
when written in the vernacular, were remarkable
for their beautiful caligraphy and grammatical in-
accuracy, and that they all seem to have been written by the same hand.   Perhaps indigence exer-
cises a peculiar and equal effect upon the hand-
writing.

I recall a few occasional mendicants whose faces
were less familiar.   One afternoon a most extraordinary Irishman, with a black eye, a bruised hat,
and other traces of past enjoyment, waited upon

me with a pitiful story of destitution and want,
and concluded by requesting the usual trifle. I
replied, with some severity, that if I gave him a
dime he would probably spend it for drink. " Be
Gorra ! but you 're roight — I wad that ! " he answered promptly. I was so much taken aback by
this unexpected exhibition of frankness that I instantly handed over the dime. It seems that Truth
had survived the wreck of his other virtues ; he
did get drunk, and, impelled by a like conscientious
sense of duty, exhibited himself to me in that
state a few hours after, to show that my bounty
had not been misapplied.

In spite of the peculiar characters of these reminiscences, I cannot help feeling a certain regret
at the decay of Professional Mendicancy. Perhaps
it may be owing to a lingering trace of that youthful superstition which saw in all beggars a possible
prince or fairy, and invested their calling with a
mysterious awe. Perhaps it may be from a belief
that there is something in the old-fashioned alms-
givings and actual contact with misery that is
wholesome for both donor and recipient, and that
any system which interposes a third party between
them is only putting on a thick glove, which, while
it preserves us from contagion, absorbs and dead-
ens the kindly pressure of our hand. It is a very
pleasant thing to purchase relief from the annoy-
ance and trouble of having to weigh the claims of

an afflicted neighbor. As I turn over these printed tickets, which the courtesy of the San Francisco Benevolent Association has — by a slight stretch of the imagination in supposing that any sane unfortunate might rashly seek relief from a newspaper office — conveyed to these editorial hands, I cannot help wondering whether, when in our last extremity we come to draw upon the Immeasurable Bounty, it will be necessary to present a ticket.

"SEEING THE STEAMER OFF."

I HAVE sometimes thought, while watching the departure of an Eastern steamer, that the act of parting from friends — so generally one of bitterness and despondency — is made by an ingenious Californian custom to yield a pleasurable excitement. This luxury of leave-taking, in which most Californians indulge, is often protracted to the hauling in of the gang-plank. Those last words, injunctions, promises, and embraces, which are mournful and depressing perhaps in that privacy demanded on other occasions, are here, by reason of their very publicity, of an edifying and exhilarating character. A parting kiss, blown from the deck of a steamer into a miscellaneous crowd, of course loses much of that sacred solemnity with which foolish superstition is apt to invest it. A broadside of endearing epithets, even when properly aimed and apparently raking the whole wharf, is apt to be impotent and harmless. A husband who prefers to embrace his wife for the last time at the door of her stateroom, and finds himself the centre of an admiring group of unconcerned spectators, of course feels himself lifted above any feeling

save that of ludicrousness which the situation suggests. The mother, parting from her offspring,
should become a Roman matron under the like influences ; the lover who takes leave of his sweet-
heart is not apt to mar the general hilarity by any
emotional folly. In fact, this system of delaying
our parting sentiments until the last moment —
this removal of domestic scenery and incident to
a public theatre — may be said to be worthy of a
stoical and democratic people, and is an event in
our lives which may be shared with the humblest
coal-passer or itinerant vender of oranges. It is
a return to that classic out-of-door experience and
mingling of public and domestic economy which
so ennobled the straight-nosed Athenian.

So universal is this desire to be present at the
departure of any steamer that, aside from the regular
crowd of loungers who make their appearance con-
fessedly only to look on, there are others who take
advantage of the slightest intimacy to go through
the leave-taking formula. People whom you have
quite forgotten, people to whom you have been
lately introduced, suddenly and unexpectedly make
their appearance and wring your hands with fervor.
The friend, long estranged, forgives you nobly at
the last moment, to take advantage of this glorious
opportunity of " seeing you off." Your bootmaker,
tailor, and hatter — haply with no ulterior motives
and unaccompanied by official friends — visit you

with enthusiasm. You find great difficulty in detaching your relatives and acquaintances from the trunks on which they resolutely seat themselves, up to the moment when the paddles are moving, and you are haunted continually by an ill-defined idea that they may be carried off, and foisted on you — with the payment of their passage, which, under the circumstances, you could not refuse — for the rest of the voyage. Your friends will make their appearance at the most inopportune moments, and from the most unexpected places, — dangling from hawsers, climbing up paddle-boxes, and crawling through cabin windows at the imminent peril of their lives. You are nervous and crushed by this added weight of responsibility. Should you be a stranger, you will find any number of people on board, who will cheerfully and at a venture take leave of you on the slightest advances made on your part. A friend of mine assures me that he once parted, with great enthusiasm and cordiality, from a party of gentlemen, to him personally unknown, who had apparently mistaken his state-room. This party, — evidently connected with some fire company, — on comparing notes on the wharf, being somewhat dissatisfied with the result of their performances, afterward rendered my friend's position on the hurricane deck one of extreme peril and inconvenience, by reason of skilfully projected oranges and apples.

accompanied with some invective. Yet there is certainly something to interest us in the examination of that cheerless damp closet, whose painted wooden walls no furniture or company can make habitable, wherein our friend is to spend so many vapid days and restless nights. The sight of these apartments, yclept *state-rooms*, — Heaven knows why, except it be from their want of cosiness, — is full of keen reminiscences to most Californians who have not outgrown the memories of that dreary interval when, in obedience to nature's wise compensations, homesickness was blotted out by sea-sickness, and both at last resolved into a chaotic and distempered dream, whose details we now recognize. The steamer chair that we used to drag out upon the narrow strip of deck and doze in, over the pages of a well-thumbed novel ; the deck itself, of afternoons, redolent with the skins of oranges and bananas, of mornings, damp with salt-water and mopping ; the netted bulwark, smelling of tar in the tropics, and fretted on the weather side with little saline crystals ; the villanously compounded odors of victuals from the pantry, and oil from the machinery ; the young lady that we used to flirt with, and with whom we shared our last novel, adorned with marginal annotations ; our own chum ; our own bore ; the man who was never sea-sick ; the two events of the day, breakfast and dinner, and the dreary in-

terval between ; the tremendous importance given,
to trifling events and trifling people ; the young
lady who kept a journal ; the newspaper, published
on board, filled with mild pleasantries and impertinences, elsewhere unendurable ; the young lady
who sang ; the wealthy passenger ; the popular
passenger ; the —

[Let us sit down for a moment until this qualm-
ishness, which these associations and some infec-
tious quality of the atmosphere seem to produce,
has passed away. What becomes of our steamer
friends ? Why are we now so apathetic about
them ? Why is it that we drift away from them
so unconcernedly, forgetting even their names and
faces ? Why, when we do remember them, do we
look at them so suspiciously, with an undefined
idea that, in the unrestrained freedom of the voyage, they became possessed of some confidence and
knowledge of our weaknesses that we never should
have imparted ? Did we make any such confes-
sions ? Perish the thought. The popular man,
however, is not now so popular. We have heard
finer voices than that of the young lady who sang
so sweetly. Our chum's fascinating qualities, somehow, have deteriorated on land ; so have those of
the fair young novel-reader, now the wife of an
honest miner in Virginia City.]

— The passenger who made so many trips, and
exhibited a reckless familiarity with the officers ;

the officers themselves, now so modest and unde-
monstrative, a few hours later so all-powerful and
important, — these are among the reminiscences
of most Californians, and these are to be remembered among the experiences of our friend. Yet
he feels, as we all do, that his past experience will
be of profit to him, and has already the confident
air of an old voyager.

As you stand on the wharf again, and listen to
the cries of itinerant fruit venders, you wonder
why it is that grief at parting and the unpleasant
novelties of travel are supposed to be assuaged by
oranges and apples, even at ruinously low prices.
Perhaps it may be, figuratively, the last offering of
the fruitful earth, as the passenger commits himself to the bosom of the sterile and unproductive
ocean. Even while the wheels are moving and the
lines are cast off, some hardy apple merchant,
mounted on the top of a pile, concludes a trade
with a steerage passenger, — twenty feet inter-
posing between buyer and seller, — and achieves,
under these difficulties, the delivery of his wares.
Handkerchiefs wave, hurried orders mingle with
parting blessings, and the steamer is "off." As
you turn your face cityward, and glance hurriedly
around at the retreating crowd, you will see a
reflection of your own wistful face in theirs, and
read the solution of one of the problems which
perplex the California enthusiast. Before you lies

San Francisco, with her hard angular outlines, her
brisk, invigorating breezes, her bright, but unsympathetic sunshine, her restless and energetic population; behind you fades the recollection of
changeful, but honest skies ; of extremes of heat
and cold, modified and made enjoyable through
social and physical laws, of pastoral landscapes, of
accessible Nature in her kindliest forms, of inherited virtues, of long-tested customs and habits, of old friends and old faces, — in a word —
of HOME!

NEIGHBORHOODS I HAVE MOVED FROM.

I.

A BAY-WINDOW once settled the choice of my house and compensated for many of its inconveniences. When the chimney smoked, or the doors alternately shrunk and swelled, resisting any forcible attempt to open them, or opening of themselves with ghostly deliberation, or when suspicious blotches appeared on the ceiling in rainy weather, there was always the bay-window to turn to for comfort. And the view was a fine one. Alcatraz, Lime Point, Fort Point, and Saucelito were plainly visible over a restless expanse of water that changed continually, glittering in the sunlight, darkening in rocky shadow, or sweeping in mimic waves on a miniature beach below.

Although at first the bay-window was supposed to be sacred to myself and my writing materials, in obedience to some organic law, it by and by became a general lounging-place. A rocking chair and crochet basket one day found their way there. Then the baby invaded its recesses, fortifying himself behind intrenchments of colored worsteds and spools of cotton, from which he was only dislodged by concerted assault, and carried lamenting into captivity. A subtle glamour crept over all who came within its influence. To apply one's self to serious work there was an absurdity. An incoming ship, a gleam on the water, a cloud lingering about Tamalpais, were enough to distract the attention. Reading or writing, the bay-window was always showing something to be looked at. Unfortunately, these views were not always pleasant, but the window gave equal prominence and importance to all, without respect to quality.

The landscape in the vicinity was unimproved, but not rural. The adjacent lots had apparently just given up bearing scrub-oaks, but had not seriously taken to bricks and mortar. In one direction the vista was closed by the Home of the Inebriates, not in itself a cheerful-looking building, and, as the apparent terminus of a ramble in a certain direction, having all the effect of a moral lesson. To a certain extent, however, this building was an imposition. The enthusiastic members of my family, who confidently expected to see its inmates hilariously disporting themselves at its windows in the different stages of inebriation portrayed by the late W. E. Burton, were much disappointed. The Home was reticent of its secrets. The County Hospital, also in range of the bay-window, showed much more animation. At certain hours of the day convalescents passed in

review before the window on their way to an air-
ing. This spectacle was the still more depressing
from a singular lack of sociability that appeared to
prevail among them. Each man was encompassed
by the impenetrable atmosphere of his own peculiar suffering. They did not talk or walk together.
From the window I have seen half a dozen sunning
themselves against a wall within a few feet of each
other, to all appearance utterly oblivious of the
fact. Had they but quarrelled or fought, — anything would have been better than this horrible
apathy.

The lower end of the street on which the bay-
window was situate, opened invitingly from a popular thoroughfare ; and after beckoning the un-
wary stranger into its recesses, ended unexpectedly
at a frightful precipice. On Sundays, when the
travel North-Beachwards was considerable, the bay-
window delighted in the spectacle afforded by unhappy pedestrians who were seduced into taking
this street as a short-cut somewhere else. It was
amusing to notice how these people invariably, on
coming to the precipice, glanced upward to the
bay-window and endeavored to assume a careless
air before they retraced their steps, whistling os-
tentatiously, as if they had previously known all
about it. One high-spirited young man in particular, being incited thereto by a pair of mischievous bright eyes in an opposite window,

actually descended this fearful precipice rather than return, to the great peril of life and limb, and manifest injury to his Sunday clothes.

Dogs, goats, and horses constituted the *fauna* of our neighborhood. Possessing the lawless freedom of their normal condition, they still evinced a tender attachment to man and his habitations. Spirited steeds got up *extempore* races on the sidewalks, turning the street into a miniature *Corso*; dogs wrangled in the areas; while from the hill beside the house a goat browsed peacefully upon my wife's geraniums in the flower-pots of the second-story window. "We had a fine hail-storm last night," remarked a newly arrived neighbor, who had just moved into the adjoining house. It would have been a pity to set him right, as he was quite enthusiastic about the view and the general sanitary qualifications of the locality. So I did n't tell him anything about the goats who were in the habit of using his house as a stepping-stone to the adjoining hill.

But the locality was remarkably healthy. People who fell down the embankments found their wounds heal rapidly in the steady sea-breeze. Ventilation was complete and thorough. The opening of the bay-window produced a current of wholesome air which effectually removed all noxious exhalations, together with the curtains, the hinges of the back door, and the window-shutters. Owing to this peculiarity, some of my writings acquired an extensive circulation and publicity in the neighborhood, which years in another locality might not have produced. Several articles of wearing apparel, which were mysteriously transposed from our clothes-line to that of an humble though honest neighbor, was undoubtedly the result of these sanitary winds. Yet in spite of these advantages I found it convenient in a few months to move. And the result whereof I shall communicate in other papers.

II.

" A HOUSE with a fine garden and extensive shrubbery, in a genteel neighborhood," were, if I remember rightly, the general terms of an advertisement which once decided my choice of a dwelling. I should add that this occurred at an early stage of my household experience, when I placed a trustful reliance in advertisements. I have since learned that the most truthful people are apt to indulge a slight vein of exaggeration in describing their own possessions, as though the mere circumstance of going into print were an excuse for a certain kind of mendacity. But I did not fully awaken to this fact until a much later period, when, in answering an advertisement which described a highly advantageous tenement, I was referred to the house I then occupied, and from which a thousand inconveniences were impelling me to move.

The " fine garden " alluded to was not large, but contained several peculiarly shaped flower-beds. I was at first struck with the singular resemblance which they bore to the mutton-chops that are usually brought on the table at hotels and restaurants, — a resemblance the more striking from the sprigs of parsley which they produced freely. One plat in particular reminded me, not unpleasantly, of a peculiar cake, known to my boyhood as " a bolivar." The owner of the property, however, who seemed to be a man of original æsthetic ideas, had banked up one of these beds with bright-colored sea-shells, so that in rainy weather it suggested an aquarium, and offered the elements of botanical and conchological study in pleasing juxtaposition. I have since thought that the fish-geraniums, which it also bore to a surprising extent, were introduced originally from some such idea of consistency. But it was very pleasant, after dinner, to ramble up and down the gravelly paths (whose occasional boulders reminded me of the dry bed of a somewhat circuitous mining stream), smoking a cigar, or inhaling the rich aroma of fennel, or occasionally stopping to pluck one of the hollyhocks with which the garden abounded. The prolific qualities of this plant

alarmed us greatly, for although, in the first trans-
port of enthusiasm, my wife planted several different kinds of flower-seeds, nothing ever came up
but hollyhocks; and although, impelled by the
same laudable impulse, I procured a copy of
"Downing's Landscape Gardening," and a few
gardening tools, and worked for several hours in
the garden, my efforts were equally futile.

The "extensive shrubbery" consisted of several
dwarfed trees. One was a very weak young weep-
ing willow, so very limp and maudlin, and so evidently bent on establishing its reputation, that it
had to be tied up against the house for support.
The dampness of that portion of the house was
usually attributed to the presence of this lachry-
mose shrub.   And to these a couple of highly objectionable trees, known, I think, by the name of
Malva, which made an inordinate show of cheap
blossoms that they were continually shedding, and
one or two dwarf oaks, with scaly leaves and a
generally spiteful exterior, and you have what
was not inaptly termed by our Milesian handmaid
"the scrubbery."

The gentility of our neighbor suffered a blight
from the unwholesome vicinity of McGinnis Court.
This court was a kind of *cul de sac* that, on being
penetrated, discovered a primitive people living in
a state of barbarous freedom, and apparently spending the greater portion of their lives on their own

door-steps.   Many of those details of the toilet
which a popular prejudice restricts to the dressing-
room in other localities, were here performed in
the open court without fear and without reproach.
Early in the week the court was hid in a choking,
soapy mist, which arose from innumerable wash-
tubs.   This was followed in a day or two later by
an extraordinary exhibition of wearing apparel of
divers colors, fluttering on lines like a display of
bunting on ship-board, and whose flapping in the
breeze was like irregular discharges of musketry.
It was evident also that the court exercised a de-
moralizing influence over the whole neighborhood.
A sanguine property-owner once put up a handsome dwelling on the corner of our street, and lived
therein; but although he appeared frequently on
his balcony, clad in a bright crimson dressing-gown,
which made him look like a tropical bird of some
rare and gorgeous species, he failed to woo any
kindred dressing-gown to the vicinity, and only
provoked opprobrious epithets from the *gamins* of
the court.   He moved away shortly after, and on
going by the house one day, I noticed a bill of
" Rooms to let, with board," posted conspicuously
on the Corinthian columns of the porch.   McGinnis Court had triumphed.   An interchange of civil-
ities at once took place between the court and the
servants' area of the palatial mansion, and some
of the young men boarders exchange playful slang

with the adolescent members of the court.   From
that moment we felt that our claims to gentility
were forever abandoned.

Yet, we enjoyed intervals of unalloyed content-
ment.   When the twilight toned down the hard
outlines of the oaks, and made shadowy clumps
and formless masses of other bushes, it was quite
romantic to sit by the window and inhale the faint,
sad odor of the fennel in the walks below.   Perhaps this economical pleasure was much enhanced
by a picture in my memory, whose faded colors the
odor of this humble plant never failed to restore.
So I often sat there of evenings and closed my eyes
until the forms and benches of a country school-
room came back to me, redolent with the incense
of fennel covertly stowed away in my desk, and
gazed again in silent rapture on the round, red
cheeks and long black braids of that peerless creature whose glance had often caused my cheeks to
glow over the preternatural collar, which at that
period of my boyhood it was my pride and privilege
to wear.   As I fear I may be often thought hyper-
critical and censorious in these articles, I am willing to record this as one of the advantages of our
new house, not mentioned in the advertisement,
nor chargeable in the rent.   May the present tenant, who is a stock-broker, and who impresses me
with the idea of having always been called " Mr."
from his cradle up, enjoy this advantage, and try
sometimes to remember he was a boy !

III.

SOON after I moved into Happy Valley I was
struck with the remarkable infelicity of its title.
Generous as Californians are in the use of adjec-
tives, this passed into the domain of irony.   But I
was inclined to think it sincere, — the production
of a weak but gushing mind, just as the feminine
nomenclature of streets in the vicinity was evidently bestowed by one in habitual communion with
" Friendship's Gifts " and " Affection's Offerings."
Our house on Laura Matilda Street looked somewhat like a toy Swiss Cottage, — a style of architecture so prevalent, that in walking down the
block it was quite difficult to resist an impression
of fresh glue and pine shavings.   The few shade-
trees might have belonged originally to those oval
Christmas boxes which contain toy villages; and
even the people who sat by the windows had a
stiffness that made them appear surprisingly unreal
and artificial.   A little dog belonging to a neighbor
was known to the members of my household by
the name of " Glass," from the general suggestion
he gave of having been spun of that article.   Perhaps I have somewhat exaggerated these illustrations of the dapper nicety of our neighborhood, —
a neatness and conciseness which I think have a
general tendency to belittle, dwarf, and contract

their objects. For we gradually fell into small ways and narrow ideas, and to some extent squared the round world outside to the correct angles of Laura Matilda Street.

One reason for this insincere quality may have been the fact that the very foundations of our neighborhood were artificial. Laura Matilda Street was "made ground." The land, not yet quite reclaimed, was continually struggling with its old enemy. We had not been long in our new home before we found an older tenant, not yet wholly divested of his rights, who sometimes showed himself in clammy perspiration on the basement walls, whose damp breath chilled our dining-room, and in the night struck a mortal chilliness through the house. There were no patent fastenings that could keep him out, — no writ of unlawful detainer that could eject him. In the winter his presence was quite palpable; he sapped the roots of the trees, he gurgled under the kitchen floor, he wrought an unwholesome greenness on the side of the veranda. In summer he became invisible, but still exercised a familiar influence over the locality. He planted little stitches in the small of the back, sought out old aches and weak joints, and sportively punched the tenants of the Swiss Cottage under the ribs. He inveigled little children to play with him, but his plays generally ended in scarlet fever, diphtheria, whooping-cough, and measles. He sometimes followed strong men about until they sickened suddenly and took to their beds. But he kept the green-plants in good order, and was very fond of verdure, bestowing it even upon lath and plaster and soulless stone. He was generally invisible, as I have said ; but some time after I had moved, I saw him one morning from the hill stretching his gray wings over the valley, like some fabulous vampire, who had spent the night sucking the wholesome juices of the sleepers below, and was sluggish from the effects of his repast. It was then that I recognized him as Malaria, and knew his abode to be the dread Valley of the shadow of Miasma, — miscalled the Happy Valley !

On week days there was a pleasant melody of boiler-making from the foundries, and the gas works in the vicinity sometimes lent a mild perfume to the breeze. Our street was usually quiet, however, — a footfall being sufficient to draw the inhabitants to their front windows, and to oblige an incautious trespasser to run the gauntlet of batteries of blue and black eyes on either side of the way. A carriage passing through it communicated a singular thrill to the floors, and caused the china on the dining-table to rattle. Although we were comparatively free from the prevailing winds, wandering gusts sometimes got bewildered and strayed unconsciously into our street, and finding an unencumbered field, incontinently set up a shriek of joy, and went gleefully to work on the clothes-lines and chimney-pots, and had a good time generally until they were quite exhausted. I have a very vivid picture in my memory of an organ-grinder who was at one time blown into the end of our street, and actually blown through it in spite of several ineffectual efforts to come to a stand before the different dwellings, but who was finally whirled out of the other extremity, still playing and vainly endeavoring to pursue his unhallowed calling. But these were noteworthy exceptions to the calm and even tenor of our life.

There was contiguity but not much sociability in our neighborhood. From my bedroom window I could plainly distinguish the peculiar kind of victuals spread on my neighbor's dining-table; while, on the other hand, he obtained an equally uninterrupted view of the mysteries of my toilet. Still, that "low vice, curiosity," was regulated by certain laws, and a kind of rude chivalry invested our observation. A pretty girl, whose bedroom window was the cynosure of neighboring eyes, was once brought under the focus of an opera-glass in the hands of one of our ingenuous youth; but this act met such prompt and universal condemnation, as an unmanly advantage, from the lips of married men and bachelors who did n't own opera-glasses, that it was never repeated.

With this brief sketch I conclude my record of

v. 17—I

the neighborhoods I have moved from. I have
moved from many others since then, but they
have generally presented features not dissimilar to
the three I have endeavored to describe in these
pages. I offer them as types containing the salient peculiarities of all. Let no inconsiderate
reader rashly move on account of them. My
experience has not been cheaply bought. From
the nettle Change I have tried to pluck the flower
Security. Draymen have grown rich at my expense. House-agents have known me and were glad,
and landlords have risen up to meet me from afar.
The force of habit impels me still to consult all
the bills I see in the streets, nor can the war telegrams divert my first attention from the advertising
columns of the daily papers. I repeat, let no man
think I have disclosed the weaknesses of the
neighborhood, nor rashly open that closet which
contains the secret skeleton of his dwelling. My
carpets have been altered to fit all sized odd-
shaped apartments from parallelopiped to hexa-
gons. Much of my furniture has been distributed
among my former dwellings. These limbs have
stretched upon uncarpeted floors, or have been let
down suddenly from imperfectly established bed-
steads. I have dined in the parlor and slept in
the back kitchen. Yet the result of these sacri-
fices and trials may be briefly summed up in the
statement that I am now on the eve of removal
from my PRESENT NEIGHBORHOOD.

MY SUBURBAN RESIDENCE.

I LIVE in the suburbs. My residence, to quote the pleasing fiction of the advertisement, "is within fifteen minutes' walk of the City Hall." Why the City Hall should be considered as an eligible terminus of anybody's walk, under any circumstances, I have not been able to determine. Never having walked from my residence to that place, I am unable to verify the assertion, though I may state as a purely abstract and separate proposition, that it takes me the better part of an hour to reach Montgomery Street.

My selection of locality was a compromise between my wife's desire to go into the country, and my own predilections for civic habitation. Like most compromises, it ended in retaining the objectionable features of both propositions; I procured the inconveniences of the country without losing the discomforts of the city. I increased my distance from the butcher and green-grocer, without approximating to herds and kitchen-gardens. But I anticipate.

Fresh air was to be the principal thing sought for. That there might be too much of this did

not enter into my calculations. The first day I
entered my residence, it blew; the second day was
windy; the third, fresh, with a strong breeze stirring; on the fourth, it blew; on the fifth, there
was a gale, which has continued to the present
writing.

That the air is fresh, the above statement sufficiently establishes. That it is bracing, I argue
from the fact that I find it impossible to open the
shutters on the windward side of the house. That
it is healthy, I am also convinced, believing that
there is no other force in Nature that could so
buffet and ill-use a person without serious injury
to him. Let me offer an instance. The path to
my door crosses a slight eminence. The unconscious visitor, a little exhausted by the ascent and
the general effects of the gentle gales which he
has faced in approaching my hospitable mansion,
relaxes his efforts, smooths his brow, and ap-
proaches with a fascinating smile. Rash and too
confident man! The wind delivers a succession of
rapid blows, and he is thrown back. He staggers
up again, in the language of the P. R., "smiling
and confident." The wind now makes for a vul-
nerable point, and gets his hat in chancery. All
ceremony is now thrown away; the luckless wretch
seizes his hat with both hands, and charges madly
at the front door. Inch by inch, the wind con-
tests the ground; another struggle, and he stands

upon the veranda. On such occasions I make it
a point to open the door myself, with a calmness
and serenity that shall offer a marked contrast to
his feverish and excited air, and shall throw suspicion of inebriety upon him. If he be inclined
to timidity and bashfulness, during the best of the
evening he is all too conscious of the disarrange-
ment of his hair and cravat. If he is less sensitive, the result is often more distressing. A valued
elderly friend once called upon me after undergo-
ing a twofold struggle with the wind and a large
Newfoundland dog (which I keep for reasons here-
inafter stated), and not only his hat, but his wig,
had suffered. He spent the evening with me,
totally unconscious of the fact that his hair presented the singular spectacle of having been parted
diagonally from the right temple to the left ear.
When ladies called, my wife preferred to receive
them. They were generally hysterical, and often
in tears. I remember, one Sunday, to have been
startled by what appeared to be the balloon from
Hayes Valley drifting rapidly past my conservatory, closely followed by the Newfoundland dog.
I rushed to the front door, but was anticipated by
my wife. A strange lady appeared at lunch, but
the phenomenon remained otherwise unaccounted
for. Egress from my residence is much more easy.
My guests seldom "stand upon the order of their
going, but go at once"; the Newfoundland dog

playfully harassing their rear. I was standing one
day, with my hand on the open hall door, in serious conversation with the minister of the parish,
when the back door was cautiously opened. The
watchful breeze seized the opportunity, and charged
through the defenceless passage. The front door
closed violently in the middle of a sentence, precipitating the reverend gentleman into the garden.
The Newfoundland dog, with that sagacity for
which his race is so distinguished, at once concluded that a personal collision had taken place
between myself and visitor, and flew to my defence. The reverend gentleman never called again.

The Newfoundland dog above alluded to was
part of a system of protection which my suburban
home once required. Robberies were frequent in
the neighborhood, and my only fowl fell a victim
to the spoiler's art. One night I awoke, and found
a man in my room. With singular delicacy and
respect for the feelings of others, he had been careful not to awaken any of the sleepers, and retired
upon my rising, without waiting for any suggestion.
Touched by his delicacy, I forbore giving the alarm
until after he had made good his retreat. I then
wanted to go after a policeman, but my wife re-
monstrated, as this would leave the house exposed.
Remembering the gentlemanly conduct of the bur-
glar, I suggested the plan of following him and
requesting him to give the alarm as he went in

town. But this proposition was received with equal disfavor. The next day I procured a dog and a revolver. The former went off, but the latter would n't. I then got a new dog and chained him, and a duelling pistol, with a hair-trigger. The result was so far satisfactory that neither could be approached with safety, and for some time I left them out, indifferently, during the night. But the chain one day gave way, and the dog, evidently having no other attachment to the house, took the opportunity to leave. His place was soon filled by the Newfoundland, whose fidelity and sagacity I have just recorded.

Space is one of the desirable features of my suburban residence. I do not know the number of acres the grounds contain except from the inordinate quantity of hose required for irrigating. I perform daily, like some gentle shepherd, upon a quarter-inch pipe without any visible result, and have had serious thoughts of contracting with some disbanded fire company for their hose and equipments. It is quite a walk to the wood-house. Every day some new feature of the grounds is discovered. My youngest boy was one day missing for several hours. His head — a peculiarly venerable and striking object — was at last discovered just above the grass at some distance from the house. On examination he was found comfortably seated in a disused drain, in company with a silver spoon and a dead rat. On being removed from this locality he howled dismally and refused to be comforted.

The view from my suburban residence is fine. Lone Mountain, with its white obelisks, is a suggestive if not cheering termination of the vista in one direction, while the old receiving vault of Yerba Buena Cemetery limits the view in another. Most of the funerals which take place pass my house. My children, with the charming imitativeness that belongs to youth, have caught the spirit of these passing corteges, and reproduce in the back yard, with creditable skill, the salient features of the lugubrious procession. A doll, from whose features all traces of vitality and expression have been removed, represents the deceased. Yet unfortunately I have been obliged to promise them more active participation in this ceremony at some future time, and I fear that they look anxiously forward with the glowing impatience of youth to the speedy removal of some one of my circle of friends. I am told that the eldest, with the unsophisticated frankness that belongs to his age, made a personal request to that effect to one of my acquaintances One singular result of the frequency of these funerals is the development of a critical and fastidious taste in such matters on the part of myself and family. If I may so express myself, without irreverence, we seldom turn out for anything less than six carriages. Any number over this is

usually breathlessly announced by Bridget as, "Here's another, mum, — and a good long one."

With these slight drawbacks my suburban residence is charming. To the serious poet, and writer of elegiac verses, the aspect of Nature, viewed from my veranda, is suggestive. I myself have experienced moments when the "sad mechanic exercise" of verse would have been of infinite relief. The following stanzas, by a young friend who has been stopping with me for the benefit of his health, addressed to a duck that frequented a small pond in the vicinity of my mansion, may be worthy of perusal. I think I have met the idea conveyed in the first verse in some of Hood's prose, but as my friend assures me that Hood was too conscientious to appropriate anything not his own, I conclude I am mistaken.

LINES TO A WATER-FOWL.

(*Intra Muros.*)

I.

Fowl, that sing'st in yonder pool,
Where the summer winds blow cool,
Are there hydropathic cures
For the ills that man endures?
Know'st thou Priessnitz? What? alack
Hast no other word but "Quack?"

II.

Cleopatra's barge might pale
To the splendors of thy tail,
Or the stately caravel
Of some "high-pooped admiral."
Never yet left such a wake
E'en the navigator Drake !

III.

Dux thou art, and leader, too,
Heeding not what 's " falling due,"
Knowing not of debt or dun, —
Thou dost heed no bill but one ;
And, though scarce conceivable,
That 's a bill Receivable,
Made — that thou thy stars mightst **thank —**
Payable at the next bank.

ON A VULGAR LITTLE BOY.

THE subject of this article is at present leaning against a tree directly opposite to my
window. He wears his cap with the wrong side before, apparently for no other object than that which
seems the most obvious,— of showing more than the
average quantity of very dirty face. His clothes,
which are worn with a certain buttonless ease and
freedom, display, in the different quality of their
fruit-stains, a pleasing indication of the progress of
the seasons. The nose of this vulgar little boy
turns up at the end. I have noticed this in several
other vulgar little boys, although it is by no means
improbable that youthful vulgarity may be present
without this facial peculiarity. Indeed, I am
inclined to the belief that it is rather the result of
early inquisitiveness — of furtive pressures against
window-panes, and of looking over fences, or of
the habit of biting large apples hastily than an
indication of scorn or juvenile superciliousness.
The vulgar little boy is more remarkable for his
obtrusive familiarity. It is my experience of his
predisposition to this quality which has induced
me to write this article.

My acquaintance with him began in a moment
of weakness. I have an unfortunate predilection
to cultivate originality in people, even when accompanied by objectionable character. But, as I
lack the firmness and skilfulness which usually
accompany this taste in others, and enable them
to drop acquaintances when troublesome, I have
surrounded myself with divers unprofitable friends,
among whom I count the vulgar little boy. The
manner in which he first attracted my attention
was purely accidental. He was playing in the
street, and the driver of a passing vehicle cut at
him, sportively, with his whip. The vulgar little
boy rose to his feet and hurled after his tormentor
a single sentence of invective. I refrain from repeating it, for I feel that I could not do justice to
it here. If I remember rightly, it conveyed, in
a very few words, a reflection on the legitimacy
of the driver's birth ; it hinted a suspicion of his
father's integrity, and impugned the fair fame of
his mother ; it suggested incompetency in his present position, personal uncleanliness, and evinced
a sceptical doubt of his future salvation. As his
youthful lips closed over the last syllable, the
eyes of the vulgar little boy met mine. Something in my look emboldened him to wink. I did
not repel the action nor the complicity it implied.
From that moment I fell into the power of the
vulgar little boy, and he has never left me since.

He haunts me in the streets and by-ways. He accosts me, when in the company of friends, with repulsive freedom. He lingers about the gate of my dwelling to waylay me as I issue forth to business. Distance he overcomes by main strength of lungs, and he hails me from the next street. He met me at the theatre the other evening, and demanded my check with the air of a young foot-pad. I foolishly gave it to him, but re-entering some time after, and comfortably seating myself in the parquet, I was electrified by hearing my name called from the gallery with the addition of a playful adjective. It was the vulgar little boy. During the performance he projected spirally-twisted playbills in my direction, and indulged in a running commentary on the supernumeraries as they entered.

To-day has evidently been a dull one with him. I observe he whistles the popular airs of the period with less shrillness and intensity. Providence, however, looks not unkindly on him, and delivers into his hands as it were two nice little boys who have at this moment innocently strayed into our street. They are pink and white children, and are dressed alike, and exhibit a certain air of neatness and refinement which is alone sufficient to awaken the antagonism of the vulgar little boy. A sigh of satisfaction breaks from his breast. What does he do? Any other boy would content himself

with simply knocking the hats off their respective
heads, and so vent his superfluous vitality in a
single act, besides precipitating the flight of the
enemy.   But there are æsthetic considerations not
to be overlooked; insult is to be added to the injury inflicted, and in the struggles of the victim
some justification is to be sought for extreme
measures.   The two nice little boys perceive their
danger and draw closer to each other.   The vulgar
little boy begins by irony.   He affects to be over-
powered by the magnificence of their costume.   He
addresses me (across the street and through the
closed window), and requests information if there
haply be a circus in the vicinity.   He makes affec-
tionate inquiries after the health of their parents.
He expresses a fear of maternal anxiety in regard
to their welfare.   He offers to conduct them home.
One nice little boy feebly retorts; but alas! his
correct pronunciation, his grammatical exactitude,
and his moderate epithets only provoke a scream
of derision from the vulgar little boy, who now
rapidly changes his tactics.   Staggering under the
weight of his vituperation, they fall easy victims
to what he would call his "dexter mawley."   A
wail of lamentation goes up from our street.   But
as the subject of this article seems to require a
more vigorous handling than I had purposed to
give it, I find it necessary to abandon my present
dignified position, seize my hat, open the front
door, and try a stronger method.

WAITING FOR THE SHIP.

A FORT POINT IDYL.

ABOUT an hour's ride from the Plaza there is a high bluff with the ocean breaking uninterruptedly along its rocky beach. There are several cottages on the sands, which look as if they had recently been cast up by a heavy sea. The cultivated patch behind each tenement is fenced in by bamboos, broken spars, and driftwood. With its few green cabbages and turnip-tops, each garden looks something like an aquarium with the water turned off. In fact you would not be surprised to meet a merman digging among the potatoes, or a mermaid milking a sea cow hard by.

Near this place formerly arose a great semaphoric telegraph with its gaunt arms tossed up against the horizon. It has been replaced by an observatory, connected with an electric nerve to the heart of the great commercial city. From this point the incoming ships are signalled, and again checked off at the City Exchange. And while we are here looking for the expected steamer, let me tell you a story.

Not long ago, a simple, hard-working mechanic

had amassed sufficient by diligent labor in the
mines to send home for his wife and two children.
He arrived in San Francisco a month before the
time the ship was due, for he was a western man,
and had made the overland journey and knew
little of ships or seas or gales. He procured work
in the city, but as the time approached he would
go to the shipping office regularly every day. The
month passed, but the ship came not ; then a month
and a week, two weeks, three weeks, two months,
and then a year.

The rough, patient face, with soft lines over-
lying its hard features, which had become a daily
apparition at the shipping agent's, then disappeared.
It turned up one afternoon at the observatory as
the setting sun relieved the operator from his
duties. There was something so childlike and
simple in the few questions asked by this stranger,
touching his business, that the operator spent some
time to explain. When the mystery of signals and
telegraphs was unfolded, the stranger had one more
question to ask. "How long might a vessel be
absent before they would give up expecting her ?"
The operator could n't tell ; it would depend on
circumstances. Would it be a year ? Yes, it
might be a year, and vessels had been given up
for lost after two years and had come home. The
stranger put his rough hand on the operator's, and
thanked him for his "troubil," and went away.

Still the ship came not. Stately clippers swept into the Gate, and merchantmen went by with colors flying, and the welcoming gun of the steamer often reverberated among the hills. Then the patient face, with the old resigned expression, but a brighter, wistful look in the eye, was regularly met on the crowded decks of the steamer as she disembarked her living freight. He may have had a dimly defined hope that the missing ones might yet come this way, as only another road over that strange unknown expanse. But he talked with ship captains and sailors, and even this last hope seemed to fail. When the careworn face and bright eyes were presented again at the observatory, the operator, busily engaged, could not spare time to answer foolish interrogatories, so he went away. But as night fell, he was seen sitting on the rocks with his face turned seaward, and was seated there all that night.

When he became hopelessly insane, for that was what the physicians said made his eyes so bright and wistful, he was cared for by a fellow-craftsman who had known his troubles. He was allowed to indulge his fancy of going out to watch for the ship, in which she "and the children" were, at night when no one else was watching. He had made up his mind that the ship would come in at night. This, and the idea that he would relieve the operator, who would be tired with watching all day, seemed to please him.   So he went out and relieved the operator every night !

For two years the ships came and went.   He was there to see the outward-bound clipper, and greet her on her return.   He was known only by a few who frequented the place.   When he was missed at last from his accustomed spot, a day or two elapsed before any alarm was felt.   One Sunday, a party of pleasure-seekers clambering over the rocks were attracted by the barking of a dog that had run on before them.   When they came up they found a plainly dressed man lying there dead.   There were a few papers in his pocket, — chiefly slips cut from different journals of old marine memoranda, — and his face was turned towards the distant sea.

LEGENDS AND TALES.

THE LEGEND OF MONTE DEL DIABLO.

THE cautious reader will detect a lack of authenticity in the following pages. I am not a cautious reader myself, yet I confess with some concern to the absence of much documentary evidence in support of the singular incident I am about to relate. Disjointed memoranda, the proceedings of *ayuntamientos* and early departmental *juntas*, with other records of a primitive and superstitious people, have been my inadequate authorities. It is but just to state, however, that though this particular story lacks corroboration, in ransacking the Spanish archives of Upper California I have met with many more surprising and incredible stories, attested and supported to a degree that would have placed this legend beyond a cavil or doubt. I have, also, never lost faith in the legend myself, and in so doing have profited much from the examples of divers grant-claimants, who have often jostled me in their more practical researches, and who have my sincere sympathy at the scepticism of a modern hard-headed and practical world.

For many years after Father Junipero Serro first

rang his bell in the wilderness of Upper California, the spirit which animated that adventurous priest did not wane. The conversion of the heathen went on rapidly in the establishment of Missions throughout the land. So sedulously did the good Fathers set about their work, that around their isolated chapels there presently arose *adobe* huts, whose mud-plastered and savage tenants partook regularly of the provisions, and occasionally of the Sacrament, of their pious hosts. Nay, so great was their progress, that one zealous Padre is reported to have administered the Lord's Supper one
• Sabbath morning to " over three hundred heathen Salvages." It was not to be wondered that the Enemy of Souls, being greatly incensed thereat, and alarmed at his decreasing popularity, should have grievously tempted and embarrassed these Holy Fathers, as we shall presently see.

Yet they were happy, peaceful days for California. The vagrant keels of prying Commerce had not as yet ruffled the lordly gravity of her bays. No torn and ragged gulch betrayed the suspicion of golden treasure. The wild oats drooped idly in the morning heat, or wrestled with the afternoon breezes. Deer and antelope dotted the plain. The watercourses brawled in their familiar channels, nor dreamed of ever shifting their regular tide. The wonders of the Yosemite and Calaveras were as yet unrecorded. The Holy Fathers noted

little of the landscape beyond the barbaric prodi-
gality with which the quick soil repaid the sowing.
A new conversion, the advent of a Saint's day, or
the baptism of an Indian baby, was at once the
chronicle and marvel of their day.

At this blissful epoch there lived at the Mission
of San Pablo Father José Antonio Haro, a worthy
brother of the Society of Jesus. He was of tall
and cadaverous aspect. A somewhat romantic history had given a poetic interest to his lugubrious
visage. While a youth, pursuing his studies at
famous Salamanca, he had become enamored of the
charms of Doña Cármen de Torrencevara, as that
lady passed to her matutinal devotions. Untoward
circumstances, hastened, perhaps, by a wealthier
suitor, brought this amour to a disastrous issue;
and Father José entered a monastery, taking upon
himself the vows of celibacy. It was here that
his natural fervor and poetic enthusiasm conceived
expression as a missionary. A longing to convert
the uncivilized heathen succeeded his frivolous
earthly passion, and a desire to explore and develop
unknown fastnesses continually possessed him. In
his flushing eye and sombre exterior was detected
a singular commingling of the discreet Las Casas
and the impetuous Balboa.

Fired by this pious zeal, Father José went forward in the van of Christian pioneers. On reaching Mexico, he obtained authority to establish the

Mission of San Pablo. Like the good Junipero, accompanied only by an acolyte and muleteer, he unsaddled his mules in a dusky *cañon*, and rang his bell in the wilderness. The savages — a peaceful, inoffensive, and inferior race — presently flocked around him. The nearest military post was far away, which contributed much to the security of these pious pilgrims, who found their open trustfulness and amiability better fitted to repress hostility than the presence of an armed, suspicious, and brawling soldiery. So the good Father José said matins and prime, mass and vespers, in the heart of Sin and Heathenism, taking no heed to himself, but looking only to the welfare of the Holy Church. Conversions soon followed, and, on the 7th of July, 1760, the first Indian baby was baptized,— an event which, as Father José piously records, " exceeds the richnesse of gold or precious jewels or the chancing upon the Ophir of Solomon." I quote this incident as best suited to show the ingenious blending of poetry and piety which distinguished Father José's record.

The Mission of San Pablo progressed and prospered until the pious founder thereof, like the infidel Alexander, might have wept that there were no more heathen worlds to conquer. But his ardent and enthusiastic spirit could not long brook an idleness that seemed begotten of sin ; and one pleasant August morning, in the year of grace

1770, Father José issued from the outer court of the Mission building, equipped to explore the field for new missionary labors.

Nothing could exceed the quiet gravity and unpretentiousness of the little cavalcade. First rode a stout muleteer, leading a pack-mule laden with the provisions of the party, together with a few cheap crucifixes and hawks' bells. After him came the devout Padre José, bearing his breviary and cross, with a black *serapa* thrown around his shoulders; while on either side trotted a dusky convert, anxious to show a proper sense of their regeneration by acting as guides into the wilds of their heathen brethren. Their new condition was agreeably shown by the absence of the usual mud-plaster, which in their unconverted state they assumed to keep away vermin and cold. The morning was bright and propitious. Before their departure, mass had been said in the chapel, and the protection of St. Ignatius invoked against all contingent evils, but especially against bears, which, like the fiery dragons of old, seemed to cherish unconquerable hostility to the Holy Church.

As they wound through the *cañon*, charming birds disported upon boughs and sprays, and sober quails piped from the alders; the willowy watercourses gave a musical utterance, and the long grass whispered on the hillside. On entering the deeper defiles, above them towered dark green

masses of pine, and occasionally the *madroño*
shook its bright scarlet berries.   As they toiled
up many a steep ascent, Father José sometimes
picked up fragments of scoria, which spake to his
imagination of direful volcanoes and impending
earthquakes.   To the less scientific mind of the
muleteer Ignacio they had even a more terrifying
significance; and he once or twice snuffed the air
suspiciously, and declared that it smelt of sulphur.
So the first day of their journey wore away, and
at night they encamped without having met a single heathen face.

It was on this night that the Enemy of Souls
appeared to Ignacio in an appalling form.   He
had retired to a secluded part of the camp and
had sunk upon his knees in prayerful meditation,
when he looked up and perceived the Arch-Fiend
in the likeness of a monstrous bear.   The Evil
One was seated on his hind legs immediately before him, with his fore paws joined together just
below his black muzzle.   Wisely conceiving this
remarkable attitude to be in mockery and derision
of his devotions, the worthy muleteer was transported with fury.   Seizing an arquebuse, he instantly closed his eyes and fired.   When he had
recovered from the effects of the terrific discharge,
the apparition had disappeared.   Father José, awakened by the report, reached the spot only in time
to chide the muleteer for wasting powder and ball

in a contest with one whom a single *ave* would have been sufficient to utterly discomfit.   What further reliance he placed on Ignacio's story is not known ; but, in commemoration of a worthy Californian custom, the place was called *La Cañada de la Tentacion del Pio Muletero*, or "The Glen of the Temptation of the Pious Muleteer," a name which it retains to this day.

The next morning the party, issuing from a narrow gorge, came upon a long valley, sear and burnt with the shadeless heat.   Its lower extremity was lost in a fading line of low hills, which, gathering might and volume toward the upper end of the valley, upheaved a stupendous bulwark against the breezy North.   The peak of this awful spur was just touched by a fleecy cloud that shifted to and fro like a banneret.   Father José gazed at it with mingled awe and admiration.   By a singular coincidence, the muleteer Ignacio uttered the simple ejaculation "*Diablo !*"

As they penetrated the valley, they soon began to miss the agreeable life and companionable echoes of the *cañon* they had quitted.   Huge fissures in the parched soil seemed to gape as with thirsty mouths.   A few squirrels darted from the earth, and disappeared as mysteriously before the jingling mules.   A gray wolf trotted leisurely along just ahead.   But whichever way Father José turned, the mountain always asserted itself and arrested his wandering eye. Out of the dry and arid valley, it seemed to spring into cooler and bracing life. Deep cavernous shadows dwelt along its base; rocky fastnesses appeared midway of its elevation; and on either side huge black hills diverged like massy roots from a central trunk. His lively fancy pictured these hills peopled with a majestic and intelligent race of savages; and looking into futurity, he already saw a monstrous cross crowning the dome-like summit. Far different were the sensations of the muleteer, who saw in those awful solitudes only fiery dragons, colossal bears and break-neck trails. The converts, Concepcion and Incarnacion, trotting modestly beside the Padre, recognized, perhaps, some manifestation of their former weird mythology.

At nightfall they reached the base of the mountain. Here Father José unpacked his mules, said vespers, and, formally ringing his bell, called upon the Gentiles within hearing to come and accept the Holy Faith. The echoes of the black frowning hills around him caught up the pious invitation, and repeated it at intervals; but no Gentiles appeared that night. Nor were the devotions of the muleteer again disturbed, although he afterward asserted, that, when the Father's exhortation was ended, a mocking peal of laughter came from the mountain. Nothing daunted by these intimations of the near hostility of the Evil One, Father José declared his intention to ascend the mountain at early dawn; and before the sun rose the next morning he was leading the way.

The ascent was in many places difficult and dangerous. Huge fragments of rock often lay across the trail, and after a few hours' climbing they were forced to leave their mules in a little gully, and continue the ascent afoot. Unaccustomed to such exertion, Father José often stopped to wipe the perspiration from his thin cheeks. As the day wore on, a strange silence oppressed them. Except the occasional pattering of a squirrel, or a rustling in the *chimisal* bushes, there were no signs of life. The half-human print of a bear's foot sometimes appeared before them, at which Ignacio always crossed himself piously. The eye was sometimes cheated by a dripping from the rocks, which on closer inspection proved to be a resinous oily liquid with an abominable sulphurous smell. When they were within a short distance of the summit, the discreet Ignacio, selecting a sheltered nook for the camp, slipped aside and busied himself in preparations for the evening, leaving the Holy Father to continue the ascent alone. Never was there a more thoughtless act of prudence, never a more imprudent piece of caution. Without noticing the desertion, buried in pious reflection, Father José pushed mechanically on, and, reaching the summit, cast himself down and gazed upon the prospect.

Below him lay a succession of valleys opening
into each other like gentle lakes, until they were
lost to the southward.   Westerly the distant range
hid the bosky *cañada* which sheltered the mission
of San Pablo.   In the farther distance the Pacific
Ocean stretched away, bearing a cloud of fog upon
its bosom, which crept through the entrance of the
bay, and rolled thickly between him and the north-
eastward ; the same fog hid the base of mountain
and the view beyond.   Still, from time to time the
fleecy veil parted, and timidly disclosed charming
glimpses of mighty rivers, mountain defiles, and
rolling plains, sear with ripened oats, and bathed
in the glow of the setting sun.   As Father José
gazed, he was penetrated with a pious longing.
Already his imagination, filled with enthusiastic
conceptions, beheld all that vast expanse gathered
under the mild sway of the Holy Faith, and peopled with zealous converts.   Each little knoll in
fancy became crowned with a chapel ; from each
dark *cañon* gleamed the white walls of a mission
building.   Growing bolder in his enthusiasm, and
looking farther into futurity, he beheld a new
Spain rising on these savage shores.   He already
saw the spires of stately cathedrals, the domes of
palaces, vineyards, gardens, and groves.   Convents,
half hid among the hills, peeping from plantations
of branching limes ; and long processions of chant-
ing nuns wound through the defiles.   So com-

pletely was the good Father's conception of the
future confounded with the past, that even in their
choral strain the well-remembered accents of Cármen struck his ear.   He was busied in these fanciful imaginings, when suddenly over that extended
prospect the faint, distant tolling of a bell rang
sadly out and died.   It was the *Angelus*.   Father
José listened with superstitious exaltation.   The
mission of San Pablo was far away, and the sound
must have been some miraculous omen.   But never
before, to his enthusiastic sense, did the sweet se-
riousness of this angelic symbol come with such
strange significance.   With the last faint peal, his
glowing fancy seemed to cool; the fog closed in
below him, and the good Father remembered he
had not had his supper.   He had risen and was
wrapping his *serapa* around him, when he perceived for the first time that he was not alone.

Nearly opposite, and where should have been
the faithless Ignacio, a grave and decorous figure
was seated.   His appearance was that of an elderly
hidalgo, dressed in mourning, with mustaches of
iron-gray carefully waxed and twisted around a
pair of lantern-jaws.   The monstrous hat and prodigious feather, the enormous ruff and exaggerated
trunk-hose, contrasted with a frame shrivelled and
wizened, all belonged to a century previous.   Yet
Father José was not astonished.   His adventurous
life and poetic imagination, continually on the

lookout for the marvellous, gave him a certain
advantage over the practical and material minded.
He instantly detected the diabolical quality of his
visitant, and was prepared. With equal coolness
and courtesy he met the cavalier's obeisance.

" I ask your pardon, Sir Priest," said the stranger, " for disturbing your meditations. Pleasant
they must have been, and right fanciful, I imagine, when occasioned by so fair a prospect."

" Worldly, perhaps, Sir Devil, — for such I take
you to be," said the Holy Father, as the stranger
bowed his black plumes to the ground ; " worldly,
perhaps ; for it hath pleased Heaven to retain even
in our regenerated state much that pertaineth to
the flesh, yet still, I trust, not without some speculation for the welfare of the Holy Church. In
dwelling upon yon fair expanse, mine eyes have
been graciously opened with prophetic inspiration,
and the promise of the heathen as an inheritance
hath marvellously recurred to me. For there can
be none lack such diligence in the True Faith,
but may see that even the conversion of these
pitiful salvages hath a meaning. As the blessed
St. Ignatius discreetly observes," continued Father
José, clearing his throat and slightly elevating his
voice, " ' the heathen is given to the warriors of
Christ, even as the pearls of rare discovery which
gladden the hearts of shipmen.' Nay, I might
say — "

But here the stranger, who had been wrinkling his brows and twisting his mustaches with well-bred patience, took advantage of an oratorical pause : —

" It grieves me, Sir Priest, to interrupt the current of your eloquence as discourteously as I have already broken your meditations ; but the day already waneth to night.   I have a matter of serious import to make with you, could I entreat your cautious consideration a few moments."

Father José hesitated.   The temptation was great, and the prospect of acquiring some knowledge of the Great Enemy's plans not the least trifling object.   And if the truth must be told, there was a certain decorum about the stranger that interested the Padre.   Though well aware of the Protean shapes the Arch-Fiend could assume, and though free from the weaknesses of the flesh, Father José was not above the temptations of the spirit.   Had the Devil appeared, as in the case of the pious St. Anthony, in the likeness of a comely damsel, the good Father, with his certain experience of the deceitful sex, would have whisked her away in the saying of a paternoster.   But there was, added to the scourity of age, a grave sadness about the stranger, — a thoughtful consciousness as of being at a great moral disadvantage, — which at once decided him on a magnanimous course of conduct.

v. 17—J

The stranger then proceeded to inform him, that
he had been diligently observing the Holy Father's
triumphs in the valley. That, far from being greatly exercised thereat, he had been only grieved to
see so enthusiastic and chivalrous an antagonist
wasting his zeal in a hopeless work. For, he observed, the issue of the great battle of Good and
Evil had been otherwise settled, as he would presently show him. "It wants but a few moments
of night," he continued, "and over this interval of
twilight, as you know, I have been given complete
control. Look to the West."

As the Padre turned, the stranger took his enormous hat from his head, and waved it three times
before him. At each sweep of the prodigious
feather, the fog grew thinner, until it melted im-
palpably away, and the former landscape returned,
yet warm with the glowing sun. As Father José
gazed, a strain of martial music arose from the
valley, and issuing from a deep *cañon*, the good
Father beheld a long cavalcade of gallant cavaliers,
habited like his companion. As they swept down
the plain, they were joined by like processions,
that slowly defiled from every ravine and *cañon* of
the mysterious mountain. From time to time the
peal of a trumpet swelled fitfully upon the breeze ;
the cross of Santiago glittered, and the royal banners of Castile and Aragon waved over the moving
column. So they moved on solemnly toward the

sea, where, in the distance, Father José saw stately caravels, bearing the same familiar banner, awaiting them.   The good Padre gazed with conflicting emotions, and the serious voice of the stranger broke the silence.

"Thou hast beheld, Sir Priest, the fading footprints of adventurous Castile.   Thou hast seen the declining glory of old Spain, — declining as yonder brilliant sun.   The sceptre she hath wrested from the heathen is fast dropping from her decrepit and fleshless grasp.   The children she hath fostered shall know her no longer.   The soil she hath acquired shall be lost to her as irrevocably as she herself hath thrust the Moor from her own Granada."

The stranger paused, and his voice seemed broken by emotion; at the same time, Father José, whose sympathizing heart yearned toward the departing banners, cried in poignant accents, —

"Farewell, ye gallant cavaliers and Christian soldiers!   Farewell, thou, Nuñes de Balboa! thou, Alonzo de Ojeda! and thou, most venerable Las Casas!   Farewell, and may Heaven prosper still the seed ye left behind!"

Then turning to the stranger, Father José beheld him gravely draw his pocket-handkerchief from the basket-hilt of his rapier, and apply it decorously to his eyes.

"Pardon this weakness, Sir Priest," said the

cavalier, apologetically ; " but these worthy gentlemen were ancient friends of mine, and have done
me many a delicate service, — much more, per-
chance, than these poor sables may signify," he
added, with a grim gesture toward the mourning
suit he wore.

Father José was too much preoccupied in reflection to notice the equivocal nature of this tribute,
and, after a few moments' silence, said, as if con-
tinuing his thought, —

" But the seed they have planted shall thrive
and prosper on this fruitful soil."

As if answering the interrogatory, the stranger
turned to the opposite direction, and, again waving
his hat, said, in the same serious tone, —

" Look to the East ! "

The Father turned, and, as the fog broke away
before the waving plume, he saw that the sun was
rising. Issuing with its bright beams through the
passes of the snowy mountains beyond, appeared a
strange and motley crew. Instead of the dark and
romantic visages of his last phantom train, the
Father beheld with strange concern the blue eyes
and flaxen hair of a Saxon race. In place of
martial airs and musical utterance, there rose upon
the ear a strange din of harsh gutturals and singular sibilation. Instead of the decorous tread
and stately mien of the cavaliers of the former
vision, they came pushing, bustling, panting, and

swaggering. And as they passed, the good Father noticed that giant trees were prostrated as with the breath of a tornado, and the bowels of the earth were torn and rent as with a convulsion. And Father José looked in vain for holy cross or Christian symbol; there was but one that seemed an ensign, and he crossed himself with holy horror as he perceived it bore the effigy of a bear.

"Who are these swaggering Ishmaelites?" he asked, with something of asperity in his tone.

The stranger was gravely silent.

"What do they here, with neither cross nor holy symbol?" he again demanded.

"Have you the courage to see, Sir Priest?" responded the stranger, quietly.

Father José felt his crucifix, as a lonely traveller might his rapier, and assented.

"Step under the shadow of my plume," said the stranger.

Father José stepped beside him, and they instantly sank through the earth.

When he opened his eyes, which had remained closed in prayerful meditation during his rapid descent, he found himself in a vast vault, bespangled overhead with luminous points like the starred firmament. It was also lighted by a yellow glow that seemed to proceed from a mighty sea or lake that occupied the centre of the chamber. Around this subterranean sea dusky figures flitted, bearing

ladles filled with the yellow fluid, which they had
replenished from its depths. From this lake
diverging streams of the same mysterious flood
penetrated like mighty rivers the cavernous distance. As they walked by the banks of this glittering Styx, Father José perceived how the liquid
stream at certain places became solid. The ground
was strewn with glittering flakes. One of these
the Padre picked up and curiously examined. It
was virgin gold.

An expression of discomfiture overcast the good
Father's face at this discovery; but there was
trace neither of malice nor satisfaction in the stranger's air, which was still of serious and fateful contemplation. When Father José recovered his
equanimity, he said, bitterly, —

"This, then, Sir Devil, is your work! This is
your deceitful lure for the weak souls of sinful nations! So would you replace the Christian grace
of holy Spain!"

"This is what must be," returned the stranger,
gloomily. "But listen, Sir Priest. It lies with
you to avert the issue for a time. Leave me here
in peace. Go back to Castile, and take with you
your bells, your images, and your missions. Continue here, and you only precipitate results. Stay!
promise me you will do this, and you shall not
lack that which will render your old age an ornament and a blessing"; and the stranger motioned
significantly to the lake.

It was here, the legend discreetly relates, that the Devil showed — as he always shows sooner or later — his cloven hoof. The worthy Padre, sorely perplexed by his threefold vision, and, if the truth must be told, a little nettled at this wresting away of the glory of holy Spanish discovery, had shown some hesitation. But the unlucky bribe of the Enemy of Souls touched his Castilian spirit. Starting back in deep disgust, he brandished his crucifix in the face of the unmasked Fiend, and in a voice that made the dusky vault resound, cried, —

"Avaunt thee, Sathanas! Diabolus, I defy thee! What! wouldst thou bribe me, — me, a brother of the Sacred Society of the Holy Jesus, Licentiate of Cordova and Inquisitor of Guadalaxara? Thinkest thou to buy me with thy sordid treasure? Avaunt!"

What might have been the issue of this rupture, and how complete might have been the triumph of the Holy Father over the Arch-Fiend, who was recoiling aghast at these sacred titles and the flourishing symbol, we can never know, for at that moment the crucifix slipped through his fingers.

Scarcely had it touched the ground before Devil and Holy Father simultaneously cast themselves toward it. In the struggle they clinched, and the pious José, who was as much the superior of his antagonist in bodily as in spiritual strength, was

about to treat the Great Adversary to a back
somersault, when he suddenly felt the long nails
of the stranger piercing his flesh. A new fear
seized his heart, a numbing chillness crept through
his body, and he struggled to free himself, but in
vain. A strange roaring was in his ears ; the lake
and cavern danced before his eyes and vanished ;
and with a loud cry he sank senseless to the
ground.

When he recovered his consciousness he was
aware of a gentle swaying motion of his body. He
opened his eyes, and saw it was high noon, and
that he was being carried in a litter through the
valley. He felt stiff, and, looking down, perceived
that his arm was tightly bandaged to his side.

He closed his eyes and after a few words of
thankful prayer, thought how miraculously he had
been preserved, and made a vow of candlesticks to
the blessed Saint José   He then called in a faint
voice, and presently the penitent Ignacio stood
beside him.

The joy the poor fellow felt at his patron's returning consciousness for some time choked his
utterance. He could only ejaculate, "A miracle !
Blessed Saint José, he lives !" and kiss the Padre's
bandaged hand. Father José, more intent on his
last night's experience, waited for his emotion to
subside, and asked where he had been found.

"On the mountain, your Reverence, but a few
varas from where he attacked you."

"How?—you saw him then?" asked the Padre, in unfeigned astonishment.

"Saw him, your Reverence! Mother of God, I should think I did! And your Reverence shall see him too, if he ever comes again within range of Ignacio's arquebuse."

"What mean you, Ignacio?" said the Padre, sitting bolt-upright in his litter.

"Why, the bear, your Reverence,— the bear, Holy Father, who attacked your worshipful person while you were meditating on the top of yonder mountain."

"Ah!" said the Holy Father, lying down again. "Chut, child! I would be at peace."

When he reached the Mission, he was tenderly cared for, and in a few weeks was enabled to resume those duties from which, as will be seen, not even the machinations of the Evil One could divert him. The news of his physical disaster spread over the country; and a letter to the Bishop of Guadalaxara contained a confidential and detailed account of the good Father's spiritual temptation. But in some way the story leaked out; and long after José was gathered to his fathers, his mysterious encounter formed the theme of thrilling and whispered narrative. The mountain was generally shunned. It is true that Señor Joaquin Pedrillo afterward located a grant near the base of the mountain; but as Señora Pedrillo was known to be

a termagant half-breed, the Señor was not supposed to be over-fastidious.

Such is the Legend of Monte del Diablo.   As I
said before, it may seem to lack essential corroboration.   The discrepancy between the Father's narrative and the actual climax has given rise to some
scepticism on the part of ingenious quibblers.   All
such I would simply refer to that part of the report of Señor Julio Serro, Sub-Prefect of San Pablo, before whom attest of the above was made.
Touching this matter, the worthy Prefect observes,
"That although the body of Father José doth
show evidence of grievous conflict in the flesh, yet
that is no proof that the Enemy of Souls, who could
assume the figure of a decorous elderly *caballero*,
could not at the same time transform himself into
a bear for his own vile purposes."

THE ADVENTURE OF PADRE VICENTIO.

A LEGEND OF SAN FRANCISCO.

ONE pleasant New Year's Eve, about forty years ago, Padre Vicentio was slowly picking his way across the sand-hills from the Mission Dolores. As he climbed the crest of the ridge beside Mission Creek, his broad, shining face might have been easily mistaken for the beneficent image of the rising moon, so bland was its smile and so indefinite its features. For the Padre was a man of notable reputation and character; his ministration at the mission of San José had been marked with cordiality and unction; he was adored by the simple-minded savages, and had succeeded in impressing his individuality so strongly upon them that the very children were said to have miraculously resembled him in feature.

As the holy man reached the loneliest portion of the road, he naturally put spurs to his mule as if to quicken that decorous pace which the obedient animal had acquired through long experience of its master's habits. The locality had an unfavorable reputation. Sailors — deserters from whaleships — had been seen lurking about the outskirts of the town, and low scrub oaks which everywhere beset the trail might have easily concealed some desperate runaway. Besides these material obstructions, the devil, whose hostility to the church was well known, was said to sometimes haunt the vicinity in the likeness of a spectral whaler, who had met his death in a drunken bout, from a harpoon in the hands of a companion. The ghost of this unfortunate mariner was frequently observed sitting on the hill toward the dusk of evening, armed with his favorite weapon and a tub containing a coil of line, looking out for some belated traveller on whom to exercise his professional skill. It is related that the good Father José Maria of the Mission Dolores had been twice attacked by this phantom sportsman; that once, on returning from San Francisco, and panting with exertion from climbing the hill, he was startled by a stentorian cry of "There she blows!" quickly followed by a hurtling harpoon, which buried itself in the sand beside him; that on another occasion he narrowly escaped destruction, his serapa having been transfixed by the diabolical harpoon and dragged away in triumph. Popular opinion seems to have been divided as to the reason for the devil's particular attention to Father José, some asserting that the extreme piety of the Padre excited the Evil One's animosity, and others that his adipose tendency simply rendered him, from a professional view-point, a profitable capture.

Had Father Vicentio been inclined to scoff at this apparition as a heretical innovation, there was still the story of Concepcion, the Demon Vaquero, whose terrible *riata* was fully as potent as the whaler's harpoon. Concepcion, when in the flesh, had been a celebrated herder of cattle and wild horses, and was reported to have chased the devil in the shape of a fleet *pinto* colt all the way from San Luis Obispo to San Francisco, vowing not to give up the chase until he had overtaken the disguised Arch-Enemy. This the devil prevented by resuming his own shape, but kept the unfortunate vaquero to the fulfilment of his rash vow; and Concepcion still scoured the coast on a phantom steed, beguiling the monotony of his eternal pursuit by lassoing travellers, dragging them at the heels of his unbroken mustang until they were eventually picked up, half-strangled, by the roadside. The Padre listened attentively for the tramp of this terrible rider. But no footfall broke the stillness of the night; even the hoofs of his own mule sank noiselessly in the shifting sand. Now and then a rabbit bounded lightly by him, or a quail ran into the bushes. The melancholy call of plover from the adjoining marshes of Mission Creek came to him so faintly and fitfully that it seemed almost a recollection of the past rather than a reality of the present.

To add to his discomposure one of those heavy sea-fogs peculiar to the locality began to drift across the hills and presently encompassed him. While endeavoring to evade its cold embraces, Padre Vicentio incautiously drove his heavy spurs into the flanks of his mule as that puzzled animal was hesitating on the brink of a steep declivity. Whether the poor beast was indignant at this novel outrage, or had been for some time reflecting on the evils of being priest-ridden, has not transpired; enough that he suddenly threw up his heels, pitching the reverend man over his head, and, having accomplished this feat, coolly dropped on his knees and tumbled after his rider.

Over and over went the Padre, closely followed by his faithless mule. Luckily the little hollow which received the pair was of sand that yielded to the superincumbent weight, half burying them without further injury. For some moments the poor man lay motionless, vainly endeavoring to collect his scattered senses. A hand irreverently laid upon his collar, and a rough shake, assisted to recall his consciousness. As the Padre staggered to his feet he found himself confronted by a stranger.

Seen dimly through the fog, and under circumstances that to say the least were not prepossessing, the new-comer had an inexpressibly mysterious and brigand-like aspect. A long boat-cloak concealed his figure, and a slouched hat hid his features, permitting only his eyes to glisten in the depths. With a deep groan the Padre slipped from the stranger's grasp and subsided into the soft sand again.

"Gad's life!" said the stranger, pettishly, "hast no more bones in thy fat carcass than a jellyfish? Lend a hand, here! Yo, heave ho!" and he dragged the Padre into an upright position. "Now, then, who and what art thou?"

The Padre could not help thinking that the question might have more properly been asked by himself; but with an odd mixture of dignity and trepidation he began enumerating his different titles, which were by no means brief, and would have been alone sufficient to strike awe in the bosom of an ordinary adversary. The stranger irreverently broke in upon his formal phrases, and assuring him that a priest was the very person he was looking for, coolly replaced the old man's hat, which had tumbled off, and bade him accompany him at once on an errand of spiritual counsel to one who was even then lying in extremity. "To think," said the stranger, "that I should stumble upon the very man I was seeking! Body of Bacchus! but this is lucky! Follow me quickly, for there is no time to lose."

Like most easy natures the positive assertion of the stranger, and withal a certain authoritative air

of command, overcame what slight objections the
Padre might have feebly nurtured during this remarkable interview. The spiritual invitation was
one, also, that he dared not refuse ; not only that ;
but it tended somewhat to remove the superstitious
dread with which he had begun to regard the mysterious stranger. But, following at a respectful distance, the Padre could not help observing with a
thrill of horror that the stranger's footsteps made
no impression on the sand, and his figure seemed
at times to blend and incorporate itself with the
fog, until the holy man was obliged to wait for
its reappearance. In one of these intervals of
embarrassment he heard the ringing of the far-off
Mission bell, proclaiming the hour of midnight.
Scarcely had the last stroke died away before the
announcement was taken up and repeated by a
multitude of bells of all sizes, and the air was
filled with the sound of striking clocks and the
pealing of steeple chimes. The old man uttered
a cry of alarm. The stranger sharply demanded
the cause. " The bells ! did you not hear them ? "
gasped Padre Vicentio. " Tush ! tush ! " answered
the stranger, " thy fall hath set triple bob-majors
ringing in thine ears. Come on ! "

The Padre was only too glad to accept the explanation conveyed in this discourteous answer.
But he was destined for another singular experience. When they had reached the summit of the

eminence now known as Russian Hill, an exclamation again burst from the Padre. The stranger
turned to his companion with an impatient gesture;
but the Padre heeded him not. The view that
burst upon his sight was such as might well have
engrossed the attention of a more enthusiastic
temperament. The fog had not yet reached the
hill, and the long valleys and hillsides of the em-
barcadero below were glittering with the light of a
populous city. "Look!" said the Padre, stretching his hand over the spreading landscape. "Look,
dost thou not see the stately squares and brilliant-
ly lighted avenues of a mighty metropolis. Dost
thou not see, as it were, another firmament below?"

"Avast heaving, reverend man, and quit this
folly," said the stranger, dragging the bewildered
Padre after him. "Behold rather the stars knocked
out of thy hollow noddle by the fall thou hast
had. Prithee, get over thy visions and rhapsodies,
for the time is wearing apace."

The Padre humbly followed without another
word. Descending the hill toward the north, the
stranger leading the way, in a few moments the
Padre detected the wash of waves, and presently
his feet struck the firmer sand of the beach. Here
the stranger paused, and the Padre perceived a
boat lying in readiness hard by. As he stepped
into the stern sheets, in obedience to the command

of his companion, he noticed that the rowers seemed to partake of the misty incorporeal texture of his companion, a similarity that became the more distressing when he perceived also that their oars in pulling together made no noise. The stranger, assuming the helm, guided the boat on quietly, while the fog, settling over the face of the water and closing around them, seemed to interpose a muffled wall between themselves and the rude jarring of the outer world. As they pushed further into this penetralia, the Padre listened anxiously for the sound of creaking blocks and the rattling of cordage, but no vibration broke the veiled stillness or disturbed the warm breath of the fleecy fog. Only one incident occurred to break the monotony of their mysterious journey. A one-eyed rower, who sat in front of the Padre, catching the devout father's eye, immediately grinned such a ghastly smile, and winked his remaining eye with such diabolical intensity of meaning that the Padre was constrained to utter a pious ejaculation, which had the disastrous effect of causing the marine Cocles to "catch a crab," throwing his heels in the air and his head into the bottom of the boat. But even this accident did not disturb the gravity of the rest of the ghastly boat's crew.

When, as it seemed to the Padre, ten minutes had elapsed, the outline of a large ship loomed up

directly across their bow. Before he could utter the
cry of warning that rose to his lips, or brace himself
against the expected shock, the boat passed gently
and noiselessly through the sides of the vessel, and
the holy man found himself standing on the berth
deck of what seemed to be an ancient caravel.
The boat and boat's crew had vanished. Only his
mysterious friend, the stranger, remained. By the
light of a swinging lamp the Padre beheld him
standing beside a hammock, whereon, apparently,
lay the dying man to whom he had been so mysteriously summoned. As the Padre, in obedience
to a sign from his companion, stepped to the side
of the sufferer, he feebly opened his eyes and thus
addressed him: —

"Thou seest before thee, reverend father, a helpless mortal, struggling not only with the last agonies of the flesh, but beaten down and tossed with
sore anguish of the spirit. It matters little when
or how I became what thou now seest me. Enough
that my life has been ungodly and sinful, and that
my only hope of absolution lies in my imparting
to thee a secret which is of vast importance to
the holy Church, and affects greatly her power,
wealth, and dominion on these shores. But the
terms of this secret and the conditions of my absolution are peculiar. I have but five minutes to
live. In that time I must receive the extreme'
unction of the Church."

" And thy secret ? " said the holy father.

" Shall be told afterwards," answered the dying man. " Come, my time is short. Shrive me quickly."

The Padre hesitated. " Couldst thou not tell this secret first ? "

" Impossible ! " said the dying man, with what seemed to the Padre a momentary gleam of triumph. Then, as his breath grew feebler, he called impatiently, " Shrive me ! shrive me ! "

" Let me know at least what this secret concerns ? " suggested the Padre, insinuatingly.

" Shrive me first," said the dying man.

But the priest still hesitated, parleying with the sufferer until the ship's bell struck, when, with a triumphant, mocking laugh from the stranger, the vessel suddenly fell to pieces, amid the rushing of waters which at once involved the dying man, the priest, and the mysterious stranger.

The Padre did not recover his consciousness until high noon the next day, when he found himself lying in a little hollow between the Mission Hills, and his faithful mule a few paces from him, cropping the sparse herbage. The Padre made the best of his way home, but wisely abstained from narrating the facts mentioned above, until after the discovery of gold, when the whole of this veracious incident was related, with the assertion of the padre that the secret which was thus mysteriously snatched from his possession was nothing more than the discovery of gold, years since, by the runaway sailors from the expedition of Sir Francis Drake.

THE LEGEND OF DEVIL'S POINT.

O N the northerly shore of San Francisco Bay, at a point where the Golden Gate broadens into the Pacific stands a bluff promontory. It affords shelter from the prevailing winds to a semi-circular bay on the east. Around this bay the hillside is bleak and barren, but there are traces of former habitation in a weather-beaten cabin and deserted corral. It is said that these were origi-nally built by an enterprising squatter, who for some unaccountable reason abandoned them shortly after. The "Jumper" who succeeded him disap-peared one day, quite as mysteriously. The third tenant, who seemed to be a man of sanguine, hope-ful temperament, divided the property into build-ing lots, staked off the hillside, and projected the map of a new metropolis. Failing, however, to convince the citizens of San Francisco that they had mistaken the site of their city, he presently fell into dissipation and despondency. He was frequently observed haunting the narrow strip of beach at low tide, or perched upon the cliff at high water. In the latter position a sheep-tender one day found him, cold and pulseless, with a map

of his property in his hand, and his face turned
toward the distant sea.

Perhaps these circumstances gave the locality
its infelicitous reputation. Vague rumors were
bruited of a supernatural influence that had been
exercised on the tenants. Strange stories were
circulated of the origin of the diabolical title by
which the promontory was known. By some it
was believed to be haunted by the spirit of one of
Sir Francis Drake's sailors who had deserted his
ship in consequence of stories told by the Indians
of gold discoveries, but who had perished by star-
vation on the rocks. A *vaquero* who had once
passed a night in the ruined cabin, related how
a strangely dressed and emaciated figure had
knocked at the door at midnight and demanded food.
Other story-tellers, of more historical accuracy,
roundly asserted that Sir Francis himself had been
little better than a pirate, and had chosen this spot
to conceal quantities of ill-gotten booty, taken
from neutral bottoms, and had protected his hiding-
place by the orthodox means of hellish incantation
and diabolic agencies. On moonlight nights a
shadowy ship was sometimes seen standing off-and-
on, or when fogs encompassed sea and shore the
noise of oars rising and falling in their row-locks
could be heard muffled and indistinctly during the
night. Whatever foundation there might have
been for these stories. it was certain that a more

weird and desolate-looking spot could not have
been selected for their theatre. High hills, ver-
dureless and enfiladed with dark cañadas, cast their
gaunt shadows on the tide. During a greater portion of the day the wind, which blew furiously and
incessantly, seemed possessed with a spirit of fierce
disquiet and unrest. Toward nightfall the sea-
fog crept with soft step through the portals of the
Golden Gate, or stole in noiseless marches down
the hillside, tenderly soothing the wind-buffeted
face of the cliff, until sea and sky were hid together. At such times the populous city beyond
and the nearer settlement seemed removed to an infinite distance. An immeasurable loneliness settled
upon the cliff. The creaking of a windlass, or the
monotonous chant of sailors on some unseen, outlying ship, came faint and far, and full of mystic
suggestion.

About a year ago a well-to-do middle-aged
broker of San Francisco found himself at nightfall the sole occupant of a "plunger," encompassed in a dense fog, and drifting toward the
Golden Gate. This unexpected termination of an
afternoon's sail was partly attributable to his want
of nautical skill, and partly to the effect of his
usually sanguine nature. Having given up the
guidance of his boat to the wind and tide, he had
trusted too implicitly for that reaction which his
business experience assured him was certain to occur

in all affairs, aquatic as well as terrestrial. "The tide will turn soon," said the broker, confidently, "or something will happen." He had scarcely settled himself back again in the stern-sheets, before the bow of the plunger, obeying some mysterious impulse, veered slowly around and a dark object loomed up before him. A gentle eddy carried the boat further in shore, until at last it was completely embayed under the lee of a rocky point now faintly discernible through the fog. He looked around him in the vain hope of recognizing some familiar headland. The tops of the high hills which rose on either side were hidden in the fog. As the boat swung around, he succeeded in fastening a line to the rocks, and sat down again with a feeling of renewed confidence and security.

It was very cold. The insidious fog penetrated his tightly buttoned coat, and set his teeth to chattering in spite of the aid he sometimes drew from a pocket-flask. His clothes were wet and the stern-sheets were covered with spray. The comforts of fire and shelter continually rose before his fancy as he gazed wistfully on the rocks. In sheer despair he finally drew the boat toward the most accessible part of the cliff and essayed to ascend. This was less difficult than it appeared, and in a few moments he had gained the hill above. A dark object at a little distance attracted his attention, and on approaching it proved to be a deserted

cabin.   The story goes on to say, that having built
a roaring fire of stakes pulled from the adjoining
corral, with the aid of a flask of excellent brandy,
he managed to pass the early part of the evening
with comparative comfort.

There was no door in the cabin, and the windows
were simply square openings, which freely admitted the searching fog.   But in spite of these discomforts, — being a man of cheerful, sanguine
temperament, — he amused himself by poking the
fire, and watching the ruddy glow which the flames
threw on the fog from the open door.   In this innocent occupation a great weariness overcame him,
and he fell asleep.

He was awakened at midnight by a loud "halloo," which seemed to proceed directly from the
sea.   Thinking it might be the cry of some boat-
man lost in the fog, he walked to the edge of the
cliff, but the thick veil that covered sea and land
rendered all objects at the distance of a few feet
indistinguishable.   He heard, however, the regular strokes of oars rising and falling on the water.
The halloo was repeated.   He was clearing his
throat to reply, when to his surprise an answer
came apparently from the very cabin he had quitted.   Hastily retracing his steps, he was the more
amazed, on reaching the open door, to find a stranger warming himself by the fire.   Stepping back
far enough to conceal his own person, he took a
good look at the intruder.

He was a man of about forty, with a cadaverous
face.   But the oddity of his dress attracted the
broker's attention more than his lugubrious physiognomy.   His legs were hid in enormously wide
trousers descending to his knee, where they met
long boots of sealskin.   A pea-jacket with exaggerated cuffs, almost as large as the breeches, covered his chest, and around his waist a monstrous
belt, with a buckle like a dentist's sign, supported
two trumpet-mouthed pistols and a curved hanger.
He wore a long queue, which depended half-way
down his back.   As the firelight fell on his ingenuous countenance the broker observed with
some concern that this queue was formed entirely
of a kind of tobacco, known as pigtail or twist.
Its effect, the broker remarked, was much heightened when in a moment of thoughtful abstraction
the apparition bit off a portion of it, and rolled it
as a quid into the cavernous recesses of his jaws.

Meanwhile, the nearer splash of oars indicated
the approach of the unseen boat.   The broker had
barely time to conceal himself behind the cabin
before a number of uncouth looking figures clambered up the hill toward the ruined rendezvous.
They were dressed like the previous comer, who,
as they passed through the open door, exchanged
greetings with each in antique phraseology, bestowing at the same time some familiar nickname.
Flash-in-the-Pan, Spitter-of-Frogs, Malmsey Butt,

Latheyard-Will, and Mark-the-Pinker, were the
few *sobriquets* the broker remembered. Whether
these titles were given to express some peculiarity
of their owner he could not tell, for a silence followed as they slowly ranged themselves upon the
floor of the cabin in a semicircle around their
cadaverous host.

At length Malmsey Butt, a spherical-bodied
man-of-war's-man, with a rubicund nose, got on his
legs somewhat unsteadily, and addressed himself
to the company. They had met that evening, said
the speaker, in accordance with a time-honored
custom. This was simply to relieve that one of
their number who for fifty years had kept watch
and ward over the locality where certain treasures
had been buried. At this point the broker pricked
up his ears. "If so be, camarados and brothers
all," he continued, "ye are ready to receive the
report of our excellent and well-beloved brother,
Master Slit-the-Weazand, touching his search for
this treasure, why, marry, to 't and begin."

A murmur of assent went around the circle as
the speaker resumed his seat. Master Slit-the-
Weazand slowly opened his lantern jaws, and
began. He had spent much of his time in determining the exact location of the treasure. He believed — nay, he could state positively — that its
position was now settled. It was true he had
done some trifling little business outside. Modes-

ty forbade his mentioning the particulars, but he
would simply state that of the three tenants who
had occupied the cabin during the past ten years,
none were now alive. [Applause, and cries of
"Go to! thou wast always a tall fellow!" and
the like.]

Mark-the-Pinker next arose.   Before proceeding
to business he had a duty to perform in the sacred
name of Friendship.   It ill became him to pass an
eulogy upon the qualities of the speaker who had
preceded him, for he had known him from "boyhood's hour."   Side by side they had wrought together in the Spanish war.   For a neat hand with
a toledo he challenged his equal, while how nobly
and beautifully he had won his present title of
Slit-the-Weazand, all could testify.   The speaker,
with some show of emotion, asked to be pardoned
if he dwelt too freely on passages of their early
companionship ; he then detailed, with a fine touch
of humor, his comrade's peculiar manner of slit-
ting the ears and lips of a refractory Jew, who had
been captured in one of their previous voyages.
He would not weary the patience of his hearers,
but would briefly propose that the report of Slit-
the-Weazand be accepted, and that the thanks of
the company be tendered him.

A beaker of strong spirits was then rolled into
the hut, and cans of grog were circulated freely
from hand to hand.   The health of Slit-the-Weaz-

and was proposed in a neat speech by Mark-the-
Pinker, and responded to by the former gentleman
in a manner that drew tears to the eyes of all
present.   To the broker, in his concealment, this
momentary diversion from the real business of the
meeting occasioned much anxiety.   As yet nothing
had been said to indicate the exact locality of the
treasure to which they had mysteriously alluded.
Fear restrained him from open inquiry, and curiosity kept him from making good his escape during
the orgies which followed.

But his situation was beginning to become critical.   Flash-in-the-Pan, who seemed to have been
a man of choleric humor, taking fire during some
hotly contested argument, discharged both his pistols at the breast of his opponent.   The balls
passed through on each side immediately below his
arm-pits, making a clean hole, through which the
horrified broker could see the firelight behind him.
The wounded man, without betraying any concern,
excited the laughter of the company, by jocosely
putting his arms akimbo, and inserting his thumbs
into the orifices of the wounds, as if they had been
arm-holes.   This having in a measure restored
good-humor, the party joined hands and formed
a circle preparatory to dancing.   The dance was
commenced by some monotonous stanzas hummed
in a very high key by one of the party, the rest
joining in the following chorus, which seemed to
present a familiar sound to the broker's ear.

"Her Majestie is very sicke,
  Lord Essex hath ye measles,
  Our Admiral hath licked ye French—
  Poppe ! saith ye weasel !"

At the regular recurrence of the last line, the party discharged their loaded pistols in all directions, rendering the position of the unhappy broker one of extreme peril and perplexity.

When the tumult had partially subsided, Flash-in-the-Pan called the meeting to order, and most of the revellers returned to their places, Malmsey Butt, however, insisting upon another chorus, and singing at the top of his voice : —

"I am ycleped J. Keyser—I was born at Spring, hys Garden,
  My father toe make me ane clerke erst did essaye,
  But a fico for ye offis—I spurn ye losels offeire ;
  For I fain would be ane butcher by'r ladykin alwaye."

Flash-in-the-Pan drew a pistol from his belt, and bidding some one gag Malmsey Butt with the stock of it, proceeded to read from a portentous roll of parchment that he held in his hand. It was a semi-legal document, clothed in the quaint phraseology of a bygone period. After a long preamble, asserting their loyalty as lieges of Her most bountiful Majesty and Sovereign Lady the Queen, the document declared that they then and there took possession of the promontory, and all the treasure trove therein contained, formerly buried by Her Majesty's most faithful and devoted

Admiral Sir Francis Drake, with the right to search, discover, and appropriate the same ; and for the purpose thereof they did then and there form a guild or corporation to so discover, search for, and disclose said treasures, and by virtue thereof they solemnly subscribed their names. But at this moment the reading of the parchment was arrested by an exclamation from the assembly, and the broker was seen frantically struggling at the door in the strong arms of Mark-the-Pinker.

" Let me go ! " he cried, as he made a desperate attempt to reach the side of Master Flash-in-the-Pan. " Let me go ! I tell you, gentlemen, that document is not worth the parchment it is written on. The laws of the State, the customs of the country, the mining ordinances, are all against it. Don't, by all that 's sacred, throw away such a capital investment through ignorance and informality. Let me go ! I assure you, gentlemen, professionally, that you have a big thing, — a remarkably big thing, and even if I ain't in it, I 'm not going to see it fall through. Don't, for God's sake, gentlemen, I implore you, put your names to such a ridiculous paper. There is n't a notary — "

He ceased. The figures around him, which were beginning to grow fainter and more indistinct, as he went on, swam before his eyes, flickered, reappeared again, and finally went out. He rubbed his eyes and gazed around him. The cabin was deserted. On the hearth the red embers of his fire were fading away in the bright beams of the morning sun, that looked aslant through the open window. He ran out to the cliff. The sturdy sea-breeze fanned his feverish cheeks, and tossed the white caps of waves that beat in pleasant music on the beach below. A stately merchantman with snowy canvas was entering the Gate. The voices of sailors came cheerfully from a bark at anchor below the point. The muskets of the sentries gleamed brightly on Alcatraz, and the rolling of drums swelled on the breeze. Farther on, the hills of San Francisco, cottage-crowned and bordered with wharves and warehouses, met his longing eye.

Such is the Legend of Devil's Point. Any objections to its reliability may be met with the statement, that the broker who tells the story has since incorporated a company under the title of " Flash-in-the-Pan Gold and Silver Treasure Mining Company," and that its shares are already held at a stiff figure. A copy of the original document is said to be on record in the office of the company, and on any clear day the locality of the claim may be distinctly seen from the hills of San Francisco.

THE DEVIL AND THE BROKER.

A MEDIÆVAL LEGEND.

THE church clocks in San Francisco were striking ten. The Devil, who had been flying over the city that evening, just then alighted on the roof of a church near the corner of Bush and Montgomery Streets. It will be perceived that the popular belief that the Devil avoids holy edifices, and vanishes at the sound of a *Credo* or *Pater-noster*, is long since exploded. Indeed, modern scepticism asserts that he is not averse to these orthodox discourses, which particularly bear reference to himself, and in a measure recognize his power and importance.

I am inclined to think, however, that his choice of a resting-place was a good deal influenced by its contiguity to a populous thoroughfare. When he was comfortably seated, he began pulling out the joints of a small rod which he held in his hand, and which presently proved to be an extraordinary fishing-pole, with a telescopic adjustment that permitted its protraction to a marvellous extent. Affixing a line thereto, he selected a fly of a particular pattern from a small box which he carried

with him, and, making a skilful cast, threw his
line into the very centre of that living stream which
ebbed and flowed through Montgomery Street.

Either the people were very virtuous that evening or the bait was not a taking one.   In vain the
Devil whipped the stream at an eddy in front of
the Occidental, or trolled his line into the shadows
of the Cosmopolitan; five minutes passed without
even a nibble.   "Dear me!" quoth the Devil,
"that's very singular; one of my most popular
flies, too !   Why, they'd have risen by shoals in
Broadway or Beacon Street for that.   Well, here
goes another." And, fitting a new fly from his well-
filled box, he gracefully recast his line.

For a few moments there was every prospect of
sport.   The line was continually bobbing and the
nibbles were distinct and gratifying.   Once or
twice the bait was apparently gorged and carried
off in the upper stories of the hotels to be digested
at leisure.   At such times the professional manner in which the Devil played out his line would
have thrilled the heart of Izaak Walton.   But his
efforts were unsuccessful; the bait was invariably
carried off without hooking the victim, and the
Devil finally lost his temper.   "I've heard of
these San-Franciscans before," he muttered; "wait
till I get hold of one, — that's all!" he added
malevolently, as he rebaited his hook.   A sharp
tug and a wriggle foiled his next trial, and

finally, with considerable effort, he landed a portly two-hundred-pound broker upon the church roof.

As the victim lay there gasping, it was evident that the Devil was in no hurry to remove the hook from his gills; nor did he exhibit in this delicate operation that courtesy of manner and graceful manipulation which usually distinguished him.

" Come," he said, gruffly, as he grasped the broker by the waistband, "quit that whining and grunting. Don't flatter yourself that you 're a prize either. I was certain to have had you. It was only a question of time."

" It is not that, my lord, which troubles me," whined the unfortunate wretch, as he painfully wriggled his head, " but that I should have been fooled by such a paltry bait. What will they say of me down there ? To have let ' bigger things ' go by, and to be taken in by this cheap trick," he added, as he groaned and glanced at the fly which the Devil was carefully rearranging, " is what, — pardon me, my lord, — is what gets me !"

" Yes," said the Devil, philosophically, " I never caught anybody yet who did n't say that; but tell me, ain't you getting somewhat fastidious down there ? Here is one of my most popular flies, the greenback," he continued, exhibiting an emerald-looking insect, which he drew from his box. " This, so generally considered excellent in election season, has not even been nibbled at. Perhaps your sagacity, which, in spite of this unfortunate *contretemps*, no one can doubt," added the Devil, with a graceful return to his usual courtesy, " may explain the reason or suggest a substitute."

The broker glanced at the contents of the box with a supercilious smile. " Too old-fashioned, my lord, — long ago played out. Yet," he added, with a gleam of interest, " for a consideration I might offer something — ahem ! — that would make a taking substitute for these trifles. Give me," he continued, in a brisk, business-like way, " a slight percentage and a bonus down, and I 'm your man."

" Name your terms," said the Devil, earnestly.

" My liberty and a percentage on all you take, and the thing 's done."

The Devil caressed his tail thoughtfully, for a few moments. He was certain of the broker any way, and the risk was slight. " Done !" he said.

" Stay a moment," said the artful broker. " There are certain contingencies. Give me your fishing-rod and let me apply the bait myself. It requires a skilful hand, my lord ; even your well-known experience might fail. Leave me alone for half an hour, and if you have reason to complain of my success I will forfeit my deposit, — I mean my liberty."

The Devil acceded to his request, bowed, and withdrew. Alighting gracefully in Montgomery Street, he dropped into Meade & Co.'s clothing

store, where, having completely equipped himself
à la mode, he sallied forth intent on his personal
enjoyment. Determining to sink his professional
character, he mingled with the current of human
life, and enjoyed, with that immense capacity for
excitement peculiar to his nature, the whirl, bustle,
and feverishness of the people, as a purely æsthetic
gratification unalloyed by the cares of business.
What he did that evening does not belong to our
story. We return to the broker, whom we left on
the roof.

When he made sure that the Devil had retired,
he carefully drew from his pocket-book a slip of
paper and affixed it on the hook. The line had
scarcely reached the current before he felt a bite.
The hook was swallowed. To bring up his victim
rapidly, disengage him from the hook, and reset his
line, was the work of a moment. Another bite and
the same result. Another, and another. In a very
few minutes the roof was covered with his panting
spoil. The broker could himself distinguish that
many of them were personal friends ; nay, some
of them were familiar frequenters of the building
on which they were now miserably stranded. That
the broker felt a certain satisfaction in being in-
strumental in thus misleading his fellow-brokers
no one acquainted with human nature will for a
moment doubt. But a stronger pull on his line
caused him to put forth all his strength and skill.

The magic pole bent like a coach-whip. The broker held firm, assisted by the battlements of the church. Again and again it was almost wrested from his hand, and again and again he slowly reeled in a portion of the tightening line. At last, with one mighty effort, he lifted to the level of the roof a struggling object. A howl like Pandemonium rang through the air as the broker successfully landed at his feet — the Devil himself!

The two glared fiercely at each other. The broker, perhaps mindful of his former treatment, evinced no haste to remove the hook from his antagonist's jaw. When it was finally accomplished, he asked quietly if the Devil was satisfied. That gentleman seemed absorbed in the contemplation of the bait which he had just taken from his mouth. "I am," he said, finally, "and forgive you; but what do you call this?"

"Bend low," replied the broker, as he buttoned up his coat ready to depart. The Devil inclined his ear. "I call it WILD CAT!"

THE OGRESS OF SILVER LAND;

THE DIVERTING HISTORY OF PRINCE BADFELLAH
AND PRINCE BULLEBOYE.

IN the second year of the reign of the renowned
Caliph Lo there dwelt in SILVER LAND, adjoining his territory, a certain terrible ogress. She
lived in the bowels of a dismal mountain, where
she was in the habit of confining such unfortunate
travellers as ventured within her domain. The
country for miles around was sterile and barren.
In some places it was covered with a white powder,
which was called in the language of the country
AL KA LI, and was supposed to be the pulverized
bones of those who had perished miserably in her
service.

In spite of this, every year, great numbers of
young men devoted themselves to the service of the
ogress, hoping to become her godsons, and to enjoy
the good fortune which belonged to that privileged
class. For these godsons had no work to perform,
neither at the mountain nor elsewhere, but roamed
about the world with credentials of their relationship in their pockets, which they called STOKH,

which was stamped with the stamp and sealed
with the seal of the ogress, and which enabled
them at the end of each moon to draw large quantities of gold and silver from her treasury. And the
wisest and most favored of those godsons were the
Princes BADFELLAH and BULLEBOYE. They knew all
the secrets of the ogress, and how to wheedle and
coax her. They were also the favorites of SOOPAH
INTENDENT, who was her Lord High Chamberlain
and Prime Minister, and who dwelt in SILVER
LAND.

One day, SOOPAH INTENDENT said to his servants, " What is that which travels the most surely, the most secretly, and the most swiftly ? "

And they all answered as one man, " LIGHTNING,
my lord, travels the most surely, the most swiftly,
and the most secretly !"

Then said SOOPAH INTENDENT, " Let Lightning
carry this message secretly, swiftly, and surely to
my beloved friends the Princes BADFELLAH and
BULLEBOYE, and tell them that their godmother is
dying, and bid them seek some other godmother
or sell their STOKH ere it becomes *badjee*, — worthless."

" Bekhesm ! On our heads be it !" answered
the servants ; and they ran to Lightning with the
message, who flew with it to the City by the Sea,
and delivered it, even at that moment, into the
hands of the Princes BADFELLAH and BULLEBOYE.

Now the Prince BADFELLAH was a wicked young man; and when he had received this message he tore his beard and rent his garment and reviled his godmother, and his friend SOOPAH INTENDENT. But presently he arose, and dressed himself in his finest stuffs, and went forth into the bazaars and among the merchants, capering and dancing as he walked, and crying in a loud voice, " O, happy day ! O, day worthy to be marked with a white stone ! "

This he said cunningly, thinking the merchants and men of the bazaars would gather about him, which they presently did, and began to question him: " What news, O most worthy and serene Highness ?   Tell us, that we make merry too !"

Then replied the cunning prince, " Good news, O my brothers, for I have heard this day that my godmother in SILVER LAND is well." The merchants, who were not aware of the substance of the real message, envied him greatly, and said one to another : " Surely our brother the Prince BADFELLAH is favored by Allah above all men " ; and they were about to retire, when the prince checked them, saying: " Tarry for a moment. Here are my credentials, or STOKH. The same I will sell you for fifty thousand sequins, for I have to give a feast to-day, and need much gold. Who will give fifty thousand ? " And he again fell to capering and dancing. But this time the merchants drew

a little apart, and some of the oldest and wisest
said : " What dirt is this which the prince would
have us swallow ? If his godmother were well,
why should he sell his STOKH ? Bismillah ! The
olives are old and the jar is broken !" When
Prince BADFELLAH perceived them whispering, his
countenance fell, and his knees smote against each
other through fear ; but, dissembling again, he said :
" Well, so be it ! Lo, I have much more than shall
abide with me, for my days are many and my
wants are few. Say forty thousand sequins for my
STOKH and let me depart in Allah's name. Who
will give forty thousand sequins to become the
godson of such a healthy mother ?" And he again
fell to capering and dancing, but not as gayly as
before, for his heart was troubled. The merchants,
however, only moved farther away. " Thirty thousand sequins," cried Prince BADFELLAH ; but even
as he spoke they fled before his face, crying : " His
godmother is dead. Lo, the jackals are defiling
her grave. Mashalla ! he has no godmother." And
they sought out PANIK, the swift-footed messenger,
and bade him shout through the bazaars that the
godmother of Prince BADFELLAH was dead. When
he heard this, the prince fell upon his face, and
rent his garments, and covered himself with the
dust of the market-place. As he was sitting thus,
a porter passed him with jars of wine on his shoulders, and the prince begged him to give him a jar,

for he was exceeding thirsty and faint. But the porter said, " What will my lord give me first ? " And the prince, in very bitterness of spirit, said, " Take this," and handed him his STOKH, and so exchanged it for a jar of wine.

Now the Prince BULLEBOYE was of a very different disposition. When he received the message of SOOPAH INTENDENT he bowed his head, and said, " It is the will of God." Then he rose, and without speaking a word entered the gates of his palace. But his wife, the peerless MAREE JAHANN, perceiving the gravity of his countenance, said, " Why is my lord cast down and silent ? Why are those rare and priceless pearls, his words, shut up so tightly between those gorgeous oyster-shells, his lips ? " But to this he made no reply. Thinking further to divert him, she brought her lute into the chamber and stood before him, and sang the song and danced the dance of BEN KOTTON, which is called IBRAHIM'S DAUGHTER, but she could not lift the veil of sadness from his brow.

When she had ceased, the Prince BULLEBOYE arose and said, " Allah is great, and what am I, his servant, but the dust of the earth ! Lo, this day has my godmother sickened unto death, and my STOKH become as a withered palm-leaf. Call hither my servants and camel-drivers, and the merchants that have furnished me with stuffs, and the beggars who have feasted at my table, and bid them

take all that is here, for it is mine no longer!"
With these words he buried his face in his mantle
and wept aloud.

But MAREE JAHANN, his wife, plucked him by
the sleeve. "Prithee, my lord," said she, "bethink
thee of the BROKAH or scrivener, who besought
thee but yesterday to share thy STOKH with him
and gave thee his bond for fifty thousand sequins." But the noble Prince BULLEBOYE, raising his head, said: "Shall I sell to him for fifty
thousand sequins that which I know is not worth
a SOO MARKEE? For is not all the BROKAH's
wealth, even his wife and children, pledged on
that bond? Shall I ruin him to save myself?
Allah forbid! Rather let me eat the salt fish of
honest penury, than the kibobs of dishonorable
affluence; rather let me wallow in the mire of
virtuous oblivion, than repose on the divan of luxurious wickedness."

When the prince had given utterance to this
beautiful and edifying sentiment, a strain of gentle
music was heard, and the rear wall of the apartment, which had been ingeniously constructed like
a flat, opened and discovered the Ogress of SILVER
LAND in the glare of blue fire, seated on a triumphal
car attached to two ropes which were connected
with the flies, in the very act of blessing the unconscious prince. When the walls closed again
without attracting his attention, Prince BULLEBOYE

arose, dressed himself in his coarsest and cheapest stuffs, and sprinkled ashes on his head, and in this guise, having embraced his wife, went forth into the bazaars.   In this it will be perceived how differently the good Prince BULLEBOYE acted from the wicked Prince BADFELLAH, who put on his gayest garments to simulate and deceive.

Now when Prince BULLEBOYE entered the chief bazaar, where the merchants of the city were gathered in council, he stood up in his accustomed place, and all that were there held their breath, for the noble Prince BULLEBOYE was much respected. "Let the BROKAH, whose bond I hold for fifty thousand sequins, stand forth!" said the prince.   And the BROKAH stood forth from among the merchants. Then said the prince: "Here is thy bond for fifty thousand sequins, for which I was to deliver unto thee one half of my STOKH.   Know, then, O my brother, — and thou, too, O Aga of the BROKAHS, — that this my STOKH which I pledged to thee is worthless.   For my godmother, the Ogress of SILVER LAND, is dying.   Thus do I release thee from thy bond, and from the poverty which might overtake thee as it has even me, thy brother, the Prince BULLEBOYE."   And with that the noble Prince BULLEBOYE tore the bond of the BROKAH into pieces and scattered it to the four winds.

Now when the prince tore up the bond there was a great commotion, and some said, "Surely the

Prince BULLEBOYE is drunken with wine"; and others, "He is possessed of an evil spirit"; and his friends expostulated with him, saying, "What thou hast done is not the custom of the bazaars, — behold, it is not BIZ!" But to all the prince answered gravely, "It is right; on my own head be it!"

But the oldest and wisest of the merchants, they who had talked with Prince BADFELLAH the same morning, whispered together, and gathered around the BROKAH whose bond the Prince BULLEBOYE had torn up. "Hark ye," said they, " our brother the Prince BULLEBOYE is cunning as a jackal. What bosh is this about ruining himself to save thee? Such a thing was never heard before in the bazaars. It is a trick, O thou mooncalf of a BROKAH! Dost thou not see that he has heard good news from his godmother, the same that was even now told us by the Prince BADFELLAH, his confederate, and that he would destroy thy bond for fifty thousand sequins because his STOKH is worth a hundred thousand! Be not deceived, O too credulous BROKAH! for this what our brother the prince doeth is not in the name of ALLAH, but of BIZ, the only god known in the bazaars of the city."

When the foolish BROKAH heard these things he cried, "Justice, O Aga of the BROKAHS, — justice and the fulfilment of my bond! Let the prince deliver unto me the STOKH. Here are my fifty

thousand sequins." But the prince said, "Have I
not told that my godmother is dying, and that my
STOKH is valueless?" At this the BROKAH only
clamored the more for justice and the fulfilment
of his bond. Then the Aga of the BROKAHS said,
"Since the bond is destroyed, behold thou hast no
claim. Go thy ways!" But the BROKAH again
cried, "Justice, my lord Aga! Behold, I offer the
prince seventy thousand sequins for his STOKH!"
But the prince said, "It is not worth one sequin!"
Then the Aga said, "Bismillah! I cannot understand this. Whether thy godmother be dead, or
dying, or immortal, does not seem to signify.
Therefore, O prince, by the laws of BIZ and of
ALLAH, thou art released. Give the BROKAH thy
STOKH for seventy thousand sequins, and bid him
depart in peace. On his own head be it!" When
the prince heard this command, he handed his
STOKH to the BROKAH, who counted out to him
seventy thousand sequins. But the heart of the
virtuous prince did not rejoice, nor did the BRO-
KAH, when he found his STOKH was valueless; but
the merchants lifted their hands in wonder at the
sagacity and wisdom of the famous Prince BULLE-
BOYE. For none would believe that it was the law
of ALLAH that the prince followed, and not the
rules of BIZ.

THE RUINS OF SAN FRANCISCO.

TOWARDS the close of the nineteenth century the city of San Francisco was totally ingulfed by an earthquake. Although the whole coast-line must have been much shaken, the accident seems to have been purely local, and even the city of Oakland escaped. Schwappelfurt, the celebrated German geologist, has endeavored to explain this singular fact by suggesting that there are some things the earth cannot swallow, — a statement that should be received with some caution, as exceeding the latitude of ordinary geological speculation.

Historians disagree in the exact date of the calamity. Tulu Krish, the well-known New-Zealander, whose admirable speculations on the ruins of St. Paul as seen from London Bridge have won for him the attentive consideration of the scientific world, fixes the occurrence in A. D. 1880. This, supposing the city to have been actually founded in 1850, as asserted, would give but thirty years for it to have assumed the size and proportions it had evidently attained at the time of its destruction. It is not our purpose, however, to

question the conclusions of the justly famed **Ma-
orian** philosopher. Our present business lies with
the excavations that are now being prosecuted by
order of the Hawaiian government upon the site
of the lost city.

Every one is familiar with the story of its discovery. For many years the bay of San Francisco
had been famed for the luscious quality of its
oysters. It is stated that a dredger one day raked
up a large bell, which proved to belong to the City
Hall, and led to the discovery of the cupola of
that building. The attention of the government
was at once directed to the spot. The bay of San
Francisco was speedily drained by a system of
patent siphons, and the city, deeply embedded in
mud, brought to light after a burial of many centuries. The City Hall, Post-Office, Mint, and Cus-
tom-House were readily recognized by the large
full-fed barnacles which adhered to their walls.
Shortly afterwards the first skeleton was discovered; that of a broker, whose position in the upper strata of mud nearer the surface was supposed
to be owing to the exceeding buoyancy or inflation
of scrip which he had secured about his person
while endeavoring to escape. Many skeletons,
supposed to be those of females, encompassed in
that peculiar steel coop or cage which seems to
have been worn by the women of that period,
were also found in the upper stratum. Alexis

von Puffer, in his admirable work on San Francisco, accounts for the position of these unfortunate creatures by asserting that the steel cage was originally the frame of a parachute-like garment which distended the skirt, and in the submersion of the city prevented them from sinking. "If anything," says Von Puffer, "could have been wanting to add intensity to the horrible catastrophe which took place as the waters first entered the city, it would have been furnished in the forcible separation of the sexes at this trying moment. Buoyed up by their peculiar garments, the female population instantly ascended to the surface. As the drowning husband turned his eyes above, what must have been his agony as he saw his wife shooting upward, and knew that he was debarred the privilege of perishing with her? To the lasting honor of the male inhabitants, be it said that but few seemed to have availed themselves of their wives' superior levity. Only one skeleton was found still grasping the ankles of another in their upward journey to the surface."

For many years California had been subject to slight earthquakes, more or less generally felt, but not of sufficient importance to awaken anxiety or fear. Perhaps the absorbing nature of the San-Franciscans' pursuits of gold-getting, which metal seems to have been valuable in those days, and actually used as a medium of currency, rendered

the inhabitants reckless of all other matters.
Everything tends to show that the calamity was
totally unlooked for.   We quote the graphic language of Schwappelfurt :—

"The morning of the tremendous catastrophe
probably dawned upon the usual restless crowd of
gold-getters intent upon their several avocations.
The streets were filled with the expanded figures
of gayly dressed women, acknowledging with coy
glances the respectful salutations of beaux as they
gracefully raised their remarkable cylindrical head-
coverings, a model of which is still preserved in
the Honolulu Museum.   The brokers had gathered at their respective temples.   The shopmen
were exhibiting their goods.   The idlers, or 'Bummers,' — a term applied to designate an aristocratic,
privileged class who enjoyed immunities from labor, and from whom a majority of the rulers are
chosen, — were listlessly regarding the promenaders from the street-corners or the doors of
their bibulous temples.   A slight premonitory
thrill runs through the city.   The busy life of
this restless microcosm is arrested.   The shop-
keeper pauses as he elevates the goods to bring
them into a favorable light, and the glib professional recommendation sticks on his tongue.   In
the drinking-saloon the glass is checked half-way
to the lips ; on the streets the promenaders pause.
Another thrill, and the city begins to go down, a

few of the more persistent topers tossing off their liquor at the same moment. Beyond a terrible sensation of nausea, the crowds who now throng the streets do not realize the extent of the catastrophe. The waters of the bay recede at first from the centre of depression, assuming a concave shape, the outer edge of the circle towering many thousand feet above the city. Another convulsion, and the water instantly resumes its level. The city is smoothly ingulfed nine thousand feet below, and the regular swell of the Pacific calmly rolls over it. Terrible," says Schwappelfurt, in conclusion, " as the calamity must have been, in direct relation to the individuals immediately concerned therein, we cannot but admire its artistic management ; the division of the catastrophe into three periods, the completeness of the cataclysms, and the rare combination of sincerity of intention with felicity of execution."

A NIGHT AT WINGDAM.

I HAD been stage-ridden and bewildered all day,
and when we swept down with the darkness
into the Arcadian hamlet of " Wingdam," I resolved
to go no farther, and rolled out in a gloomy and
dyspeptic state. The effects of a mysterious pie,
and some sweetened carbonic acid known to the
proprietor of the " Half-Way House " as " lemming
sody," still oppressed me. Even the facetiæ of the
gallant expressman who knew everybody's Christian
name along the route, who rained letters, news-
papers, and bundles from the top of the stage, whose
legs frequently appeared in frightful proximity to
the wheels, who got on and off while we were
going at full speed, whose gallantry, energy, and
superior knowledge of travel crushed all us other
passengers to envious silence, and who just then
was talking with several persons and manifestly
doing something else at the same time, — even this
had failed to interest me. So I stood gloomily,
clutching my shawl and carpet-bag, and watched
the stage roll away, taking a parting look at the
gallant expressman as he hung on the top rail with
one leg, and lit his cigar from the pipe of a running

footman. I then turned toward the Wingdam
Temperance Hotel.

It may have been the weather, or it may have
been the pie, but I was not impressed favorably
with the house. Perhaps it was the name extend-
ing the whole length of the building, with a letter
under each window, making the people who looked
out dreadfully conspicuous. Perhaps it was that
" Temperance" always suggested to my mind rusks
and weak tea. It was uninviting. It might have
been called the " Total Abstinence " Hotel, from
the lack of anything to intoxicate or inthrall the
senses. It was designed with an eye to artistic
dreariness. It was so much too large for the settlement, that it appeared to be a very slight improvement on out-doors. It was unpleasantly new.
There was the forest flavor of dampness about it,
and a slight spicing of pine. Nature outraged, but
not entirely subdued, sometimes broke out afresh in
little round, sticky, resinous tears on the doors and
windows. It seemed to me that boarding there must
seem like a perpetual picnic. As I entered the
door, a number of the regular boarders rushed out
of a long room, and set about trying to get the
taste of something out of their mouths, by the ap-
plication of tobacco in various forms. A few immediately ranged themselves around the fireplace,
with their legs over each other's chairs, and in that
position silently resigned themselves to indigestion.

Remembering the pie, I waived the invitation of the landlord to supper, but suffered myself to be conducted into the sitting-room. " Mine host " was a magnificent-looking, heavily bearded specimen of the animal man. He reminded me of somebody or something connected with the drama. I was sitting beside the fire, mutely wondering what it could be, and trying to follow the particular chord of memory thus touched, into the intricate past, when a little delicate-looking woman appeared at the door, and, leaning heavily against the casing, said in an exhausted tone, " Husband ! " As the landlord turned toward her, that particular remembrance flashed before me in a single line of blank verse. It was this: " Two souls with but one single thought, two hearts that beat as one."

It was Ingomar and Parthenia his wife. I imagined a different *dénouement* from the play. Ingomar had taken Parthenia back to the mountains, and kept a hotel for the benefit of the Alemanni, who resorted there in large numbers. Poor Parthenia was pretty well fagged out, and did all the work without "help." She had two " young barbarians," a boy and a girl. She was faded, but still good-looking.

I sat and talked with Ingomar, who seemed perfectly at home and told me several stories of the Alemanni, all bearing a strong flavor of the wilderness, and being perfectly in keeping with the house.

How he, Ingomar, had killed a certain dreadful
" bar," whose skin was just up " yar," over his bed.
How he, Ingomar, had killed several "bucks,"
whose skins had been prettily fringed and em-
broidered by Parthenia, and even now clothed him.
How he, Ingomar, had killed several " Injins," and
was once nearly scalped himself. All this with
that ingenious candor which is perfectly justifiable
in a barbarian, but which a Greek might feel inclined to look upon as " blowing." Thinking of
the wearied Parthenia, I began to consider for the
first time that perhaps she had better married the
old Greek. Then she would at least have always
looked neat. Then she would not have worn a
woollen dress flavored with all the dinners of the
past year. Then she would not have been obliged
to wait on the table with her hair half down. Then
the two children would not have hung about her
skirts with dirty fingers, palpably dragging her
down day by day. I suppose it was the pie which
put such heartless and improper ideas in my head,
and so I rose up and told Ingomar I believed I'd
go to bed. Preceded by that redoubtable barbarian
and a flaring tallow candle, I followed him up
stairs to my room. It was the only single room
he had, he told me; he had built it for the con-
venience of married parties who might stop here,
but, that event not happening yet, he had left it
half furnished. It had cloth on one side, and large

cracks on the other. The wind, which always swept over Wingdam at night-time, puffed through the apartment from different apertures. The window was too small for the hole in the side of the house where it hung, and rattled noisily. Everything looked cheerless and dispiriting. Before Ingomar left me, he brought that " bar-skin," and throwing it over the solemn bier which stood in one corner, told me he reckoned that would keep me warm, and then bade me good night. I undressed myself, the light blowing out in the middle of that ceremony, crawled under the " bar-skin," and tried to compose myself to sleep.

But I was staringly wide awake. I heard the wind sweep down the mountain-side, and toss the branches of the melancholy pine, and then enter the house, and try all the doors along the passage. Sometimes strong currents of air blew my hair all over the pillow, as with strange whispering breaths. The green timber along the walls seemed to be sprouting, and sent a dampness even through the " bar-skin." I felt like Robinson Crusoe in his tree, with the ladder pulled up, — or like the rocked baby of the nursery song. After lying awake half an hour, I regretted having stopped at Wingdam ; at the end of the third quarter, I wished I had not gone to bed ; and when a restless hour passed, I got up and dressed myself. There had been a fire down in the big room. Perhaps it was still burning. I opened the door and groped my way along the passage, vocal with the snores of the Alemanni and the whistling of the night wind; I partly fell down stairs, and at last entering the big room, saw the fire still burning. I drew a chair toward it, poked it with my foot, and was astonished to see, by the upspringing flash, that Parthenia was sitting there also, holding a faded-looking baby.

I asked her why she was sitting up.

"She did not go to bed on Wednesday night before the mail arrived, and then she awoke her husband, and there were passengers to 'tend to."

"Did she not get tired sometimes?"

"A little, but Abner" (the barbarian's Christian name) "had promised to get her more help next spring, if business was good."

"How many boarders had she?"

"She believed about forty came to regular meals, and there was transient custom, which was as much as she and her husband could 'tend to. But *he* did a great deal of work."

"What work?"

"O, bringing in the wood, and looking after the traders' things."

"How long had she been married?"

"About nine years. She had lost a little girl and boy. Three children living. *He* was from Illinois. She from Boston. Had an education

(Boston Female High School, — Geometry, Alge-
bra, a little Latin and Greek). Mother and father
died.   Came to Illinois alone, to teach school
Saw *him* — yes — a love match." ("Two souls,"
etc., etc.)   "Married and emigrated to Kansas.
Thence across the Plains to California. Always
on the outskirts of civilization. *He* liked it.

   " She might sometimes have wished to go home.
Would like to on account of her children. Would
like to give them an education. Had taught them
a little herself, but could n't do much on account
of other work. Hoped that the boy would be like
his father, strong and hearty. Was fearful the
girl would be more like her. Had often thought
she was not fit for a pioneer's wife."

   " Why ? "

   " O, she was not strong enough, and had seen
some of his friends' wives in Kansas who could
do more work. But he never complained, — he
was so kind." (" Two souls," etc.)

   Sitting there with her head leaning pensively on
one hand, holding the poor, wearied, and limp-
looking baby wearily on the other arm, dirty,
drabbled, and forlorn, with the firelight playing
upon her features no longer fresh or young, but
still refined and delicate, and even in her grotesque
slovenliness still bearing a faint reminiscence of
birth and breeding, it was not to be wondered that
I did not fall into excessive raptures over the bar-

barian's kindness. Emboldened by my sympathy, she told me how she had given up, little by little, what she imagined to be the weakness of her early education, until she found that she acquired but little strength in her new experience. How, translated to a backwoods society, she was hated by the women, and called proud and " fine," and how her dear husband lost popularity on that account with his fellows. How, led partly by his roving instincts, and partly from other circumstances, he started with her to California. An account of that tedious journey. How it was a dreary, dreary waste in her memory, only a blank plain marked by a little cairn of stones, — a child's grave. How she had noticed that little Willie failed. How she had called Abner's attention to it, but, man-like, he knew nothing about children, and pooh-poohed it, and was worried by the stock. How it happened that after they had passed Sweetwater, she was walking beside the wagon one night, and looking at the western sky, and she heard a little voice say "Mother." How she looked into the wagon and saw that little Willie was sleeping comfortably and did not wish to wake him. How that in a few moments more she heard the same voice saying "Mother." How she came back to the wagon and leaned down over him, and felt his breath upon her face, and again covered him up tenderly, and once more resumed her weary journey beside him, praying to God for his recovery. How with her face turned to the sky she heard the same voice saying "Mother," and directly a great bright star shot away from its brethren and expired. And how she knew what had happened, and ran to the wagon again only to pillow a little pinched and cold white face upon her weary bosom. The thin red hands went up to her eyes here, and for a few moments she sat still. The wind tore round the house and made a frantic rush at the front door, and from his couch of skins in the inner room — Ingomar, the barbarian, snored peacefully.

"Of course she always found a protector from insult and outrage in the great courage and strength of her husband?"

"O yes; when Ingomar was with her she feared nothing. But she was nervous and had been frightened once!"

"How?"

"They had just arrived in California. They kept house then, and had to sell liquor to traders. Ingomar was hospitable, and drank with everybody, for the sake of popularity and business, and Ingomar got to like liquor, and was easily affected by it. And how one night there was a boisterous crowd in the bar-room; she went in and tried to get him away, but only succeeded in awakening the coarse gallantry of the half-crazed revellers. And how, when she had at last got him in the room with her frightened children, he sank down on the bed in a stupor, which made her think the liquor was drugged. And how she sat beside him all night, and near morning heard a step in the passage, and, looking toward the door, saw the latch slowly moving up and down, as if somebody were trying it. And how she shook her husband, and tried to waken him, but without effect. And how at last the door yielded slowly at the top (it was bolted below), as if by a gradual pressure without; and how a hand protruded through the opening. And how as quick as lightning she nailed that hand to the wall with her scissors (her only weapon), but the point broke, and somebody got away with a fearful oath. How she never told her husband of it, for fear he would kill that somebody; but how on one day a stranger called here, and as she was handing him his coffee, she saw a queer triangular scar on the back of his hand."

She was still talking, and the wind was still blowing, and Ingomar was still snoring from his couch of skins, when there was a shout high up the straggling street, and a clattering of hoofs, and rattling of wheels. The mail had arrived. Parthenia ran with the faded baby to awaken Ingomar, and almost simultaneously the gallant expressman stood again before me addressing me by my Christian name, and inviting me to drink out of a mysterious black bottle. The horses were speedily watered, and the business of the gallant expressman concluded, and, bidding Parthenia good by, I got on the stage, and immediately fell asleep, and dreamt of calling on Parthenia and Ingomar, and being treated with pie to an unlimited extent, until I woke up the next morning in Sacramento. I have some doubts as to whether all this was not a dyspeptic dream, but I never witness the drama, and hear that noble sentiment concerning "Two souls," etc., without thinking of Wingdam and poor Parthenia.

THE END.

3772